Montana FREEDOM

JOSIE JADE

Chapter 1

Daniel Clark

The early morning was still cool despite the late spring season. The sun was up but hadn't yet made its way over the mountains. It would heat up later, and then I would once again long for the sun to set so we could get some relief from the heat.

But right now? It was beautiful.

And peaceful. I usually liked to sleep a little later than this, but today, I needed to clear my head, and walking was the best way to do it. I could go to the gym and burn off steam, but that didn't feel right. I just…needed to move and let my mind wander and try to let go of the images in my head.

It wasn't as if nightmares were uncommon among those of us who lived and worked at Resting Warrior. That was kind of the whole point of the ranch, a place where those with PTSD—both military-centric and not—could come to recover in the peace and beauty that was Montana.

I'd had nightmares since I'd left the service, but those had been repetitive and manageable. After a while, though they were still bad, they seemed like a simple part of life. The ones I was having now were different. They brought me out of sleep, covered in sweat and panting with adrenaline, reaching to save someone who wasn't there because I didn't have the closure of knowing whether they were all right.

Every night for the last six months had felt like some variation on the same theme. Bursting into the house we'd raided all those years ago, trying to free people who'd been captured, but when I went to let them out of the cage, it was *her*.

Brown hair and big eyes, one brown and one blue, staring at me, desperate and grateful as I freed her from that fucking rusted metal cage. And then she was gone.

Or she was already there, in the cages with all the other people, looking at me and calling out for help, and I was stuck in place, knowing what was about to happen and that it was already too late for me to save her.

I stopped, pressing the heels of my hands into my eyes. I couldn't get the sight of her out of my head. She was real. I was the one who'd let her out of that cage six months ago. I'd led her to the paramedics, and then she disappeared entirely. As if she'd never existed and I'd made her up.

Now she was my own personal ghost.

Logically, I knew she was probably fine. I'd missed her leaving or being taken somewhere. She was a trauma victim. Getting out of that place as soon as possible would have been good for her. But no one knew where she went. I'd checked. None of the Resting Warrior men had seen her go anywhere, none of the paramedics or police. If she'd vaporized right in front of me, she would be just as missing as she was right now.

Still, it was all too similar to my past, and I was

exhausted, constantly waking up in a panic and reaching for her, trying to get her out before the explosions hit.

Not once had I been successful in my dreams, and lately, those were shaking me more than I wanted to admit.

After all this time, I'd thought I was better. I'd moved on, done the work, rebuilt myself, and accepted my self-imposed punishment as a way of life. I'd let people die, and nothing in the world could make up for it. So I helped them now. I didn't take things for myself. Some people, Dr. Rayne included, thought my minimalism, celibacy, and denial were too much. Maybe they were.

But that way of life was the only thing that felt right all these years.

How could I let myself indulge in any kind of pleasure when my mistakes had robbed twenty people of their ability to do the same? Atrocities happened in war, and I could do nothing to stop them, but I could make up for my part in them. For me, I didn't think there was another way forward.

The soft sound of crunching dirt made me look up from where my gaze was focused on the ground, and I saw Liam walking toward me. He was farther out on the ranch than I was, and earlier. He didn't live on the property, and it was a bit of a running joke on the ranch that Liam always showed up at the exact last minute for everything. So why was he here so early?

All this time, focusing outward gave me the ability to read people. I could simply look at them and figure out what they were feeling, and, if I pushed, get them to open up or admit what was really bothering them. Liam's shoulders were hunched, gaze as focused on the ground as mine had been moments ago. It didn't seem like he realized he wasn't alone.

"And here I thought I'd be the only one out here this morning."

I was glad I said something. Liam stopped and startled, suddenly focusing on me. It took him a few seconds to come back from wherever he was in his thoughts and place me here. Then he smiled, but it wasn't a normal Liam smile.

He was the joker of the ranch—the man who brought lightness and levity to everything, no matter the situation. Sometimes a little too much. The man standing in front of me right now was anything but light.

"I needed to get out and clear my head."

I nodded. "Know the feeling."

We stopped when we reached each other, standing and turning to look at the still-brightening sky on the other side of the mountains.

Among the men who lived and worked here, Liam and I weren't particularly close. He was younger than me by nearly a decade, and a world of age, experience, and trauma stretched between us. There were similarities too, as with all of us, but our pairing felt the least natural.

"You all right?" I asked him.

"Sure."

I chuckled. "That's an answer I'm certain everyone would accept."

"I'll be fine, I'm sure," he said. "Just feeling a little lost at the moment."

"Anything you need to talk about?"

Liam shrugged. "No. Not yet anyway. Thank you for the offer, though. You?"

I couldn't stop the instinctual grimace, and Liam grinned. "That bad?"

"Yes and no," I admitted with a sigh. "It's something I probably shouldn't be worrying about, and also something I can't *stop* thinking about. Someone."

His eyebrows rose. "Who?" Then he pulled it back. "Sorry, you don't need to tell me."

I didn't blame him for his surprise and curiosity. It wasn't exactly a secret I kept to myself and lived simply. Not everyone knew the reasons why I chose to stay alone and direct all my intentions outward, nor did they need to. We all knew enough about one another's trauma to work around what we needed, but we also had a policy of not digging too deep into one another's pain. We were here for support and help, but not to be assholes. Liam was trying to respect the rule. But at this point? I was going to have to tell someone.

"The woman," I clarified. "From the night of the Riders raid. The one I let out of the cage who then disappeared."

Liam's face shifted in recognition. "Ah. Yeah, I remember."

Sighing, I shoved my hands into my pockets. "The whole 'people in cages' thing, without going too deep for such a nice morning, hits a little close to home for me. And I know she's probably fine, but no one remembers where she went, and I just want to know she didn't run away, only to die from her injuries or something worse."

It was the first time I'd really voiced it out loud. I had no closure where she was concerned. She was a person in trouble, and I'd helped her, but not enough. I hadn't really *saved* her.

My gut twinged, and I made a note of that thought for my next therapy session. My instincts and drive to save people had been the subject of more than one of those sessions, and it looked like I needed to devote some more attention to that front.

"I keep having nightmares about it. About her calling out for help and not making it. And frankly, it's gotten a lot worse than I feel it should be. Hence why I'm out here at dawn when my perfectly warm and comfortable bed is waiting."

"Was it the cage, or was it her?"

I looked at him. "What do you mean?"

Liam shrugged and took a turn back toward the main ranch. I fell in step beside him, and we walked slowly. "You said people in cages was a thing for you. And I get that. It's awful. But I'm guessing if that's true, you've had nightmares about it before."

"I have," I acknowledged.

"So, maybe I'm wrong, I'm not Dr. Rayne…" He grinned. "But if the cages were the part of it that was bothering you, I would think it would amplify the old nightmares. Maybe it wouldn't be so specific as *her* reaching out."

I froze in my tracks for a second. He wasn't wrong. The nightmares that now haunted me were about saving her, getting to her, erasing the pain in those bicolored eyes. They were all about her. I hadn't noticed the subtle differences between those things, but then again, that was the beauty of getting an opinion outside your own head.

"And besides," Liam said, "I was there too. Things were hectic in the aftermath. You did what you needed to do—you got her out of the cage and free. You made sure she was safe before you moved on to your next duty. I know it might not feel like it, but there was nothing else you could have or should have done."

I'd been told as much by others. If only my mind and my heart would actually listen instead of telling me I hadn't and there was still work to do.

Find her. The words were like a rhythm in my chest now, along with my pulse. Find her.

But I had no way to do that, and finding her might mean bringing up things she never wanted to relive. I could handle this. I'd handled worse, and living with the constant thrum of wanting to find her would eventually fade into the chaotic backdrop of the many things I was still paying for.

"Thank you," I said to Liam, not voicing the last bits of

my thoughts. It wasn't that I thought he wouldn't be sympathetic, but things looked different after another decade of life. I wasn't as hopeful as I'd once been, and the constant wear of those scars was taking its toll.

Whether the toll was deserved was a question I still wrestled with.

"You going to the opening?" Liam asked, shifting away to a lighter topic. That was more like him, sensing when the mood needed to be lifted.

"I wouldn't miss it. And I'll be eager to hear how it goes tonight."

Garnet Bend's favorite coffee shop was having a grand reopening today after nearly five months of being closed. Lena Mitchell, the vibrant, spunky owner of the small shop, had been targeted by a man with a grudge, and she had almost died as a result.

She was also our colleague's girlfriend. And hopefully, after tonight, not just girlfriend but fiancée.

Liam laughed, the sound loud in the quiet morning. "No shot in hell Lena says no."

I laughed with him. "No, probably not."

Jude and Lena had circled each other for far too long, and now that they were together, you had to be blind not to see how truly happy they were.

We were approaching the break in the road where I needed to split off for my house, so I clapped a hand on Liam's shoulder.

"Thank you for this, and if you need to talk about it—"

He held out a hand. "I'll let you know. See you in a bit."

I couldn't respond. He was already jogging toward the main lodge, where I assumed he'd left his truck.

I still had plenty of time before the opening, so I moved slowly on the way back to my small house in a far corner of the property. It was simple, but it suited me. And while I was walking, I tried to puzzle out a little more of what Liam had mentioned. What was it about this woman specifically that had drawn me in?

She was beautiful, no denying it, but there were plenty of beautiful women in the world, and none of them called to me like she did. Was it her? Or was it my own issues rising up to bite me in the ass yet again?

That was quite enough wallowing for one day, so I put it aside as I showered and went to the lodge to take care of a few things before going into town.

By the time I reached Garnet Bend, the line outside Deja Brew spanned several blocks in both directions. I laughed knowing Lena—sweet person that she was—was still probably freaking out at the idea of so many people waiting for her to open the doors.

I found Lucas in line near the front. "You're telling me Evie didn't get you in early?"

He snorted. "No. I told her I'd be manual labor and whatever else they needed, but she said I needed to wait like everyone else. Jude is the only one in there with them."

"Hi!" Cori said, coming up to us with Grant. The local vet and Grant had had their own brush with death, and they were equally as in love as Jude and Lena. The flush on Cori's cheeks told me enough about what they'd been doing before they arrived.

"We thought we were going to be late."

"If I know Lena," Grace called from across the street, "she's stalling."

I looked at the patrons behind us in line and smiled. It was good this was a small town with people who knew everyone, so our growing cluster of friends wouldn't be upsetting to those waiting. The way Deja Brew and Resting Warrior were tangled together was well known by now.

Grace hugged Cori quickly before getting pulled back

into Harlan's arms. An unexpected lurch in my gut had me looking away from them. The men of Resting Warrior were my brothers in every way that mattered, and I was happy for them. But I couldn't ignore the way their happiness contrasted with the emptiness in my own life.

"What's up, Daniel?" Lucas asked quietly.

"What do you mean?"

He smirked, holding back a laugh. "I mean that you're usually dark and broody, but you seem to have taken an extra dose of it this morning."

I made a show of a big smile. "Better?"

"Sure thing." Then again, but quieter, he asked, "Seriously, is something wrong?"

"Nothing I can't handle."

He nodded once. "Let me know if there's anything I can do."

"Of course."

Cori looked around. "Where are Noah and Kate? I assumed they would be here."

"I'm sure they will be," Harlan said. "I think Noah's still feeding the animals and will be by in a bit."

Ahead of us, the doors to Deja Brew opened inward, and the line surged forward. We were barely outside the entrance when it stopped. Just inside, Jude was managing the line and making sure they didn't immediately have a fire code violation on their hands, but the smile on his face told me he didn't care.

A person suddenly came flying out the doors, past the crowd, and nearly crashed into Lucas. It was Evelyn, Lucas's fiancée, out of breath and eyes filled with both anxiety and joy. The shirt she wore showed her scarred arms, remnants from her brutal stalker of an ex. She now wore her scars as proud marks of her survival and not of shame.

"Remember when I told you we didn't need help and everything was fine?"

Lucas laughed, wrapping an arm around her. "Yes, I do remember that."

"How much groveling will I have to do if I tell you I was wrong and we literally need *all* the help we can get?"

"No groveling at all," he said, leaning down and kissing her forehead. "Tell us where you need us."

All of us followed her into the shop, weaving around people patiently waiting in line to receive coffee or the baked goods for which Lena was renowned—even after a smear campaign tried to convince the town otherwise.

Evie handed us each an apron as we moved behind the counter. "Lucas, I need at least one more person handling the line and keeping them happy. I need someone filling the pastry orders as they come over the counter, and the rest of you, I'll yell what I need."

Grace saluted her. "Yes, Boss."

Evie rolled her eyes, but she was smiling. I glanced at Lucas and Grant, who were all smiles too. This was what it meant to be a part of the Resting Warrior family, and it was the very thing we'd wanted to build when we'd started our place.

Breaking into the roles Evie assigned, we went to work.

Chapter 2

Emma Derine

I pinned another piece of paper to the wall. This one had phone numbers on it. Or at least, it did in my mind. Phone logs of numbers. I had no idea who they belonged to or how they connected yet, but a bunch of numbers were repeated multiple times, and that felt significant.

Cracking my neck, I stepped back and looked at my creation, groaning.

What had started as one corner of a wall, trying to get all my thoughts out in a place where I could *look* at them, had now become nearly two full walls of the cabin. Some fishing line and nails were my makeshift pushpins and string, and it looked like one of those boards you found in crime dramas when they were trying to figure out the killer.

And that's what it was. Kind of.

Trying to figure out where my killer was, what he was doing, and how to take him down. Or rather, the man who would have been my killer—and still would be if he ever saw me again.

I flopped down on the couch in the center of the room. I'd moved it so it faced the wall of clues that, to anyone else, would look like nonsense. Blank pages or scribbled notes that only made sense to me.

That was the hard part about having a perfect photographic memory but not having the smarts to go with it. I was sure I had all the information I needed to figure this out, but I couldn't see the solution. The only other possibility was to ask for help, and I couldn't do that. I knew now how deep his influence went, and I wasn't about to risk putting a target on my back.

Outside, the light was fading, getting dark early in the shadows of the large trees on this mountainside.

That was the other reason I'd moved the couch to the center of the room. I needed as much space around me as possible so I didn't go mad thinking the walls were closing in.

Living in a cage for more than a month would do that to you. Small spaces made me panic, and the little side room in this cabin that held a bed and not much else was too cramped. I'd barely set foot in it after the first night when I'd thought I was going to die because I couldn't breathe.

The couch had been my home ever since.

Every night, I slept here, waking at the slightest sound from outside and wondering if this night was the night Simon or his men came crashing in, not expecting me, and finding me anyway. At least if that happened, it would be quick.

Then there was the other part of my nights. The dreams. I dreamed of being in the cage, but not only that—I dreamed of being pulled out of it. The man who saved me and took my hand, offering me freedom. His was the face I saw the most. Thick black hair, dark, kind eyes, and a sympathetic smile that was never far from my thoughts.

If I could figure it out, *he* would believe me. I knew it. He would listen and try to understand. Maybe he would even help me if I asked. But I didn't know where to find him. I'd left the mystery man behind when I fled the house and never looked back.

For now, I was content to have him help in my dreams. It was a comfort when I woke in a panic, remembering the too-tight space and the choking fear. A small comfort, but a comfort nonetheless.

I closed my eyes, not wanting to do what I knew I had to. This cabin was a hideout, and it had been stocked with food when I got here, thanks to my remembering an address on one of the pieces of my wall of notes.

But it had been nearly six months, and I was down to scraps. My stomach growled, as if it knew what I was thinking and agreed. I needed to get more food somehow.

The idea of stealing made me curl up into a ball with guilt and anxiety, but I didn't see any other way around it. I had no money and no ID, no way to buy what I needed unless I wanted to put myself on the grid again, and that was something I couldn't do.

I was probably already wanted for stealing the car. Though it was stolen already before I stole it again.

There was gas in the car. I hadn't started the thing since the night I'd fled here, so at least I wasn't at risk of running out of gas and being stranded.

The town I'd passed through to get to this place wasn't far. I remembered it exactly, like everything. And frankly, it was close enough I was surprised I hadn't seen anyone around the cabin. But it was well hidden. Simon wouldn't have anything in his name that wasn't as perfect as possible. He stayed off the grid, and I'd learned from the best.

If only I could *find him.*

Once I knew where he was, I could take what I knew to the police and trade the information for my safety.

My stomach rumbled again. Covering my face with my hands, I breathed deeply. The anxiety was rising, like it did whenever I thought about leaving this place and being seen. It was so strong and so sudden, I'd given up on the thought of leaving the cabin a week after I got here.

But I didn't have a choice now. If I didn't leave and go get food, I was eventually going to starve. I couldn't survive on water alone.

I traced the route in my head. Down the rocky, treacherous mountain path and to the main road, past ranch after ranch and open fields that somehow made me feel just as anxious as enclosed spaces, and finally to the town. On my way through it, I'd spotted a small grocery store that would do the job. Smaller likely meant less security, which was perfect.

I'd found a laptop here, along with a rickety Wi-Fi network that seemed about as slow as I'd heard dial-up internet was in the nineties, but it worked. I was careful not to do anything that would identify me, though every time I logged on was a risk if Simon had someone watching for blips from his safe houses.

Still, I checked every couple of days and scanned the news stories just to see if he'd been caught. Nothing so far.

I did my usual sweep of those headlines as I waited for it to get darker. This far north, it took forever for the sun to finally set and even longer for the sky to go completely black. I couldn't wait that long, but when the sun finally sank below the horizon, I grabbed one of the ski masks in the closet full of hunting and winter clothes, took a deep breath, and forced myself to leave the cabin, locking the door behind me.

Out here, there was too much noise. Every shivering leaf and snapping twig made me jump, and I barely got the keys into the door of the old car because my hands were shaking.

"Breathe," I told myself once I was in the car. "It's okay. Keep breathing."

I'd always been an anxious person, and none of this helped. Desperation was my only driver at the moment. She was going to be the one getting me through the next couple of hours.

Once I crept down the mountain road—calling it a road was gracious—I waited for long minutes to make sure no cars were visible in either direction before pulling out onto the road and heading for the town. The ranches I passed were peaceful and quiet, even though I didn't like the wide-open space. There was even one ranch with walls like I'd never seen before. It looked more like a fortress or a jail than a ranch, but I knew full well some of the people here wanted to protect what was theirs at any cost.

The lights of the town came into view, and I slowed down. Not too much. I didn't want to attract attention for being too careful, just like I didn't want to speed through like I was a NASCAR driver.

The grocery store was exactly where I'd remembered, of course. Arrowhead Grocers. Small and very clearly closed, which was what I'd hoped.

A narrow alley between the buildings was just wide enough for me to pull the car in. Luckily, it was late enough no one was around on the streets either.

The alley behind the store was dark, but I could just make out a window into the back of the store. Perfect. If I was lucky, there would be no security tied to that window. Frankly, I didn't know enough about security systems to have an accurate guess, but in a small town with a small grocery store, I guessed—I hoped—they were more worried about the front door than a back window.

Pulling on the ski mask, I moved quickly. I had to. Otherwise, I was going to lose my nerve. I'd already remembered to grab the tire iron from the trunk that I'd spotted when I'd first taken the car after that night when everything happened. In the chaos, when they thought I was going to get checked out by the paramedics, I was slipping out the opposite door and getting the hell out of there.

The window smashed under the metal, and I ducked away from the shattering debris, protecting my eyes. I kept myself crouched low, waiting for any sign of an alarm or someone noticing the crash. Nothing. After a couple minutes, my lungs began to ease, and I needed to move. I couldn't discount a silent alarm, but it was already too late to worry about that.

Using the tire iron, I knocked the rest of the glass out of the frame so I wouldn't impale myself, and I looked around. A couple of trash cans and boxes. A dumpster. The dumpster looked the safest. I pulled it over as quickly and as silently as possible, hoisting myself up onto the lid. For once, I was glad to be tiny. It made not breaking the dumpster lid and fitting through the window a lot easier.

Peeking inside, I saw a small stock room. Perfect. Getting in would be fairly easy. I would collect what I needed, then use the back door. By the time any alarm was answered, I would be gone.

I hoped.

Carefully, I maneuvered myself through the window feet first.

It was awkward with nothing below the window to catch me, but I couldn't do anything about it. Pain bloomed down my torso, and I cursed, dropping the rest of the way and feeling a sickening pull in my side. Glancing up, I saw the source—an old piece of the metal window frame bent out of shape, which I'd just shoved myself onto.

"Fuck." Gritting my teeth, I pressed a hand to my shirt, already feeling wetness beneath it. Adding bandages and alcohol to the list of things I needed, I forced the injury out of my head. It wasn't a deep wound. Instinctually, I knew this wasn't life-threatening. I could make it until I got back to the cabin and treat it there. Getting in and out of here with the supplies I needed as quickly as possible was far more important.

I found a light, and I flipped it on. My clothes were nondescript, and both my face and hair were hidden by the ski mask. If there were cameras—and I didn't see any—I would simply be a small person in jeans and a long-sleeved black shirt that was way too big.

I scanned the shelves of the stock room so I could know what was here if I needed to come back later. And then I went to work. I moved to the front of the store, quickly and quietly. If I moved too fast, I could make a mess, and that would slow me down.

I spotted an alarm at the front of the store, blinking and armed. I wasn't sure why it hadn't been connected to the back window, but I counted my blessings.

I picked up a plastic basket and started to fill it. Bandages, alcohol, ibuprofen, and antibiotic cream. Cans of condensed soup. Instant potatoes. Things I could cook with my limited resources at the cabin—a camp stove and water.

Protein bars. Chicken and tuna packets and some pepperoni. Soon, the first basket was full. I put it by the back door and grabbed a second one. It was all I would be able to carry to the car.

Nuts, peanut butter, some small boxes of pasta, and a couple cans of sauce. Oatmeal and Pop-Tarts. I grabbed a loaf of bread and a few pieces of fruit too, knowing I would have to eat those first.

I was a small person. If I was careful, the food I had in the baskets could last me two weeks. Three, if I was very, very careful. And I would be. The food in the cabin had probably only been meant to last for three months, and I'd stretched it to double that time.

Putting the second basket by the back door, I swallowed the knot in my stomach and went to the counter. I'd worked enough retail in college to know how to work the cash register. There probably wouldn't be much in the drawer since they were closed, but a girl could try.

Wincing at the pull in my side, I silently promised I would find a way to pay them back once Simon was out of the picture and I wasn't a target anymore. Whoever owned this store didn't deserve this.

But then again, neither did I.

I was right—there wasn't much in the drawer, but it was enough. Maybe a hundred dollars in petty cash, which I could use to actually *buy* food the next time I needed it. I was still hopeful I could somehow crack the puzzle of where Simon had gone and not need the money, but I was trying to be realistic too.

Shoving the cash in my pocket, I groaned when I picked up the baskets. Fuck, my side hurt. I was glad it wasn't too far of a drive back to the cabin. I needed to clean it and get a bandage on it.

The back door let out a shriek when I pushed it open, the alarm finally activating with a noise that was too loud and too shrill. Adrenaline burst through my system, and I sprinted to the car, barely stopping to shove the baskets into the back seat before I was sliding behind the wheel. I drove straight forward down the alley and to the next road, doubling around in a different direction before turning back toward the cabin—and safety.

By the time I heard the sirens, I'd already reached the edge of town, and for the first time since I stepped out of the cabin, I felt like I could finally breathe.

Chapter 3

Emma

Everything was hazy.

I tried to roll over on the couch, but I'd already forgotten that was a fucking terrible idea. The cut in my side was so sensitive, just having any clothing on it was too much. Right now, I was in my jeans and the only bra I had, trying to minimize the agony.

When I'd gotten home from my thieving and brought all the food inside, the first thing I did—besides immediately opening a protein bar—was clean the cut and put one of the big bandages on it.

The medicine helped the first night to take away the pain, and yesterday it had seemed okay, until it started getting worse. A sharper pain, and my skin growing hot around it. I put on more cream and a new bandage, but nothing helped.

Now it was red and angry, aching and stabbing, and I knew I had a fever. Ever since I woke, I'd been shifting between hot and cold, and I was shivering no matter what temperature I felt like.

The wall of clues swam in front of my eyes, allowing me to pull out pieces I'd seen but never noticed before. Payments and shipments to Chicago and Detroit. Some of the repeating phone numbers were from there too—I Googled the area codes. Was that where he'd gone?

Maybe he had someone willing to take him in if he was shipping guns and drugs there. But the whole reason he was here in Montana—and the northern states in general—was the desolation. There was so much empty space out here, as well as a bunch of people who would rather mind their own business than anything else. He'd said as much. So I didn't think he would go to a city.

I shook my head and got dizzy. What was I thinking right now? I wasn't smart enough to figure this out. It was the same crap every time. I could recite anything I'd ever seen in full from memory, but when it came time to actually analyze it, it slipped out of my grasp like a live fish.

A shudder took me, chills running from my scalp all the way down my spine. I didn't have a thermometer, but I felt the fever getting worse. My body wasn't quite moving the way I wanted it to.

The laptop.

I blinked. It was on the floor where I guessed I'd left it, but I didn't remember putting it there. Medicine. I searched for medicine. I needed some sort of antibiotic. Would they sell that to me without a prescription? Hopefully. I didn't have another choice.

Fear gripped my lungs as I thought about going into the town in full daylight. But if I didn't do this, it would be too late. In the same way I knew the initial cut wasn't life-threatening, I could sense this situation was. I hadn't cleaned the wound well enough, or whatever had been on that rusty piece of metal had gone deeper than I'd been able to reach.

It was infected. I wasn't a doctor or a nurse, but given the way even television shows and movies treated infections, I knew it was bad.

I found a list in my search for natural antibiotics. Honey, garlic, and a bunch of things I didn't think your average grocery store might have.

Were they looking for me by now? I couldn't walk into Arrowhead Grocers and buy medicine with a side wound without giving away who I was and what I'd done. But the town had at least one other grocery store, and no one knew my face. It would be fine.

It had to be fine.

As if I was outside of myself, I recognized I was only so calm about it because I was becoming delirious, and the delirium was stronger than my fear.

I didn't bother to be quiet when I slipped on a clean dark shirt. All the clothes here were for a much larger person, and a man, but I couldn't wear the shirt that was torn and bloody. The cloth drifting over the wound hurt so bad I almost screamed, and having this much fabric on me only made my skin hotter. I pushed up the sleeves as much as I could and fumbled with the car keys.

They fell to the floor, creating an incredibly painful journey for me to bend down and grab them again.

The terrible, paralyzing thought slipped into my mind—I might have waited too long. I should have faced my fear and gone into the town yesterday and gotten something to stop this.

The money. I needed the money. Grabbing it off the table, I somehow was able to get it into my pocket.

I shut the door behind me, feeling unsteady on my feet. It

was so hot out here; I was going to combust. If I actually made it down the mountain, it would be a miracle.

My hands were sweating, slipping on the steering wheel, but I did make it down the mountain and onto the main road. I wasn't going as fast as I should, but it didn't matter. As long as I *stayed* on the road, I didn't care.

One of the other grocery stores was off the main road through town, and I lurched into the parking lot, not fully bothering to park between the lines. I got close enough.

"Garlic and honey," I muttered to myself. "Garlic and honey."

First though, I would go to the pharmacy. The worst they could say was no. I leaned heavily on the shelves as I waited behind the two people in front of me. Standing on my own would make me look crazy, swaying back and forth on my feet. I couldn't afford to look crazy, even if I felt like it.

A red-haired woman smiled from behind the counter. "How can I help you?"

Focus, Emma. "I was wondering if there were any…" My mind blanked, and I had to pull it back. "Antibiotics you could sell me over the counter? My sister cut her arm, and we can't see the doctor for a few days."

She frowned, and I saw her looking me up and down. Had I sounded convincing? I had no idea. "Unfortunately, I can't. I have some cream we can sell you, but if you come back in a couple of hours, the pharmacist will be here. That's one of the things they can prescribe, but you'll have to bring your sister with you."

"I'll take the cream," I said, my throat dry. "And come back."

Crap. I didn't have that kind of time. Maybe I could try the last grocery store in town and see if their pharmacist was in. Otherwise? I was out of options, because a hospital wasn't one.

Seemed like maybe Simon might get what he wanted—me, dead, and he didn't even have to do it himself.

She gave me the box of cream, and I managed to pay her and grab the change. "Hey, wait—"

I didn't. I tried to remain focused—remain *conscious*—as I part walked, part stumbled out of the pharmacy and down the block to the grocery store. I made it inside, forcing back the gray along the edges of my vision.

"Garlic and honey," I muttered.

What kind of garlic did I need? Shit, I hadn't read that on the website. I searched my memory. Because of the fever, I hadn't fully processed the page and therefore couldn't remember what it had said.

I pulled a jar of minced garlic off the shelf, knowing I wouldn't have the strength to crush it. A small bottle of honey, too. The lights in the store were blowing out, brighter than they had any right to be. Everything that had a reflection seemed to swim.

Was this what it was like to be on acid? If it was, I couldn't recommend it. Every breath hurt, and my pulse pounded in the cut so it marked out the time in painful heartbeats.

The cashier took one look at me and did a double take. "Whoa, lady. Are you okay?"

"I'm fine." I nearly dropped the bottle of honey onto the belt, knocking over the garlic with it. "Promise."

He was a kid. A teenager, maybe. Black hair and bright eyes. He reminded me of me when the world wasn't so bad. Hopefully he'd have a good life.

It took me way too long to count out the money, focusing on every individual movement I had to make. "Keep the change."

"Seriously, ma'am, are you sick? Do you need me to call someone?"

"I'm fine." I grabbed the plastic bag and held it to my chest. "I'm fine, thanks."

It was a lie. I was very much not fine. My balance was nearly gone. My head felt huge and heavy, and my feet felt like they were both feathers and weights at the same time. Everything was reduced to echoes of pain radiating through the wound in my side.

True, cold fear struck me to the core as a single thought penetrated my fever.

I wasn't going to make it.

There wasn't any coming back from this now. I wouldn't make it to the hospital. Hell, I was barely going to make it to my car. At least if I made it to the car, I could lie down.

But I could lie down on the pavement too. Wouldn't that be nice? The world began to tilt, and it no longer seemed like a bad thing. Somewhere, I heard shouting.

My vision darkened, and pain exploded through me as something struck my side. But it wasn't pavement. It was warm, living, and breathing. Someone caught me.

"Whoa, hey. Hey, I've got you. Are you okay?"

I cracked open my eyes, and I knew I was already gone, because it was him. The man from my dreams. He had let me out of one cage, and now he was going to let me out of another.

That was nice of him.

It's you, I thought at him, trying to smile before the world went dark.

Chapter 4

Daniel

I stared down at the woman in my arms in shock, horror, and disbelief.

It was *her*.

The woman from the cage, the same woman who'd been haunting my dreams for months. Part of me wondered if I was hallucinating, but I knew her face as well as my own. Hell, I saw her face more often than I looked in a mirror.

Her face was red, and she was sweating. The way she'd swayed on her feet, she was sick. One touch of my fingers to her forehead confirmed that.

She was here.

I shook my head, forcing myself out of shock and into action. My years of training clicked into place, replacing emotion with logic and the mission, which was to finally be able to save this woman's life.

Shifting, I moved my hand and saw blood. What the hell?

Undressing someone in a parking lot wasn't my style, but I didn't need to peek under her shirt far to see the problem. A gash across her ribs. Red, inflamed, and now bleeding. She had one hell of an infection, and if it was that far along…

This woman would not die on my watch. Not after all these months wondering where she was.

She shifted in my arms, not fully unconscious. "Hey," I said evenly, trying to be comforting as I moved, lifting her up and starting toward my truck. "My name is Daniel, and I've got you."

I heard a whisper of a moan in response.

"You're very sick. I need to get you to a hospital."

"No." It was the only clear thing about what she said, all other words unintelligible. She wasn't even fully awake, but she fought me, twisting to get away from me even as I fought to hold on so she wouldn't injure herself falling to the pavement. "No hospital."

That explained why her infection was this bad in the first place, if she refused to go to the emergency room.

What could I do? She was delirious and needed medical attention. But my instinct also told me if she was fighting me this badly to get away from me when she likely knew she was dying, she had a good reason.

Fine. We wouldn't go to the hospital. The hospital would come to her. I set her on the passenger side of the truck, letting her slump down until her torso lay across it, making sure nothing was pressing on the injury. I made the seat belt as loose as I could manage, and then my phone was in my hand.

I called Liam as I started the truck. He was in the lodge now and could set things in motion.

"Hello?"

"Listen closely, because we don't have a lot of time. I'm

incoming with a woman who's very sick and refuses to go to the hospital, but if she doesn't get medical attention, she's not going to make it. Call Dr. Gold. I don't care if she's at the hospital or not. Get her to the ranch. I'll pay whatever it takes.

"Have someone go to the Rattlesnake cabin and make sure the bed is made and there's enough room for the doctor to work. Get the emergency medical equipment over there too. And have someone ready to go to the grocery store on Everett and Main to get her car. I have the keys, and I'll be there in ten minutes."

"Daniel—"

"Liam. Do it. You can ask me everything later."

"Got it."

The line went dead, and I focused everything on driving. She was moving and breathing, but barely. I reached over and pressed my fingers to her pulse, just under her jaw, and my gut tightened. It was way too fast.

Way too fucking fast.

The mission was still in the forefront of my mind, but I couldn't fully ignore the growing terror in my gut. She couldn't die. She *couldn't* die. I couldn't have one more person who'd been locked in a cage die because I hadn't done enough.

Fuck, maybe I should turn around and take her to the hospital anyway.

By all rights, I probably should have done that to begin with. But my instincts said to trust her when she said she couldn't go there. Given my history, I found it hard to trust those instincts now, but I clenched my teeth and pressed down on the accelerator.

The smallest whimper came from the passenger side, and I glanced away from the road only to make sure she was still breathing and wasn't about to fall off the seat. "Almost there," I told her. "Hang on. We're going to take care of you. Promise."

In my gut, I hoped it was a promise I would be able to keep. If it wasn't, I would live with that statement for the rest of my life.

The walls of Resting Warrior came into view, and I barely slowed turning through the open gate. Another truck pulled in behind me on the road down to the cabins. Noah's truck. I saw both him and Kate in the rearview mirror. Liam must have called them.

I didn't bother to park well. Just as close to the stairs as possible.

Noah jumped out of his truck, and I tossed him the keys. "Take Liam," I called. "When he gets out here. Go for the car."

"What the hell is going on?" he asked, snatching the keys out of the air.

I ignored him, circling my own truck and yanking the passenger door open. The seat belt had kept her in place, but she'd slid a little, leaning forward off the bench. I tried to be gentle as I freed her and lifted her out of the passenger seat. The door to the cabin behind me opened.

"It's ready," Liam said, and I didn't look at anyone else as I carried her inside.

She was here.

I still wasn't fully comprehending the fact that it was her and somehow the world had put her in my path at exactly the right moment. "Is Dr. Gold coming?"

"She is," Liam called from behind me. "She wasn't at the hospital, so she'll be here shortly. Wasn't exactly pleased to be summoned, but I told her what you said."

The bed was made but turned down, and I laid her down on it. She was too hot to cover her with the blankets, and Dr. Gold needed access to her anyway.

Those of us who lived and worked here essentially considered Dr. Gold *our* doctor. She'd been there through most of our trials, and she was less than surprised now when one of our large family appeared with some kind of injury. After Evelyn, almost nothing was a shock.

My medical training was limited, but I knew enough to take her vitals so I could give them to the doctor when she arrived. I started with her temperature.

One hundred and four. Fuck.

"Oh my god." Kate's voice sounded from behind me. "It's her."

"Who?" Noah asked.

"The woman who was in the cages with me."

"No," Liam said. "Really?"

He would understand why I was panicking after what I'd told him the other day. Kate, too, had wondered about this woman's well-being. We'd spoken about it several times. Though I didn't think Noah's girlfriend had this woman starring in her nightmares with the same regularity.

Pulse nearly 140. She was in a bad state.

"Why didn't you take her to the hospital, Daniel?" Noah asked.

"I tried." I stood, running a hand through my hair. "While barely conscious, she tried to *fight me* to keep from going. After what we pulled her out of, I thought there might be a good reason she didn't want to go."

He didn't look sure, and I wasn't either, but now wasn't the time to voice my own doubts.

"Get the car," I said. "I'll wait for the doctor, and we'll talk about it when you get back."

Liam nodded. "Why the insistence on the car?"

"We don't know where she's been. It could tell us something if we need to know." I also didn't want her to feel trapped once she recovered. And she *would* recover.

"All right. We'll be back shortly. Call if you need something." Noah looked behind me at the unconscious woman with worry before he left the cabin, and I walked with Liam toward the door.

He lingered for a moment. "Are you all right? Because… Holy shit. You were just saying…"

"I know." I shook my head. "Am I all right? I have no idea. All I know is I need to keep her alive. Anything else can come later. Thank you for doing everything so quickly."

"No problem. Like Noah said, we'll be back soon. You should call everyone else and get them here. Not because she's here, but because of where we found her."

He had a point. The Riders had dropped off the radar, but we still had our ears to the ground for any information that might come our way, as did our friends. We didn't discount the threat Simon had leveled at us before he'd tried to murder Noah. That kind of threat didn't disappear simply because the person went to ground.

Regardless, when she was well enough to speak, we needed to talk to her. Gently, of course, but any information she had would be valuable.

"Yeah. I'll get them in."

A car—a sedan—was driving down the road toward us. Most of us had trucks, which meant this was Dr. Gold. The relief I felt was palpable.

Liam clapped me on the shoulder, and I waited for her to get out of the car. She didn't look happy, and I wouldn't be either if I were rudely summoned on my day off. Not that I really had any days off.

"Daniel," she said. "What's going on?"

She grabbed a bag from the back seat and met me on the porch. "A woman. She has a wound on the right side of her torso, clearly infected. Temperature of 104 and a heart rate of 140."

"Jesus." The word was muttered under her breath. As soon as we entered the room, she got to work, confirming my facts.

Kate was still here, too, and pale as a sheet. "You all right?"

"Yes. Just…everything."

Seeing this woman again would bring up painful memories for Kate. Noah had nearly died, and she certainly would have been next if we hadn't made it in time to intervene. "Step out if you need to," I said.

"Daniel, help me get her shirt off so I can see this."

I only hesitated for a second. It felt wrong to undress someone when they weren't conscious, but if we didn't do this and she died—

It was easy to lift her up and help Dr. Gold slip the shirt over her head. The woman moved in response to the fabric brushing the wound, and Kate gasped as it came into view. It wasn't pretty.

Not particularly long, but a decent depth. It was so inflamed it looked much larger than it was. "Daniel, she needs to be in a hospital. I'll call an ambulance."

"No," I said.

She looked at me, shocked. "Excuse me?"

I told the doctor briefly how I'd found her—caught sight of her walking across the parking lot and did a double take at seeing the woman I'd been searching for. Noticing her about to fall and barely catching her before she cracked her head on the pavement.

"She wasn't completely out, and when I told her I was taking her to the hospital, she fought me like a wildcat." I didn't like to say the words out loud, but I did. "I think she would have let herself die instead of going to the hospital. If she was that desperate, she has to have a good reason."

"That's not always my experience."

Slowly, I took a breath in and out. "If there's no other way, fine. But whatever it takes. I'll pay whatever needs to be paid to have her fully taken care of here."

Dr. Gold closed her eyes. "I'll do my best, given those are her current wishes. But if she gets any worse, there will be an ambulance here, and I won't ask permission before calling it. You have emergency fluids?"

I pointed to the crate in the adjacent kitchen filled with our emergency supplies, which included far more than the average first aid kit. Fluids and antibiotics were only part of the contents.

She got the line of fluids started and cleaned and dressed the wound faster and more efficiently than I could have, but the antibiotics we had weren't in liquid form. "I need more than you have," Dr. Gold said. "Watch her. If her pulse gets faster or her temperature rises any more before I get back, *bring her in*, Daniel. And if she shows any sign of consciousness, get those pills in her. The fever reducer too." She pulled a sample of blood from the woman's arm. "I need to run some tests and get antibiotics. I'm also stating once again, keeping her here is a bad idea. And when I can talk to her, I will make that very clear."

"We won't leave her," I said.

Everything Dr. Gold said was true. But the desperation in this woman's voice when she'd begged me not to take her to the hospital was still so vivid in my mind, I couldn't escape it.

I glanced at Kate, who said nothing. I seriously hoped I was making the right decision.

Dr. Gold already had her phone to her ear as she walked out the door.

As soon as she was gone, I picked up the woman's limp wrist and felt her pulse. It was a little slower but still felt as fast as a hummingbird's. She made a sound, moving a little, and I looked at Kate. "Water?"

She was back in under a minute with a glass of water. I squeezed the wrist I was holding gently. "Can you hear me?"

She didn't give a direct response, but she seemed to be surfacing. I wished she could stay unconscious since she was clearly in pain, but this would help her. "If you can hear me, can you open your eyes? We need to give you some medicine to help you."

She made a sound, something like a moan, and her eyelids fluttered. But then, nothing.

"I know it's hard." I took her hand. "If you think you could swallow some pills, just squeeze my hand."

She did. It was brief and weak, but distinct.

"Good. Okay, that's good." I took the water from Kate. "We'll do one at a time."

Leaning forward, I scooped my hand under her head, lifting her gently so she was more upright. I couldn't do everything, holding her like this. "Kate, the pills."

She was already there, and it was agonizing. One pill and then another, letting enough water into her mouth for her to swallow, and watching to make sure it all made it down. When all of them were safely taken, I felt like I could breathe a little easier. The antibiotics would start to work on whatever had injured her side, and the rest would begin to lower her temperature.

I eased her back down onto the bed and heard the slam of a car door. "Will you stay with her?"

"Of course."

Noah and Liam were back, Jude and Lucas in tow. I pulled out my phone and dialed Harlan. "Someone call Grant."

Jude called him, and soon all seven of us were there in one way or another. "Fill us in?" Noah asked.

"Yeah." I was still reeling, but I told them everything. I told them about the dreams too, though not in quite as much detail as I'd given Liam. But I needed to explain how I'd recognized her so immediately.

Everything.

I finished, and the guys with me were watching me carefully. Jude leaned back against the porch railing. "What can we do?"

"Dr. Gold will hopefully be back soon. As long as this woman's here, she can't be alone. Even once she's conscious, I think I want someone here on the porch so she doesn't run without us knowing she's up to it. And I just…" I sighed. "I want to make sure she's okay. You know enough about why."

Noah inclined his head. "Yes. Can't say I disagree. But we need to be careful, too. If having her here will draw the Riders' attention."

"Maybe that's why she didn't want to go to the hospital," Grant said through the phone.

I'd had the same thought. "We'll stay alert. Thank you, guys. I'll be the one to stay with her for a while. I don't think I could make myself stay away anyway."

Noah smiled, and it was a knowing smile. He'd felt the same way about Kate, and now Kate was a part of the family. But it wasn't the same. Was it?

"I'll come back later," Liam said. "So you can sleep."

"Thanks."

I went back inside. "I'll stay with her now. Noah is outside."

"Okay. Let me know how she is?" Kate asked.

"I will."

It was quiet with everyone gone. Pulling one of the chairs from the kitchen table, I sat on it heavily. She was so still. Breathing, but no other signs of life. And she was pale. When I checked her pulse, it was better.

I thought about Noah's smile, and I looked at her. She

was beautiful. Younger than I remembered, but beautiful even in this state.

But even if that were in the cards for me, this wasn't the time to think about it. If—*when*—she woke up, we didn't know what we'd find or who she'd be. All I knew was the world had offered me a second chance to protect this woman, and I was going to give *everything* I had to do it.

Chapter 5

Emma

I'd had this dream before. Coming out of the cage and feeling his hand on mine.

"You're okay." His voice echoed in my head. "We've got you."

Kind, dark eyes and a concerned smile. I wanted to curl up in that smile and the sound of his voice. This was where the dream usually shifted. He pulled away, just like he had that night. Handed me off to a man with a vest and a gun to take me to the ambulance.

But this time, he didn't let go. I tripped over my own feet, and he caught me. "Can you hear me?"

I could hear him. Voice warm like butter and the gentle sun of a spring afternoon. It bathed me in gentle heat. But the heat didn't stop, and it was too much.

There were other words, but I was dizzy. This dream no longer made any sense. Where was I? Where were we? Why did everything hurt, and why could I hear my pulse in my ears?

I didn't know—I just wanted it all to stop.

It was forever and not long at all before I suddenly felt awake. Not fully, but I was in my body. This wasn't a dream, and *man,* that hurt. I was still so hot I was sweating.

I was at the grocery store, and I'd been going to the car…

My eyes flew open, and I was in a dim room, and *he* was sitting there. The man from my dream was sitting in a chair, looking at his phone. He was literally three feet away from me, and I didn't know what to do. Where was I, and how the hell did I get here?

Did I misjudge him completely and I was captive once again? My mind felt fuzzy. "Where am I?"

He startled, looking up and realizing I was awake. I shrank back instinctually. Even now, sudden movements made me jumpy. "Why am I here?" My words came out in a voice that wasn't fully focused.

There was an IV in my arm, and my stomach dropped. What were they doing to me? The logical part of my brain told me this was helping. I'd collapsed in the parking lot, and he'd somehow found me there. But the logical side of my brain wasn't the one driving.

He held out his hands like he was surrendering. "It's good to see you awake. My name is Daniel. What's your name?"

Why did my heart sink at those words? I knew who he was, of course. You never forgot the face of the person who saved your life. But he didn't know who I was. There was no recognition in the face I was looking at now.

Okay. This was a good thing. If he didn't know who I was, he wouldn't be worried about Simon or the rest of them. And the selfish part of me didn't want him to know that side of me.

This could also be an opportunity to find out what he knew about Simon. I had no idea if he knew anything, but on the off chance he did and it could help me solve the mess of a puzzle back at the cabin…? I would take the chance.

"Can you tell me your name?" he asked again, and I loved the tone of his voice. It was soft, gentle, and felt like safety. But I couldn't tell him anything.

"I—" I swallowed. Everything was still hazy. Pain throbbed in my side and in my head, and I was covered with a blanket. No wonder I was sweating. "I don't know."

I tried to sit, and the blanket slipped down, revealing the fact that my shirt was gone. I was in my pants and bra. "What? Why?"

Daniel held out a hand. "The doctor was here to see you, and she needed to reach your wound. That's the only part of you we touched. I promise."

I looked around too quickly. This didn't look like what I thought a hospital room should look like, but this far out in the country, maybe it was different. "Is this a hospital? I'm not in a hospital, right?"

"No," he said quickly. "You made it very clear you didn't want to go. Nearly jumped out of my arms and straight onto the asphalt. You don't remember your name?"

Shaking my head immediately made me dizzy and hurt. The room spun. "Whoa. Dizzy. Wow." I let the question about my name pass by.

"So you don't remember what happened to you?"

"No. I mean, I remember cutting myself, but I don't remember anything else. I've been in a cabin in the woods trying to figure it out. I just kind of…showed up there." The lie wasn't a solid one, but he didn't seem to question it.

What I did see was a shade of disappointment. Why? He didn't remember me, so why would *my* memories matter?

I needed to go back to sleep. Or leave. Whichever made it easier to *think*. It felt like my brain was stuffed with cotton, and my thoughts were moving in complete slow motion.

"Can you drink something?"

Daniel picked up a glass of water and held it toward me, and all my instincts made me back the hell up, pressing myself into the far corner of the bed even though I knew he wasn't going to be the one to hurt me.

"It's okay. It will be here when you want it." He put the glass down on the table at the side of the bed.

We stared at each other, and I took the time to look at him. Really look at him. All these months, I'd been living off a half-formed dream of his face, and now, every detail was here for me to drink in and remember. Now my dreams would be much more vivid. That was nice.

"How did I get here?"

"I brought you," he said. "You were about to fall in the parking lot of a grocery store. Do you remember that?"

I did remember that. The last few moments of consciousness came back to me with clarity. I'd seen it was him, and I'd known. Had I said it out loud? If I had, this lie I was telling wouldn't hold up.

"Yeah."

"A doctor I know is helping take care of you, but she would like you to go to the hospital, if you're willing."

"No." Even in this state, I managed to make the word forceful. "No hospitals."

"I figured you'd say that. Which is why we're taking care of you here."

I frowned. "Where is here?"

"Resting Warrior Ranch. We're a little way outside Garnet Bend, to the north."

That was the right direction, at least. If I needed to get out of here.

He leaned forward, and I was briefly distracted by the way his shirt stretched over his arms and chest. It would be a lie to say the dreams of him had always stayed innocent. They hadn't. Now that he was here, I was thinking about them, and I was out of my mind enough to imagine stretching across the space between us and kissing him.

"What do you remember? If you don't mind my asking. We'd like to help you if we can."

I swallowed. How much did I tell him? The lie I'd already told was delicate. I wasn't well enough to keep track of the threads. "I…guess I woke up in a cabin. There was food, and I just stayed there, trying to remember and figure out what was going on."

The only part that was a lie was my waking up there. I had stayed there, searching my memory and trying to figure out where Simon had gone.

"Do you remember me?"

Shock hit me first. So, he *did* remember me? I was suddenly dying to know what he remembered and what he thought of me, but I'd already told the lie. I couldn't turn back now.

It hurt to slowly shake my head. That was a lie I might regret later, but I needed to be safer than sorry. I hoped he would understand that if I ever had to tell him the truth.

"Do you remember your name?" he asked again.

"Emma." I immediately winced. Probably should have given him a fake name, but the pain and the heat and the dizziness…

I sank back down onto the bed, resting my head. That felt better.

"Emma," he said. "It's nice to meet you."

The way he said my name would stay with me. I knew that much.

"We're giving you fluids and antibiotics. Whatever cut you gave you a nasty infection. You need to rest for a while. The doctor made it clear to stay off your feet."

My hand went to my side, feeling the new bandage there. It still hurt like a bitch when I touched it, but it wasn't quite as hot. An improvement, at least.

"Thank you."

Daniel's phone buzzed in his hand, and he smiled a little. "I'll be right back. If you can stomach trying to remember, I have some questions I'd like to ask you?"

"Sure. I don't know what good it will do, though."

"That's all right. We can still try." He stood and left the room. Someone was out there, and their voices were low, but with the cracked door I could still hear them.

"She's awake?" It was a second male voice.

"Yeah. Still clearly groggy. I don't expect her to stay awake for long. Her body is exhausted."

A sigh. "Have you asked her yet? About the—"

"About the Riders?" My whole body went still with fear, just the word causing all my senses to fire. "Not yet. She claims not to remember anything."

"Do you believe her?"

I couldn't see Daniel's face, but a long silence followed the question. "I don't have a reason not to. We have no idea what they did to her. If there was a trauma, her mind could have blocked it entirely. She said I can ask her questions, but if she really doesn't remember anything…"

"Yeah."

"Dinner's here. Take a break for a minute and eat it. You've been sitting in here for hours."

A shuffle of footsteps. "Hold on one second."

I went limp, falling back onto the pillows and letting my

eyes close. I evened my breathing and made it seem as if I was asleep.

The door closed softly, and the footsteps retreated. Now his voice was muffled. "I was right. She's already out again. I guess food it is."

I opened my eyes. He was bothered I didn't remember him, and a small piece of my heart started to hope for all the wrong reasons. The one-in-a-million chance he'd been thinking about me the same way I'd been thinking about him.

In the end, it didn't matter. Even if Daniel was a good man—and despite my dreams and them trying to take out Simon, I had no actual proof of that—I couldn't stay here. Sure, this wasn't a hospital, but being around any people at all was a risk. I'd given him my real name, *and* he knew about the Riders.

It was too risky. It put my life in danger, and possibly theirs too.

Fuck.

I leaned my head back and shut my eyes for a second. Leaving was the last thing I wanted to do. Having someone take care of me and actually give a damn if I made it? That sounded nice.

Too bad I didn't have room for *nice* in my life anymore.

Slowly, I looked around the room. It had a couple windows, and outside, the light told me the day was fading. There was still plenty of light left, but if I wanted to make it back to the cabin before it was pitch black outside, I needed to go now.

I reached for the needle in my arm and paused. Taking it out was not a good idea. I'd planned on taking the bag with me, but I didn't have a way to put the needle back in. I'd have to make do.

My shirt was at the end of the bed. I slipped it on, being

careful of the IV line. My shoes were still on, proving what Daniel had said was true—the shirt was the only part of me they touched.

Moving so slowly I felt like a sloth, I eased myself off the bed and unhooked the bags of fluids from the stand by the bed. At the very least, I would get the rest of these in me. Then I could try again at a different pharmacy. Or drive to a different town altogether.

My car.

Crap, I didn't have my car. Not like the car wouldn't make them notice me anyway. But it wasn't enough to make me stop. These guys had had the police with them when they came for Simon. If they said my name in connection with the Riders in front of the police, questions might get asked about the car and me in the parking lot. Simon could already know I was here.

I'd figure out the car thing later.

Pain flared in my side as I moved, and I fought down the cry of distress that wanted to come out of my mouth. I needed to stay quiet. Only the low hum of voices came from the other room; anything more than a whisper, and they'd hear me.

The window opened easily, and it wasn't so high that I would hurt myself going out of it.

I've got to stop climbing through windows.

It wasn't easy to maneuver myself holding two delicate bags of liquids, but I got my butt on the windowsill and dropped the couple of feet to the grass below.

My vision went white with the pain, and I groaned softly. It was okay. I could still make it.

Alarm bells went off in my mind, telling me I was making a mistake, but I couldn't stop moving. My fear was greater than the instinct to stay, and whatever the case, I was already out.

This was a wide-open space, and the *exposed* feeling of it was just as bad as driving down that road. A road I would have to walk down to get to the cabin. It was fine. I could make it. I would get back there to all my notes, eat something, let the medicine heal me, and everything would be clearer.

Please, I thought, my mind still at war with itself, *please let me be right.*

Every step jostled the wound, and somehow it seemed to hurt more now that I wasn't as delirious. That had been masking some of the pain.

In the distance, I saw a familiar wall, and I suddenly realized where I was. The intimidating ranch with walls that had seemed strange to me.

That was good. Closer to the cabin than I'd actually hoped. It was still far on foot, and I would be dragging when I got there, but I could make it.

I kept glancing around, but I saw no one as I made it to the wall and down to the gate. No one as I slipped through it and along the road to the north.

One good thing about my memory—I never needed directions.

I took a deep breath, wincing, holding the bags up to my chest so they could still flow, and I started walking.

I could make it.

Steeling myself, I blocked the pain from my mind.

I *would* make it.

Chapter 6

Daniel

The pizza Liam brought was completely demolished. He'd rightly pointed out that I'd forgotten to eat today. I hadn't even thought about it. When I'd spotted Emma across the parking lot of the grocery store, I'd been there to pick up some things for myself. Obviously, that didn't happen.

I rolled her name over in my mind again. *Emma.* A pretty, simple name. Her eyes were still so fascinating, one blue and one brown. No wonder I'd never forgotten her. She was truly striking.

Her fever had come down to a manageable level, and her heart rate had eased enough that when Dr. Gold came back for the second evaluation and to drop off the needed medication, she'd seemed much more confident in letting Emma rest here. Though she left more strict instructions on what signs to watch for and when we should bring her in if we saw any of them.

"That was good," Liam said. "Probably should have

brought two. I didn't realize you were going to turn into a vacuum."

"I'll probably regret it later."

"Ah, yes." Liam's grin told me what was coming. "I hear that happens when you get old."

I smirked. "Something to look forward to, then? Ten years goes faster than you think."

"True." He was silent for a moment before he looked at me. "Can I ask you something?"

"Sure." His face was uncharacteristically serious, and I wondered if it had anything to do with his walk the other morning.

Liam laid a palm on the table, hand flexing and closing a couple of times like he was arranging his thoughts. "If you were in a position like Jude was with Lena…where you'd liked someone for a long time, except they didn't know about it, what would you do?"

My brain automatically flipped through the roster of people we knew, wondering who he was talking about. Whoever it was, he'd hidden it well. "Do you think they'd be open to it?"

"I don't know. She's not exactly…talkative." He smiled sheepishly, knowing the clue gave it away.

My eyebrows rose into my hairline. "How long?"

"A while," he shrugged. Which likely meant longer than he was comfortable saying.

Mara had been a quiet and steady presence at the ranch nearly since the beginning. Just recently, she'd started to talk more, and the night of the fire and Riders' raid, she'd surprised the hell out of me by calling me and saying more than I'd heard from her in the last three years.

"You seem worried about it."

He sighed. "We've talked a little. I go out of my way to do it when I can. But I know enough about where she came from. I don't want to overstep any boundaries. And if she doesn't want the advance, I don't want to turn Resting Warrior into a place that feels unsafe for her. It's her home too."

I smiled. Liam might goof off and be the joker of the bunch, but he had a good heart. His considerations alone proved that. "I understand the hesitation. But if she said no—"

"That would be that. Of course."

"Then I wouldn't worry too much about making this place feel unsafe for her. But I still get the risk, with her background. Let me think on it? Maybe there's a way to approach it and get your answer and keep everything well insulated."

"I appreciate it."

I chuckled. "You've certainly hidden it well."

"Not well enough. Jude and Noah have both figured it out. I thought Jude was going to spit it out at Thanksgiving when I was giving him and Lena shit."

That made me laugh fully. We'd noticed Liam had backed off the jokes he'd long promised to make about the pining couple. But what he'd just admitted was nowhere near the reason I'd assumed. "I don't think Jude would do that."

"Probably not, but I'll be on my best behavior, regardless."

"Noted."

I weighed Liam and Mara together in my mind. It wasn't the first pairing I'd single out, but it did make sense in a way. Much of Liam's bluster and joking was to hide exactly how much he cared about others and a shield against getting too close to anyone who could hurt him.

Mara had been hurt too, and the past few years of seeing her slowly heal and become more confident, and even talk a little bit, had been nice. Maybe not an easy path to pursue, but if she was open, I could see them being a good match.

He certainly talked enough for the both of them.

"You should go get some rest, Daniel," he said finally. "You've been here all day, and you and I both know this means more to you than you're willing to admit. Which also means you won't leave unless I make you leave, and you'll be back here at the ass-crack of dawn."

"Am I that transparent?"

"People get more obvious as they get older."

I raised an eyebrow. "Don't push your luck."

He laughed.

"I'll just look in on her and make sure she's not awake."

"Sure. You can leave the door open a little. I don't want to scare her if she wakes up to another strange man in the room, but that could let her know someone's here."

A good plan. I eased the door open, and the knob pulled out of my hand with suction. I saw the open window first, and my stomach plummeted. The bed was empty, the IV bags were gone, and Emma had disappeared entirely.

I cursed, grabbing for my phone. How long had she been gone? Between the pizza and talking, I'd left her alone for at least an hour. She could be practically anywhere at this point.

Especially if she hitched a ride.

Don't think about that.

I should have expected this. She'd literally fought to get away when she was practically dead on her feet. Why wouldn't she run now? She wasn't well enough to be on her feet—both of us knew that—and she'd still left.

"What happened?" Liam asked, already on his feet.

"She's gone. Out the window."

He cursed too.

I froze, trying to think this through.

If someone didn't want to get well, I couldn't force them. One of the things about managing a place like this was learning you couldn't help people who weren't ready. Maybe Emma wasn't ready, but I also couldn't simply let her go.

She was sick, alone, and she was confused about who she was. The connection I felt to her completely aside, I couldn't stomach the thought of another person dying when I could prevent it.

Had I frightened her? Made her feel unsafe?

I shook my head. There were a hundred reasons she could have felt the need to leave. Her inexplicable fear of hospitals, or perhaps medical staff in general, was one of them.

She'd taken the bags of fluids with her, though, which told me she didn't have a death wish.

Grant was at the lodge and closest to the security room. But he was also working on a plan of action for a new client arriving next week and not constantly watching the cameras.

"Yeah?"

"I need you to roll back the tapes on the gate for the last hour. The woman—Emma—is gone. If she left the property, tell me which way she went."

There was silence on the other end of the line. "If she doesn't want to be here, we can't force her, Daniel."

Frustration bubbled under my skin. "I know. But before I let her go, I'd like to make sure she's not dead in a ditch or on the side of the road, given she shouldn't even be walking."

"Yeah, that's fair," he said, and I heard the hesitancy in his voice. "She went north, and yeah, she doesn't seem like she should be on her feet. But moving at a decent pace in spite of that."

"Thanks." I headed for the front door. "Let's go."

"Are you okay to do this?" Liam asked.

I stopped and looked at him, trying to be objective and examining myself. "I know this means more to me than the average case that walks through our gates, but I'm still me. I will treat Emma with the respect she deserves. I'm not sure why anyone thinks differently."

He held out his hands. "That's not what I meant, Daniel. Not at all."

"Then let's go."

He looked like he wanted to say something more, but he didn't. The trucks were all back at the lodge, and I jogged there, Liam in tow. It was getting dark now, the sun nearly below the horizon. If she'd made it far enough to get into the foothills—which I doubted—it would be much harder to find her.

I spotted footprints in the dirt as I turned out of the gate, confirming her direction, and my heart was in my throat as I kept an eye on the side of the road for a crumpled body. But we didn't find her lying dead, which was a relief.

She got a hell of a lot farther than I expected, given her condition. Nearly to the break in the farmland, where it would have been easy to lose her in the woods at the base of the mountains.

On the ground, leaning against a fence post, Emma looked as white as paper. It was disconcerting to see someone a color so unnatural.

"Shit, is she still alive?" Liam asked.

"I can only hope so."

I pulled the truck over to the side of the road, leaving a good distance between her and me. The last thing we needed was for me to spook her and for her to run into the road.

She startled at the sound of my door closing, head jerking toward me, and the only thing I saw was fear.

"Liam," I said. "Stay there, please."

Her eyes were locked on me as I approached, wild as a

cornered animal, and so, so afraid. It cracked my heart open to see that fear, so similar to how she'd looked all those months ago when I'd pulled her out of the cage.

"Emma," I said, keeping my voice low and gentle. "Are you all right?"

She shook her head no. "You don't understand. I had to leave. I had to leave, okay?"

About ten feet away, I crouched, so I was on her level. "I'm not angry." I wasn't sure why those were the words I said, but they felt right. "And I'm not here to drag you anywhere you don't want to go. I just want you to be well. You're sick."

"I have to go."

"Tell you what," I said. "When you're better, I'll take you wherever you want to go, no questions asked. I promise. All we want to do is help you get better."

She stared at me for a long time. Long enough the light shifted, everything around us darkening noticeably. Finally, she moved, and I heard a small sound of pain she tried to hide. "I don't want to die."

"I'm not going to let you die." It was a promise as well. "Will you let me help you?"

Emma nodded once, and it was good enough for me. I went to her, still keeping every movement smooth, steady, and visible. Even if she didn't remember, Emma was reacting to her trauma, and I needed to be careful. The bags of fluids were cradled in her lap.

"I'm going to pick you up and carry you to the truck. Can you put your arm around my neck?"

She did, clumsily. It wasn't ideal to lift her on the side with her wound, but I didn't want to risk tangling the tubes she miraculously still had in her arm. Now that she was in my arms, she felt light. Instinctually, she curled into me, and I forgot myself for a moment.

That implicit trust was something I craved. Caring for someone who needed me, in the same way I did at Resting Warrior. But I didn't interact with the clients much. Emma was far more personal, and helping her was soothing some of the rough edges of my tattered soul.

If things were different, and I were different, Emma was someone I could see myself caring for forever. I shouldn't notice the way she fit in my arms like she was meant to be there. I shouldn't notice how beautiful she was when she was so close to death's door.

But I did notice those things.

"It's not safe," she said quietly. "It's not safe for me. Or you."

"It's okay," I promised. "You are safe. You are."

"No." She shook her head, but the movement was barely perceptible. "Not safe for *you*." Her body went limp as she lost consciousness, and I tried not to let the words strike home. She wasn't thinking straight.

Liam was already on the passenger side of the truck, holding the door open. "She all right?"

"For now. Let's get her back to where she can actually rest."

Where she could rest and get better, and I could keep my promise of taking her wherever she wanted to go. It had to end there. Because I already knew myself. And once she was healed, Emma was better off on her own.

Chapter 7

Emma

I didn't run away again. I couldn't. The rational, non-feverish part of my brain knew if I ran again, I wouldn't make it. And gradually, as I let myself sink into the bed they gave me, and after some rest, my mind became clearer. I still wasn't one hundred percent, but I wasn't dying anymore.

The fact that I *had* been dying and stubbornly refused to acknowledge it scared me more than I chose to admit. Was the fear of Simon finding me still present? Yes. Absolutely. But deep in my gut, I didn't believe anyone at Resting Warrior would turn me over to someone like that.

Especially not Daniel.

There were other people too. I saw the doctor—a kind but stern woman who believed I needed to be in a hospital but relented when I was the one who insisted and not Daniel. The woman who'd been in the cages with me, Kate. I pretended not to remember her either, but that didn't seem to bother her nearly as much as it bothered Daniel. Her partner, Noah, who Simon had almost killed, stopped by. He seemed like a kind man, and I was glad Simon had been stopped before shooting him.

It was strange how much I didn't like being still. I'd been still for six months up in that cabin, but that was a much bigger space than this room. I was able to get up and walk around this cabin and such, but I was still too weak to get far. And every hour, it felt like the walls closed in more and more. Soon, I was sure I would go mad.

The only thing that stopped that feeling was Daniel. He'd saved me not once, not twice, but three times now. Every day, he came to visit and sat with me. We talked about everything and nothing, and when he was with me, I couldn't take my eyes off him.

The way he paid attention to me, like he saw everything, was intoxicating. And after months of imagining him closer than he was now, I found it hard to control the urge to lean forward and touch him whenever he sat on the bed.

Only a few days had passed, but when he knocked on the door softly as he always did, I was ready. "Hello."

"Hello." He smiled as he came in. "How are you feeling today?"

"Like I desperately, *desperately* want to get out of this room."

He laughed softly and glanced at the fluids and medication still connected to my arm. "That sounds about right. Would you like to see more of the ranch?"

When Dr. Gold had been here, she'd put in a little port in my arm, so it was easier for the people here to refresh the bags that hung beside my bed. So I could go outside, if they let me. "Really?"

Concern passed over Daniel's face. "Of course. You're not a prisoner here. I hope you know that."

"Yeah." I did know it, but after having been a prisoner,

and given their level of protectiveness, it was sometimes hard to remember. "Of course."

Kate had brought me some clothes that didn't belong to some anonymous member of Simon's organization and fit me a hell of a lot better. Which was good. If I was still wearing my original clothes, I'd probably smell awful by now. "And yes, I'd like that."

He smiled again. "All right, I'll meet you on the porch."

He had no need to provide me privacy—I was only putting on my shoes—but I still appreciated it. If he thought I felt like a prisoner, then he was attempting to give me space, and it was sweet.

The wilder part of my mind wished he weren't giving me space in the distinctively sexy way, but I pushed the thought aside. At the moment, it didn't seem like he was even aware I was a woman. He was kind and attentive and everything I'd imagined, but I was a rescue case. Someone he'd saved and was looking after—like an injured puppy.

Daniel was older than I was. I didn't care about that, but I wondered if he'd see me as someone he could like that way, and I played out those situations in my dreams.

I gently disconnected the lines from my arm and met him on the porch. The tank top I wore was thin, which was good because it was hot, even in the early afternoon.

"I've seen this bit." I gestured to the area in front of the cabin. "I mean, I was delirious when I saw it, but I remember enough."

A car sat next to the cabin, and I startled. It was *my* car. The one I'd stolen from Simon. I hadn't realized they'd brought it back, but I didn't have a reason to know since I hadn't been outside since I'd run the first time.

"We'll go the other way, then," Daniel said, leading me around the car and away from the gates. I saw some buildings in the near distance, but honestly, the openness of this place was refreshing. Even with the high walls around the perimeter, I didn't feel at all like I was being hemmed in or trapped.

"We have horses, dogs, alpacas, and Noah and Kate have a pair of adorable kittens who are both growing way too fast. I expect them to start terrorizing the horses soon."

"That's an interesting combination of animals."

"It is," he acknowledged. "But there's a good reason. Resting Warrior is a therapeutic ranch. People who suffer from trauma and PTSD come here to recover and heal. We work with a therapist who can help with the psychological aspect, and we have animals well known to help with empathy and healing."

I stopped in my tracks. That's what this place was? No wonder everyone was so kind and worried about me. I wasn't merely a charity case or a stray. This was what they did. Helping me….

A wave of relief crashed over my head. I hadn't realized until that second how much I'd been walking on eggshells, wondering why they were helping me and if there was some extra motive to their efforts. Guilt, too, had been part of it. But if that was what they did…why had they shown up at the house where Simon was headquartered? It didn't seem like the thing for a bunch of ranchers to do. Especially ones who did trauma therapy work for a living.

"Are you all right?"

Daniel turned, observing how I'd stopped completely. With the way he looked at me, all concern but no pity, I realized I couldn't keep up the ruse. Every thought I had was screaming at me to trust this man, and if I didn't, I would never have any chance at getting closer to him. It already might be impossible, but I still wanted to try.

"I'm good," I said. "Just not what I expected."

We kept walking, reaching a large, barn-like structure,

pale walls and a dark roof with wide doors that opened into a shaded interior. Before we even entered, I heard the soft movement of animals and the whickering of horses.

I found something comforting about the semi-darkness. Not nearly as bright as the midday sun, and less exposed.

"This is Cinnamon," he said, leading me to one of the stalls. "One of our therapy horses."

The animal hung its head over the stall, and Daniel stroked down its nose. I did the same, not realizing until our hands were so close, fingers brushing together. I glanced at him, and Daniel was already looking at me.

I needed to tell him, and I needed to do it now. "I have to tell you something."

His eyebrows rose in surprise and curiosity, but he didn't speak, waiting for me to continue.

Swallowing, I forced myself to continue, ignoring the risk still screaming in my mind. "I lied. I know who you are, and I do remember you from that night."

I saw the shock roll through his body, hand freezing where it was still petting Cinnamon's nose.

"I've wanted to know who you were for months. And…" I hesitated, not sure if this was too much, but I was already taking the risk. Might as well go all the way. "I've been dreaming about you. That night and…other things. When I woke up and saw you by the bed, I thought I was hallucinating. I had the same thought when you caught me."

Daniel just stared at me for a moment. He was still as a statue, and for a moment I wondered if I'd broken him completely. "Why?"

I blinked at the question. "What?"

He cleared his throat. "Why did you lie?"

"I didn't know if I could trust you. You were there, but I didn't know who you were or what your real motive was. It seemed safer until I knew more. I'm sorry."

A quick smile appeared. "I can't exactly argue with that. Will you tell me how you came to be in that cage?"

I still harbored some hesitancy. I could tell him some of it. But everything? That would take too long, and I didn't want him to look at me differently once he knew. It wasn't something I could either control or take back.

"I went to school for computer science, and I got cocky. I started toying around with things, hacking places I shouldn't have, and I came across the Riders' operation." A gross simplification, but it would have to do. "I didn't realize they'd noticed, but they came for me so I didn't go to the authorities."

Daniel gestured toward the other door of the barn, and I walked with him, wrapping my arms around myself. "Simon told me he didn't have time to deal with me because he was already fighting someone else. But once they finished the move to North Dakota, they were going to make me disappear."

There was no doubt about it. Simon basically told me to my face he was going to find out what I knew and who I'd told before he killed me and buried me in an unmarked grave. That was why I was terrified for him to know I was here. If he was looking for my name and found it at some place like a hospital? It wouldn't stop him from coming and killing me.

Together we approached a fence, and Daniel hadn't lied. I saw alpacas beyond it, fluffy and curious, with beady eyes fixed on us. One came over immediately and didn't balk at all when I reached out to pet it.

"His name is Al Pacacino."

I laughed. "That's amazing."

"How long?"

Looking over at Daniel, I caught the desolation in his gaze. It was so stark it stole my breath. "How long…?"

"How long did they have you in the cage?"

Oh. I swallowed. "A month. They let me out once a day to relieve myself. Never alone for more than a couple minutes, though."

He swore, turning away for a second. "I'm very sorry that happened to you."

"You didn't lock me up, Daniel." I put my hand on his where it rested on the fence. "You let me out. And I'm really thankful for it. It's why I thought I was crazy when you were suddenly saving me *again*. I assumed I'd dreamed you up." I smiled. "Because my mind already sees you as my protector."

A shadow I didn't expect fell over his face before it cleared. Something about what I said bothered him, but it was different from when I'd said I didn't remember. This was darker, but he promptly schooled his face again.

My hand was still on top of his on the fence, and I didn't pull it back. Daniel made no move to either. My stomach tumbled with butterflies and foolish hope.

"I never forgot you," he finally said, voice so quiet I had to lean forward to hear it. "The reason I recognized you in that parking lot is because I know your face almost better than my own. You disappeared, and I couldn't stop imagining something bad had happened that I wasn't able to stop. I hoped you were all right, but my dreams kept telling me you weren't."

The little gasp that came out of me was completely involuntarily. He'd dreamed about me.

"Running into you felt like a goddamn miracle."

I tried to breathe, and it was hard, the air thick in my throat with how much tension was in the atmosphere and the urge to step closer. "Seems like you're my guardian angel." I laughed lightly to brush it off, but it didn't work.

This thing between us built. I was staring into those dark eyes and marveling at the depth of them, now that I could truly see them. The ambient light of the sun glancing through them made it clear they were a rich, chocolate brown.

And the look in them… It was heaven. Something beyond his gaze told me it wasn't only worry that kept him dreaming about me. It was so much more, and I wanted to explore every part of that.

I took a step forward, and he didn't move away.

A high-pitched, snuffling chirp sounded next to us as Al Pacacino shoved his head in between us, looking for the pets we'd stopped giving him, and the tension snapped like a too-taut rubber band. I laughed. "Guess you need some more attention, huh?"

Daniel was still looking at me, though, in the quiet, thoughtful way I'd come to know over the last few days. "I have to ask, Emma. I understand why you're nervous now. But will you talk to our police chief here in Garnet Bend? He's a good friend, and all of us here would trust him with our lives. We *have* already trusted him with them. Whatever you remember could be useful, even if it doesn't seem like it."

Fear seized me, and I opened my mouth to say no before he held out a hand.

"It doesn't have to be right away. If you need to think about it, take your time. But soon."

I took a deep breath and let it out. Nothing in me wanted to talk to someone in authority until I knew exactly where Simon was and what he was doing. But I also didn't want to seem like I had anything more to hide. Not until I'd figured out the way to take him down. "Okay."

Daniel seemed relieved. "Thank you."

A shrill ringing pierced the air, and we both startled before realizing it was his phone. "Sorry," he said, checking the screen and answering. "Yeah?" A long pause followed. "Thanks, I'll be right there."

Ending the call, he smiled at me. "There's a new client here to check in, and I need to go meet them. I'll walk you back to your cabin."

"That's okay." I waved a hand and laughed, stomach swooping at his smile. I could think of a lot of things I'd do to see his smile all the time. "Not like it's that far. I'll be fine."

"You're sure?"

I nodded. "Very."

"All right." Daniel's eyes roved over me like he needed to make sure all of me was good before he would even consider leaving me. The attention—and the idea of someone caring for me like that at all—had me flushing pink. "I'll see you later."

The words were light, but the intent was not. It settled in my gut like a comfortable weight. He would see me later, and that was that.

I watched him walk away toward the main ranch lodge, admiring the broadness of his shoulders and what his jeans did to him, just like I had when I was delirious.

Apparently delirious me was just as much of an ass woman as I was when I was alert and of clear mind.

The cabin wasn't far, and when I started back after petting Al Pacacino a little longer, I had every intention of going back and resting. Then I got to my cabin, and I saw the car. The urge to head back and look at my notes now that I wasn't dying was too much. If I had the keys—

I froze. The keys were in the ignition. The cabin wasn't far from here, and I was going to come back, but I needed to see it.

Snorting, I slid into the driver's seat and groaned at the heat of a car that had sat in the sun for too long. I didn't *need* to see the notes at all. I could remember every word on every piece of paper—and every word I'd placed on the blank ones, too.

But being there, seeing it the same way I'd stared at it for months, was an urge and a comfort I couldn't fight. Everything was different, and everything had the potential to be dangerous now—even with someone as steady and kind as Daniel. Just for a little while, I wanted to be in the place that had kept me safe and alive.

The car started easily, and no one stopped me on my way out of the gate.

The cabin was exactly how I left it. No one had been here or touched anything—my memory confirmed it. And all my notes and papers were exactly where I'd left them. Not that I was any closer to figuring out the truth.

Maybe being at Resting Warrior, I would find the missing pieces so I could destroy Simon's business entirely. In the end, *that* was what I really wanted.

I would leave the notes here. No one would be able to make sense of them but me anyway, and bringing them back to the ranch would only raise questions I wasn't ready to answer. But I would still be thinking about it. Part of my mind was pretty much always working on it, like a pot simmering on a stove.

After a little while of sitting on the couch and staring at my conspiracy wall while munching on some of my stolen Pop-Tarts, I went back to the ranch. I was starting to drag, and I needed to get back to my little cabin before my limited stamina ran out. Just because I felt better didn't mean I was out of the woods completely.

Daniel was sitting in the chair on the porch when I pulled the car back into the spot where I'd found it. My stomach dropped, and I made sure to put the keys in my pocket and not leave them in the ignition. He didn't look mad.

Immediately, I pushed the thought aside. It wouldn't matter if he were. It wasn't his business.

"Hey."

His eyes met mine. "Hey."

Even though he wasn't mad, my stomach still fluttered with nerves. "Everything okay?"

"For the most part. You'll have a neighbor now. If you see him out and about, don't worry." He gestured farther down the row of cabins.

"Okay."

"And…" He rose, crossing the small distance to where I stood. "I meant what I said. You're not a prisoner here. You can feel free to come and go as you like. But considering you *are* in danger, I would like you to tell me when you're leaving. For now."

I bristled, and he reached out, catching my elbow and pulling me closer instinctively. Suddenly, I was in his orbit, and my breath was short for an entirely different reason.

"You don't have to tell me where you're going," he said. "But I would rather not have to track you down and find you nearly dead on the ground again." His mouth quirked. "I don't think I could take it."

It wasn't an unreasonable request. It still irritated me to have a limitation put on me, but if I looked at it logically, I didn't want him to have to come rescue me again either.

There were plenty of other things I wanted him to do.

"All right," I said. "I will."

"Thank you."

We stayed there, the previous tension between us building again. God, I wanted him to kiss me.

He didn't, but I didn't imagine the way his fingers tightened ever so slightly on my arm. "I'm very glad you're here—and safe," he said, finally releasing me and moving past me down the porch steps.

I felt like I was left in a vacuum because he took all my breath with him.

"Oh, and Emma?" When I turned, he was walking backward down the path, smiling wider than I'd ever seen. "If you need to leave, come borrow one of the ranch trucks. I don't want to have to bail you out for driving a stolen car either."

He turned around without missing a beat and left me gaping after him.

Chapter 8

Daniel

"Look," I said, pointing to the grass. "Signs of deer. We try to keep them off the property, but sometimes they sneak in."

Emma looked down at the ground. "How can you tell? It just looks like grass to me."

"There're patterns to the way animals walk," I told her. "Ways the grass bends under weight, and once you've been out here long enough, you get to know them. Of course, it's easier if whatever you're tracking leaves you a trail. Broken branches, footprints. If it's human, scraps of cloth. But you use whatever you need to in a rescue."

She looked pensive. "Why were you there?"

I looked over at Emma, who rode Cinnamon a few feet away. She'd told me she'd never ridden a horse, and I couldn't let it stay that way. So we were riding by the small lake on the property, and I was having trouble keeping my eyes off her. Over the last week, I'd seen Emma bloom.

The fear that had permanently etched on her face had eased, and she was smiling more. Right now, her head was tilted back toward the sky, the sun shining through her hair and turning brown to gold.

She was beautiful.

There was no point in forcing myself to ignore it. Everything from the way she smiled to her unusual eyes to the way she seemed to look up at me from under her lashes even when we were at the same level as we were now. I found myself glancing at her lips more often than was healthy.

Then I'd begin to recite the reasons it was a bad idea in my head. It was the only real thing holding me back in those moments—which seemed to happen at least once a day—when we were in proximity and kissing her would be so fucking easy.

I was dying to find out what those lips tasted like.

She was staring at me, and I realized I hadn't answered her question. The small, victorious smile on her face told me she knew why too. We were playing a game, she and I. And she was the only one winning. "Why was I where?"

"When you…" She swallowed, and a shadow fell over her face. "When you rescued me. Why were you all there? Ranching and rescuing don't seem like they go hand in hand."

"Ah." It was a valid question. "We were there to rescue Noah and Kate, which you knew. But to answer your real question, the seven of us who work here are all retired Navy SEALs. We found one another through recovering from our own traumas and decided we wanted to create a place where others could do the same. No matter if they were in the military or not."

Emma's face went slack with realization, and her gaze roved over me, suddenly taking in my whole body in an entirely different way. I would be a fucking liar if I said the way she looked at me didn't affect anything. It did.

The list of reasons why I should ignore the power of her gaze began rolling through my head. She was here to recover and was a victim of trauma—it was inappropriate. Emma was easily a decade younger than me. I was a terrible fit for her.

And yet even with those reasons, my body reacted to the way she looked at me and *loved* it. Like she was suddenly seeing me as a powerful warrior.

"I guess I should have noticed. It feels obvious now."

I smiled. "No reason you should have known."

"Do you do that kind of thing often?"

Swinging down off the saddle, I led Thunder over to one of the nearby trees and quickly knotted the reins around the thin trunk with plenty of room for him to wander.

Emma tried to dismount too, but she wasn't nearly as practiced at it. She slipped, and I made it just in time to catch her.

But catching her put her close to me, pressed up against my body so we were face-to-face. Looking into Emma's eyes was like coming home to this place after being away for far too long.

And holding her like this? My mind acknowledged how good it felt to touch someone—really touch them—after years of being alone. And damn if I didn't want to let her go, even if I had to.

"Do we go around rescuing people?"

"Yeah." Emma's voice was breathy as we were caught in the moment, the tension that sang between us whenever we got too close.

Put her down, Daniel.

I didn't.

"When you live lives like we have, it's easy to attract trouble. Do we do it all the time? No. We do it when we have to. Because we're a family, and we don't let *anyone* take or hurt what's ours."

The intensity in my voice wasn't something I intended, nor was the implication she was a part of that, but I didn't regret it. Right now, with her in my arms? I felt like I would and could do anything for her.

Finally, I forced myself to release her. She slid to the ground, body gliding against mine, and it was an act of sheer will not to kiss her.

"Guess I got lucky." She led Cinnamon over to the same tree.

"I don't know if I'd classify living in a cage for a month to be lucky."

Slowly, she sat down and looked out across the water. A gentle breeze stirred the surface and painted the world in blurry watercolor hues. Her voice was so soft, I wasn't sure she intended me to hear. "Better than being buried in an unmarked grave in the middle of nowhere."

She was right.

Later, when we'd come back to the occupied portion of the ranch, Emma told me she was leaving and drove out of the ranch in the truck she'd come to use. She'd kept her promise and told me whenever she left, even though I could tell it bothered her to have any kind of monitoring.

By the same token, it drove me crazy not knowing where she went every day. Where and why?

Part of my concern was for her health. Dr. Gold had taken out the port, and Emma was only on oral medication now. Soon, she wouldn't be on any medication at all.

But I knew damned well her health wasn't the full scope of my concern. I pushed into the lodge after watching her head back to her cabin to get the truck and made myself a cup of coffee.

Liam came out of the security office and looked at me. "You okay?"

I frowned. "Yeah, why."

"Because you were treating the coffee cup like it did something to piss you off and you were going to break it in revenge," he chuckled.

Looking down, I ran through the motions I'd made, and he was right. So in my own head thinking about Emma and her disappearing act, I'd barely noticed myself slamming the cup down. "Sorry."

"Got Emma on the mind?"

I looked at him sharply and found him smirking. "What makes you say that?"

"Of all of us, you're the steadiest. Even above Jude. But that woman brings something out in you we've never seen before. When you brought her back? I thought you were losing your mind."

"It's fine," I said. "It's none of my business where she goes."

It wasn't. But that fact conveniently didn't stop my instincts from going fucking crazy whenever she drove out of our gates.

"If it bothers you so much, just follow her."

"I shouldn't."

Liam shrugged. "Maybe not. But it's probably better you do it now and satisfy the itch before the same itch makes you snap and do something you should do even *less*."

I shoved a hand through my hair. Fuck, he was right. Outside the lodge, I heard tires on dirt. If I was going to do it, it had to be right now. My resolve was formed before I registered pouring the coffee down the sink and striding to the door.

Liam laughed behind me, but I ignored him. I only wanted to make sure she was all right—and nothing more. That's what I told myself as I jogged down the stairs to my truck, started it, and pulled out just as I glimpsed her turning left out of the gate.

The same direction she'd gone when she'd run on foot. At least she had some consistency there. I kept my distance, making sure I was far enough behind her she wouldn't mark me following her.

Guilt was still churning in my gut, warring with the instincts tingling at the back of my neck. She'd hidden her memory from me already. I understood it, but it also raised questions I couldn't answer. Maybe this would solve some of them.

It wasn't long before she turned off the main road, but nowhere I recognized as being a driveway. No, if anything, this was a rough dirt path which headed up into the foothills and woods. I could just make out the ranch truck bouncing up the hill through the trees, and I waited.

Out here, following her would be a lot more obvious than on a main road. So I took my time guiding the truck up the barely visible path. It wasn't long before I saw it. A well-hidden cabin, the truck sitting outside it, and nothing else.

An entire bucket of relief poured down on my head. I hadn't known what to expect, but this must have been the cabin she'd found and stayed in. It was her home for six months and probably felt a lot more like home than the ranch. It made sense she'd want to come back here and spend some time alone.

Throwing the truck into reverse, I turned around and left. I didn't need to know anything more than that, and I was glad it was something so innocent. Seeing the cabin didn't entirely erase those tingling instincts, but then again, those had been going since the night I pulled her out of the cage and she disappeared. For all I knew, the extra awareness was because Simon, the leader of the Riders, had promised to take revenge on all of us and then disappeared.

Hopefully we wouldn't have to wait forever for some kind of resolution.

With that in mind, I didn't turn back into the ranch drive —I continued into town. It was time to talk to Charlie.

Though Charlie didn't look particularly happy to see me. He sighed when they ushered me into the police chief's office. "Daniel, I like you and your crew as people, but I'll tell you something. I'm getting tired of y'all visiting with emergencies."

I laughed and waved a hand. "No emergencies this time, promise. But I have something connected to the Riders."

He perked up when I said it. "Well, in that case, I'm listening. That's a puzzle I damn well want to solve, but as long as there aren't any new puzzles for a while, okay?"

"We'll do our best."

Charlie finally cracked into a laugh. "This town has seen more excitement since you moved in than in the tenure of the last three police chiefs. And I'm not saying that as a compliment."

"At least we're not dropping trouble on your doorstep and leaving you to clean up the mess alone."

"That's true," he sighed. "You guys can hold your own. What did you find?"

I paused, figuring out how best to say it. "Not a what. A who."

Charlie's eyebrows rose.

"Did you hear about a woman who collapsed in the grocery store parking lot a little less than two weeks ago?"

"Yeah, I heard about it. Caused quite the stir."

"I happened to be in the parking lot. I caught her before she could smash her head on the pavement, and she outright refused to go to the hospital. So we brought Dr. Gold to the ranch, and she's been staying with us. She finally told me she was the woman in the cage that night—the one beside Kate who disappeared into thin air."

"No shit?"

"No shit," I said with a laugh. "Her name is Emma. I don't know if she'll have anything useful, and she's skittish as all get-out, but she said she'd be willing to talk to you. I don't know how solid her answer will be if I have to bring her down here."

He leaned back in his chair. "For the Riders? I don't mind coming to you. When do you want me?"

"Whatever's good for you."

"Let's do tomorrow afternoon. I'll give you a call before I head over."

I stood and shook his hand. "Sounds good. Thank you, and I promise Resting Warrior is doing its best to stay out of your hair."

Charlie didn't laugh. "I appreciate that."

It was good he'd be by tomorrow. I wanted a chance to warn Emma he was coming and make sure she didn't fall apart.

The next morning when I visited, Emma's face went pale, even though she was safely ensconced in a blanket on the couch.

"Today?"

I nodded, sitting down on the coffee table in front of her. "He'll be here soon. We'll bring you to the main lodge. I won't ask you to bring him into this space. I want you to keep feeling safe here."

Some of her color came back at that statement, and I wondered again what she hadn't told me. And I knew she was holding back. No one survived a brutal month as a prisoner and didn't have things to get off their chest. Her story of events so far was very clean and simple; I doubted the reality was the same.

"I promise I'll be there with you the entire time. If you want Kate or another woman present as well, we'll make it happen."

"No," she said. "That's okay. I trust you."

The guilt came flooding in, and I did my best to push it back. She shouldn't trust me—no one should—but I was going to do everything in my power to make sure she could.

"Thank you for that."

Her smile lit up the room. Like the sun coming out *again,* even though it was fully bright outside.

"There was something else I wanted to ask. While you're here, if you want to, we work with a therapist. Completely private. No one would know anything about what you said but her. However, I thought I would offer it to you in case you felt you needed it."

That smile faded. "I…I appreciate the offer, but I'm already so much of a burden. I have no money to pay you for my general room and board, much less anything else. Everybody must think so poorly of me."

I shook my head. "No, nobody thinks that. And you don't need to worry about money. Not right now. Part of our mission here at Resting Warrior Ranch is to help provide for people even if they can't pay."

She didn't respond.

"Just think about it. I'm going to go." I stood up. "I'll come back when Charlie's on his way."

"No." She sat up, halfway reaching for me. "No, stay."

That good kind of tension spun between us again, and I smiled, sitting back down. "All right."

"I like you being here," she said, looking down at the blanket. "I know I'm safe here, but you make me feel safer. It's why I liked having dreams about you so much. Even when I didn't know who you were or why you were there, you were still the man who saved me." She smiled, though she still wasn't meeting my eyes. "I never said thank you for it."

"There's no need to thank me."

"I want to, though." She looked at me now, and she suddenly leaned forward all the way, capturing my hand where it rested on my knee. "Truly. Thank you. For everything."

"You're welcome."

We stayed in the breathless moment, hands touching, and I thought about all the ways you could interpret the words *you're welcome.*

Emma was welcome here. She was welcome to so many things. I didn't know her well, but every moment I'd spent with her so far had been refreshing. She was honest and kind, even through her fear. And she was far, far braver than she knew.

The heavy sound of footsteps on the porch pulled us apart, and Jude knocked on the doorframe a minute later. "Camera on the far west wall busted. I don't have what I need to replace it, so Lena and I are heading down to Missoula. We might spend the night, but we're not sure yet."

I nodded. "Call if you need anything."

He smirked, knowing he wouldn't. Jude knew exactly what he was doing, and though the camera might have been busted, we had plenty of cameras. They might not have been the exact model to replace the one that broke, but it would be sufficient while he ordered another one.

The man wanted an excuse to spoil Lena, and I wasn't about to stop him from doing that. After pining for each other for so long, the two of them deserved every happiness they could find.

"Does everyone here let you know when they leave?" Emma asked. She was smiling as she did it, teasing me.

"Usually."

"Seems a little like a cult."

Her voice was still teasing, but I saw the test in her eyes. I needed to answer this carefully. "Like I said yesterday, we're a family here—everyone who works here, and everyone who's related to us. We've gone through a lot, individually and apart. I tell people when I'm leaving, too. It's not about keeping tabs on one another, it's about making sure we know where everyone is in case we need help.

"More than once, we've…" I sighed. "We've had situations where we've almost been too late because we *didn't* know. And after everything, it makes us feel better to share that with one another."

She looked at me, wonder in her eyes, and I kept going. "We were almost too late to save Noah, Kate, and you. It was closer than we would have liked."

"I didn't think of it that way," she said quietly and with longing. "It sounds lovely."

My phone vibrated in my pocket, and I glanced at it. Charlie was en route. "Okay, he's on his way. Want to head over?"

Emma smiled, but it was more like a wince. "Sure."

I helped her stand. She was slow, but moving. Even though it had been almost two weeks, seeing her get around on her own so easily was a small miracle.

We headed toward the lodge, but she was quiet. Quieter

than she normally was when we walked together, and all I felt from her was nerves. I knew she was frightened, but the way her hands were shoved in the pockets of her jeans and her shoulders were hunched made her look smaller.

By the time we were approaching the lodge, Charlie was pulling in with his cruiser. I gave him a gesture to wait for a second, and he inclined his head. Emma needed to be settled in the room first and feel comfortable before he entered. For once, I was grateful to my instincts for reading people to know exactly what she needed.

"Something I haven't asked you." I kept my voice light. "Are you a tea or coffee person? We have both."

"Coffee," she said. Then she smiled. "Though I can't remember the last time I actually had a good cup of coffee. The cabin didn't have much, and what it did have was instant."

"I promise our coffee has real beans," I chuckled. "What do you like in it?"

Emma shrugged. "A little cream, a little sugar. Nothing too overboard."

I led her to one of the armchairs. It faced the door and allowed her to sit alone, without me or Charlie on the same couch. "I'll grab you some."

"Thanks." She rubbed her hands on her jeans. Another nervous gesture. I wanted to comfort her, but I didn't know how I could allow myself to. If I did, I'd be letting her *and* myself think this tension between us was something we could explore.

I set the coffee on the table in front of her and waved outside to Charlie, who was waiting at the bottom of the stairs. He shook my hand as he came inside.

"Hello, Emma," he said. "Thank you for talking with me."

"Sure." The single word was tight.

He sat down, and I stood back behind the couch where Emma could still see me. If I made her feel safe, then I wanted to make sure she knew I was here for her.

"Daniel mentioned you were with the Riders the night we raided that house. Is that right?" To Charlie's credit, his voice was gentle.

"I was, yes."

"Can you tell me about that? What you told Daniel?"

Emma's entire body was shrinking in on itself, but she nodded. She repeated what she'd told me almost verbatim. I couldn't help but notice how nervous she was. A little too nervous for what she was doing right now, but I wasn't about to tell someone how they could feel while reliving traumatic memories.

When she finished, she seemed a little better, but still so tense I wanted to cross the room and help her undo the knots.

"Thank you for telling me that," Charlie said. "I also heard about what happened to you in the parking lot."

She nodded. "I had an infection."

"And how did you get that?"

This was why she was nervous. Charlie didn't have to be my level of observant to see the way she tensed. "I…" Her head fell. "I ran out of food at the cabin where I was staying, and I didn't have any money. So, I broke in to Arrowhead Grocers late one night after they closed."

Shock rolled through me. I wasn't angry—desperation made people do things—but I was surprised. From everything she'd told me so far, Emma seemed fairly straitlaced.

"I broke a window, and I didn't see the piece of metal sticking out of the frame until it was cutting me. I took what I needed, and I'm planning to pay it all back when I can."

I felt Charlie's shock too.

"Well," Charlie said with a soft laugh. "That solves that mystery. The store had insurance, but—"

"I'll cover it, Charlie," I interrupted him. "Whatever the damages were, I'll cover it in the interim."

As far as I was concerned, she never had to pay me back, but I already knew she wasn't the kind of woman to let that stand.

He nodded. "Good. I'll let the owners of Arrowhead know what happened and the unique circumstances. They're pretty reasonable, so hopefully they won't want to press charges. I'll do my best to handle it without using your name publicly."

Emma wilted in relief. "Thank you."

That was the source of her fear. She was terrified Simon was going to find her because she'd spoken to Charlie. Given the way she's said he'd found her before, it wasn't an unreasonable fear.

"Need anything else, Charlie?"

He shook his head. "I don't think so. If I have any questions, I'll pass them on to you."

"Great."

He stood, and I followed him outside with a backward glance at Emma. She'd melted into the chair, seemingly exhausted, clutching the cup of coffee to her chest.

I shut the door behind us. "Thank you for coming out."

"No problem." His face was more tense than he'd been inside. "I don't think she's telling the whole story."

"I don't either, but I'm not exactly shocked. Hopefully she'll take me up on my offer to go see Rayne."

Hands on his hips, Charlie looked at the ground. "Yeah. Can't argue with that logic. Keep an eye on her for me."

I smiled. "Will do." As if I could force myself to do anything else. Even now, I wanted to go back inside to make sure she was okay. Talk to her. Feel the way she looked at me and revel in the feeling of someone's trust, misplaced as it possibly was.

Charlie retreated to his cruiser, and I watched him until he disappeared down the drive, past the trees. I stayed outside for a few minutes longer, trying to wrap my head around my thoughts. And reconcile the fact that Emma was cracking the shell I'd carefully built around myself, and I wasn't as determined as I should to keep it solid.

I was in *so* much trouble.

Chapter 9

Daniel

The cage door *slammed* closed on Emma, and I lunged for her, trying to break her free. But the sound of the slamming didn't stop. Over and over and over, the sound knocked through my skull while I watched her disappear into nothing.

Still, the sound kept going, and I sat up in my bed, my body finally understanding whatever the hell the sound was, it wasn't coming from within my own mind.

"Fuck," I muttered the word, scrubbing the last of the sleep from my eyes. The dream had been frantic—even more so than normal. Like my subconscious mind was racing to save Emma from something, even though she was safe here.

The banging sounded again, harsh and insistent. Someone was at the door, and they weren't being kind about it. I glanced at my phone. I'd overslept, and there were half a dozen missed calls.

What the hell?

I didn't even bother putting on a shirt as I went to the

door, pushing it open to find Liam standing there. "What the hell is going on?"

"You didn't answer your phone, so Lucas sent me to get you. He's keeping the FBI at the lodge so they don't come get you themselves."

"What did you just say?"

Liam gave me an exasperated look. "Yeah, it's why we've been calling you. Two special agents are here, demanding to see who's in charge and also asking where Emma Derine is."

For the second time this morning, I cursed. "All right. Give me five minutes to put on some clothes."

I would rather have had more time to put my head on straight, but the FBI didn't always take kindly to waiting. If I took too much time, they might assume we had something to hide, and that wasn't the way to start off a potential working relationship.

Hell of a morning for me to sleep in.

Fresh jeans and one of my nicer long-sleeved T-shirts later, I rinsed my mouth with mouthwash, shoved my feet in my boots, and hopped in Liam's truck.

"Emma Derine?" I asked.

"That's what they said."

It was news to me. Emma hadn't volunteered her surname, and because we were originally under the impression she'd lost her memory, I hadn't asked.

"How did they even know she was here?"

Liam snorted inelegantly. "It's the FBI, Daniel. They haven't been forthcoming. Maybe you can get them to talk, but they're cagey. And one of them is a real asshole."

"Great."

"I'm surprised Lucas hasn't taken a solid swing yet."

It was a good thing Lucas was dealing with them, then. The man could get hot under the collar when it was necessary, but he was also one of the most patient of our team. It was why he worked on the troubled animal cases that came to us.

"Park behind the lodge," I told him.

"Really?"

I nodded. "I don't want us to come spinning around the corner and give them the impression we're rushing to do their bidding. If they're already trying to exert pressure, we need to try to keep it even."

This wasn't a game. Whatever it was, a woman's life hung in the balance, and I wasn't going to play fast and loose with it. But in order for us—*for me*—to have any leverage and keep Emma safe, none of us could look weak.

Liam pulled the truck up to the back stairs of the wrap-around porch, and I hopped out. "Sorry if I made y'all panic."

"No." He laughed once. "I mean, you're usually up earlier, but it's not like I'm going to complain about you taking a rest once in a while. Have you taken a vacation since we started this place?"

"I don't know what you mean." I clapped him on the shoulder as we climbed the steps. "We live in one of the most beautiful places, doing what we love. Every day is a vacation."

"Sure. That's not a cop-out," he said quietly, and I laughed again. I had a feeling I'd been giving Liam less credit than he was due since I hadn't gotten to know him the way I should have. I was glad that was changing.

As promised, two men in sharp, dark suits stood on the porch, facing across from Lucas. "They didn't want to go inside?" I asked quietly.

"Nope." Liam popped the *p* in the word intentionally.

They were both looking at me as I approached. "Gentlemen. My apologies for keeping you waiting. I'm Daniel Clark, and I manage Resting Warrior. How can I help you?"

"You could have helped us already by being readily available during business hours."

So he was the one Liam pegged as an asshole. A whole straitlaced package. Trimmed hair and beard in the classic FBI way. I didn't doubt being on the ranch was about as alien as coloring outside the lines. He gave off the air of loving the city and feeling out of place here in nature.

"As I said, sorry for the wait. If you'd told us you were coming, we could have made sure things were available to you. Now, can I see some ID?"

The one who'd already spoken pulled out his badge first. "Special Agent Cole Phillips. This is my partner, Eric Jones." The other man held out his badge as well. "We're here looking for Emma Derine."

"May I ask why?"

"No, you may not."

I slipped my hands into my pockets and stared at them both. "Then if you have neither an arrest nor a search warrant, I'll have to ask you to leave. Though Resting Warrior is a therapeutic facility, we are privately run, and none of our staff are mandatory reporters. I can't give you any information on whether someone is a guest here."

"Hold on, Mr. Clark." The second agent held out a hand. "I think there's been some kind of misunderstanding. We're not here to arrest Ms. Derine, harm her, or anything else. All we want to do is talk to her. She may have information about the location of a known fugitive, and it could help our case. That's all."

I looked at both of them, trying to get a good read. Agent Phillips was harsh, but I also didn't immediately get the feeling he was trying to force the issue in a way that was illegal or inappropriate. It felt more like he was eager to track down this lead for a break in the case. Which, I assumed, had something to do with the Riders.

Agent Jones made me feel easier. If they only wanted to talk to her, I could ask. She might say no, but if she said yes, I knew there would be someone on her side.

"We have an Emma staying here. I can't confirm her surname is Derine. I will ask if she'd like to speak to you, but whatever her answer is, it will be final. Please, wait inside. Help yourself to coffee or tea, and I'll be with you shortly."

I glanced at Lucas, and he nodded. They weren't to be left alone. None of us at Resting Warrior had problems with the branches of law enforcement, but by nature, they took whatever they could. We were used to it. But this was our place, and we would protect it.

"Stay here," I said to Liam. "Outside. Go in if Lucas needs you, but keep an eye on things."

He nodded once, leaning almost too casually against the railing. "Got it."

I walked away on purpose.

The special agents could wait.

I sighed, knowing Emma probably wasn't going to like this. Probably? Who was I kidding? She barely wanted to talk to Charlie, and in the grand scheme of things, Charlie was a little fish compared to the FBI. I needed to find out how they knew, because Charlie had promised to keep it quiet, and if the FBI had some kind of surveillance on us, I wanted to know.

"Emma?" I knocked on the door. "I know it's earlier than usual, but something's come up."

No answer. It was possible she was still sleeping, but that didn't feel right. The silence behind the door was the kind of silence that accompanied absence…or true unconsciousness.

Panic welled up in my chest. She seemed to be doing fine now that her infection was under control. But what if she wasn't? Her eyes and the sounds of her yelling for me while the cage slammed shut filled my mind, and it wasn't just panic anymore. It was raw need. I had to make sure she was all right. She *needed* to be all right.

"Emma?" I knocked again. "If you're in there and you're fine, I need to hear from you. Otherwise, I'm coming in to make sure you're okay."

I made myself wait sixty full seconds before I pulled out my keys and unlocked the cabin. Every moment was agony. "Emma?"

She wasn't in the bedroom. The door was open, the bed empty. The bathroom door was open too, with no sign of her. Relief took the place of panic in my chest, but another kind of worry gnawed at me now. She hadn't told me she was leaving this time. Granted, whatever time it was she'd decided to go, I would have been sleeping. But was it different this time?

Usually she left in the afternoon. Was this her leaving permanently?

The stolen car I'd found her with was still outside, so my gut instinct told me no. If she were planning to run away, I didn't think she would take the ranch truck. Her remorse over having to steal from the grocery store was genuine. I didn't think she wanted to do it again—especially with another vehicle.

If she wasn't back by this afternoon, then there would be real cause for worry.

Entering the lodge, I glanced at the rack of keys. The ones to her preferred truck were gone. I found a measure of comfort in that.

"Unfortunately, Emma is not on our property right now. If you'd like to speak to her, you'll have to come back later."

Agent Phillips stood, eyes wary. "Where did she go?"

"I'm not going to tell you that."

"You will—"

"Agent Phillips," I cut him off. "If the Emma you're

looking for is the same Emma who has sought shelter here, she is a woman who has experienced trauma and needs a safe space for it. I'm not going to give you her location so you and your partner can go terrify her. The people who stay at Resting Warrior aren't prisoners. They are free to come and go as they choose. So, unless you give me a good reason why (a) you believe she has anything to do with what you're looking into, and (b) why you thought she was here in the first place, you can give me your phone number and I'll call you if she's willing to talk to you."

I knew why they wanted to talk to her, but as with anything this sensitive, I wasn't going to tip our hand first. If these men were knee-deep into investigating the Riders, I wasn't opposed to helping them. The threat of the gang had been hanging over our heads without any movement for months.

But I also wasn't simply going to hand Emma over to them like an offering for slaughter. Simon and the Riders clearly wanted her dead. Speaking to the FBI wasn't going to make them want her dead any less.

Agent Phillips pulled out his phone and turned away from me in disgust. Agent Jones stood up from the table with an apologetic look on his face. "Ms. Derine's name came up in connection with a case. We've had an alert for anything with a tie to a gang called the Riders. There was a new internal report from the local police that mentioned an Emma. So close in proximity to some trouble a few months ago made us curious. That's why we're here."

I looked over at Lucas. If they wanted to talk to Emma, they would probably also want to speak to Noah and Kate. I knew Charlie had reported everything that happened in November to the FBI, but we hadn't heard anything about it.

Lucas nodded, and I agreed. We should tell them. "We're familiar with them."

The statement made them pause. Agent Jones looked at me closer. "You are?"

"I would have thought you would already have known. Everything was reported to you guys through our police chief. We were part of the raid that took them down. Or… made them pause, I guess. One of our employees had infiltrated their dog-fighting events in the course of helping a friend."

Phillips crossed his arms. "I'm guessing you are the 'independent ex-military assets'?"

"If that's what they called us," Lucas said, "then yeah."

Liam smirked too. "I'm going to get it put on a business card."

"We're all SEALs," I told them. "Former."

That sent Phillips's eyebrows rising. "I guess we do have something in common, then."

Interesting.

Jones looked over at his partner. "We're cleared to tell them." Then he looked at me. "If you're actually interested in helping to fully dismantle the Riders, then you need to tell us where Emma Derine is. Right now."

"Why?" His tone made me bristle.

"Because Emma Derine is Simon Derine's daughter. And he's the leader of the Riders."

My stomach plummeted through the floor. Both Liam and Lucas looked at me, and it was only years of training and practice that kept the shock off my face. No one we'd spoken to knew Simon's last name. He'd just been "Simon," and the moniker had enough power on its own.

Now I wondered if Emma had hidden her last name on purpose in case she thought we might know about the connection. She could have made up an identity if she was so worried about being found, but if she'd truly spent all this time in the cabin, she wouldn't have had to worry about it.

"If Emma is still in contact with her father, and potentially helping him, it makes it very important for us to find her and question her."

"She's not."

Agent Phillips smirked. Though I was a SEAL, I considered myself to be a nonviolent man unless the occasion called for it. The look on his face made me question my stance. "You think you know her well enough to tell? One of the most prolific arms and drug dealers in the northwest, and she didn't learn anything from him? I find it unlikely."

"And I'm telling you, the chances of her helping him are next to zero."

"How do you know?" He tossed the accusation at me, and I kept my lips sealed. "Fine. You don't leave me a choice. If you don't tell us what you know and where to locate Emma Derine, I'll have no choice but to arrest you for obstruction of justice."

Liam scoffed. "Seriously?"

"For hindering an investigation to take down someone like Simon Derine and the Riders? Absolutely."

I crossed my arms in an attempt to keep my hands from curling into fists. "Remember when I said you could speak to her when she came back? That offer still applies."

"So do my handcuffs."

"Phillips," Agent Jones said quietly, but his partner ignored him, looking at me expectantly.

Fuck, I wished I could tell him I had no idea where she was. If I'd kept a hold on myself and my curiosity, I wouldn't know. But if I lied and told them I didn't know and they found out later, it could be worse for both her and me.

"Fine. The reason I hardly find it likely she's helping Simon is because he had her locked in a fucking cage, and she told us he was planning to kill her and bury her once his operation moved. She disappeared the night of the raid.

Said she spent the last few months in a cabin in the woods not far from here, and what I've seen confirms it. I know where the cabin is, but I haven't gone in."

"A cage?" Agent Jones asked. He looked sick.

"Yes. For more details, you'll have to ask her. I'm not going to disrespect her more by telling you her story on her behalf. But if Simon is as bad as we both know he is, this can't be a surprise."

He shook his head. "It's not, no. But hearing someone locked their own daughter in a cage is always shocking."

In that, I agreed with him.

"Take us to the cabin."

"She will come back," I told them. "She was locked in a fucking cage. Let her answer your questions on familiar territory, and you will get a lot further."

"Do you know when she'll be here?"

"No."

Agent Phillips shook his head. "Then we don't have time to wait. Take us there."

"Or you'll arrest me?" I made sure he heard the sarcasm in my tone.

"You got it."

Sighing, I looked at Liam. "Okay to take your truck? Mine is still at the house."

"Of course."

He tossed me the keys, and I looked over my shoulder. "I'll pull around."

Lucas followed me outside onto the porch and walked with me. "Did you have any idea?"

"No," I said, and I wasn't really in a place to think it all through. On the one hand, I wished she'd been up front about who she was. No one here wished her harm or had been given the impression she was anything but a victim in more than unfortunate circumstances.

But at the same time, I understood why she hadn't said anything. Being that monster's daughter? Unthinkable. Especially if she'd told the truth about the way Simon was going to kill her.

She didn't have any reason to lie about it. Once she knew we weren't involved with Simon at all, she had no reason to deceive us or trick us. Unless she was part of his revenge.

I shook my head. No, that didn't make sense. Even Simon couldn't have known to put her in a cage purely to engender sympathy. She was his prisoner—I didn't doubt it.

"What are you going to do about it?"

"What can I do?" I asked, circling the truck. "If I were in her position, I can't say I wouldn't have done the same."

He placed a hand on the hood. "Keep an eye out. There's something off here."

"Like Phillips being a jackass? I agree."

Lucas chuckled. "Don't get yourself arrested before you get back, okay?"

"I'll do my best."

The special agents were already in their vehicle, and they followed me down the ranch drive. I didn't feel good about this, but they were forcing my hand. Hopefully Emma would forgive me for it.

I realized with a start that was the thing I was most concerned about. Not her actual connection to Simon, though it was concerning, but whether she'd still look at me the same after I brought two FBI agents storming into her life.

Once on the mountainside, I stopped a little way away from where she'd parked the truck. She already had a tendency to run, and I didn't want her to think Simon's men had finally found her. She was much better, but still not quite fully healed.

They met me between the trucks. "That cabin. She isn't

a threat, but she is skittish. I can announce myself, and she'll be less likely to run."

"No, thank you," Agent Phillips said. "We'll take it from here."

I waited for them to pass me before I pressed the heels of my palms to my eyes. "Fuck."

When I turned, my stomach dropped for the second time this morning. They were approaching the cabin with their guns drawn. Damn it, I'd told them she wasn't a threat.

If calling out to them wouldn't put her in more danger right now, I would do it. So, I followed a distance behind. If this was going to happen, I wanted Emma to see me as soon as possible, so she knew everything was going to be all right.

I realized I was more than merely protective of Emma. She was young, but she was intelligent and kind. She was funny and beautiful, and the way my entire body was tensed at the thought of her being afraid or harmed told me I'd already gotten myself in too deep.

But right now? At that moment? I couldn't worry about it.

Agents Phillips and Jones were flanking the door. Jones reached out and pounded on it three times. The booming sound echoed through the trees.

"*FBI. Open the door.*"

If there *were* any of Simon's men in the area, which I thankfully doubted, they would easily hear that.

A few seconds later, Emma opened the door. She was pale and shaking, a bowl of food still in her hand. Her eyes locked on me first. "Daniel?"

"It's going to be okay," I told her. "I didn't have a choice, but things are fine."

"Step inside," Agent Phillips said.

She did as she was told. Clearly, since two men had guns

trained on her. Even when she was nearly dying from infection, she hadn't been this pale.

I followed them inside despite the glares Agent Phillips was sending my way. And then he wasn't looking at me at all. He wasn't looking at Emma either.

All three of us were looking at the centerpiece of the cabin—two walls covered with nearly blank pieces of paper, and a spiderweb of fishing line.

What the hell?

They holstered their weapons. "This wasn't what we were expecting."

To Emma's credit, she was standing despite her fear. "What were you expecting? To come in and find me planning something? Or hiding someone you're looking for?"

"Are you?"

"No." She gestured to the wall. "If I'd figured it out already, then I would have come to the police or to you guys. Whoever would have believed me first. But I can't put all the pieces together, so I'm still just sitting here staring at everything."

Agent Jones cleared his throat. "At a wall of blank paper?"

She waved a hand. "I have perfect recall. They're not blank to me. It just helps to have a specific 'space' to put things so I can see it all laid out in my head instead of all the information piled on top of each other."

"Okay." He sounded skeptical, and I understood.

This looked…well, I didn't like to use the word crazy, but it looked crazy. All the inconsistencies in her stories, the things she hid. Was it possible there were deeper issues here?

Unfortunately, yes. It was very possible. Especially for someone with the kind of PTSD Emma was carrying.

"Your name is Emma Derine?" Agent Phillips asked. His

tone had barely softened despite it being clear that Emma was no threat.

Her face flushed, and she looked at me before looking at the floor. "Yes."

Part of me sank. I hadn't realized I'd hoped it wasn't true. She'd lied about her connection to him. Now seeing these walls, how much of what she'd said to me so far was even factual?

I hated questioning her, and I wanted to believe her. But now…

Shoving the questions and doubts in my head aside, I focused on the moment. I could deal with my own feelings later. Emma still needed me now, and no matter how I felt, I wasn't letting either special agent bulldoze her into something she didn't want.

"Do you know where your father is?"

Once again, she gestured to the wall. "I just told you I've been trying to figure it out." Her voice held a tremble I now recognized. She was terrified. Not nervous in the way she'd been with Charlie and admitting to breaking in to the grocery store. This was terror about the man who wanted to take her life. "I have no idea. I wish I did."

Emma sat down on the couch, and both men moved out of instinct, circling to make sure they could still see her whole body.

"We need you to tell us everything you know about Simon and his organization. If you have the memory you say you do, it could help."

She stiffened. "I said I would do it when I was ready. Isn't that enough?"

"No. And with your connection to Simon, we can arrest you and bring you in either way." Agent Phillips was already reaching for his cuffs, but if he thought Emma would make it easy for him, he was wrong. "So, we can do this the easy way…or the hard way."

"Don't worry, Emma," I said. "Agent Phillips threatens to arrest people as a sign of affection. He's already done it to me once today."

A flicker of a smile crossed her face, but she still didn't quite look at me.

"What does the easy way involve?"

"Coming to the field office in Seattle and telling us everything you know. After that, we'll see."

She sat still for a moment, considering. "I want Simon taken down as much as you do. Probably more, considering he wants to kill me. I don't trust you, but I'll help you."

"Good—"

"On one condition," she interrupted.

Agent Jones slid his hands into his pockets. "And what's that?"

Emma pointed straight at me. "He comes with me."

Chapter 10

Emma

I've never been anywhere.

It was the thought that kept circling in my head as I looked out the plane window and watched Seattle appear. My whole life was Montana. Born and raised, school and college, my mom's death, and meeting Simon. The only thing that wouldn't have been in Montana was my death, if Simon had his way.

Oh, and my mom took me on a road trip to see Mount Rushmore once when I was younger, but that was it.

I glanced over at Daniel. His arms were crossed, head leaning back on the headrest and eyes closed.

The FBI had booked us flights under false names, and everything had been a whirlwind since they'd barged into the cabin yesterday. The fake names made me feel better. Simon hadn't been heard from or seen since that night, but I knew just as well as the FBI he still had resources, and I was glad they were being careful.

I was also glad Daniel was here.

How happy he was to be here, I wasn't sure. He was still kind and attentive, but I could tell a difference between now and before the cabin. I didn't know if it was because I hadn't told him the truth about Simon, or because I was Simon's daughter, he didn't trust me anymore? Either way, I felt a distance I didn't like.

I'd already known I was attracted to him, but I'd convinced myself it was just me. I had no expectations. It was simply my brain painting him with hero status because he saved my life and was kind to me. The ache in my chest whenever I tried to catch his eye and he couldn't quite meet mine told me differently.

While his eyes were closed, I looked at him. I'd slept in front of him before, but I'd never seen him like this. Watching someone sleep was a different kind of intimacy. I was able to trace the slope of his nose with my eyes and admire the line of his jaw. Little things it might seem strange to examine when you were talking with someone.

Daniel had a little scruff on his face. Since the FBI showed up yesterday, he'd been so busy he'd forgotten to shave.

I was watching him, and I was desperately trying not to look at the special agents on the opposite side of the aisle. Missoula to Seattle was barely a hop, and this wasn't a big plane. There were only two seats on either side. Thankfully, I was in the window seat, so Daniel was a buffer between us.

My nerves were steadier than I thought they would be. Mostly because they already knew so much. I couldn't disappoint them the way I could Daniel and the police chief. I might be able to surprise the FBI with what I remembered, but they already thought I was tainted by association.

Something about it was relieving, as fucked up as the thought was. If they already thought I was a criminal, I had nothing to lose. And after losing everything more than once, I was tired of being in that position.

The flight attendant's voice came over the speaker, announcing how close we were to the ground, and Daniel's eyes opened. Instantly, they locked on mine, and I realized I was still staring at him, lost in thought.

"Are you all right?"

The sound of his voice roughened with sleep did things to my insides I couldn't fully explain. I swallowed. "Yeah. We're about to land."

He looked over at our dark shadows before scrubbing a hand over his face. "Okay."

"Daniel?"

"Yeah." He turned to look at me.

"I'm sorry. For not telling you. Again."

He pressed his lips together, and I could tell he was thinking it over. "I'm trying to wrap my head around it. You don't know a lot about me, Emma. Trust is something… It's difficult on a good day. But can I fault you for not telling me about something that isn't my business? If my father wanted to kill me, I wouldn't want to claim him either."

"He's not my father," I said softly. "Not in any real way, and I certainly don't think of him with any love."

Agent Phillips leaned across the aisle. "Stop talking about the case."

I flushed and sat back in my seat. The man had hard eyes and a harder demeanor. I wasn't exactly a fan. But fine. I'd wait until I'd told them everything, and then Daniel and I could talk about it. Because things weren't right between us, and I wanted to fix it.

"I'm sorry," I said again under my breath. "I hope you'll let me talk about it later. When I'm done with Agent Asshole."

Daniel chuckled, and I smiled. At least I could still make him laugh. But the unease didn't leave my gut.

Both agents had only flown with overnight luggage, and I'd borrowed a small suitcase. Daniel had his own bag also, so none of us had to wait for luggage. We went straight to the back of a black sedan that swept us away into the city. Neither of the agents said much, Phillips on his phone and Jones tapping his fingers on his leg while he looked out the window.

The driver was anonymous.

After the past weeks of seeing nothing but open space on the ranch, the city felt too big and too close. So many people, and the sky was gray with clouds instead of a clear blue. It became a blur. The nerves I'd thought were fine sprung back to life the closer we got to our destination.

The location wasn't as clandestine as I imagined. Just another building. A visitor's badge and people glancing in our direction, but nothing too over the top.

"In here, please."

Daniel made to follow and was stopped. "Not you. We're going to interview you elsewhere, Mr. Clark, and you'll meet her when she's finished."

He didn't obey them immediately, instead looking at me. The look stole my breath. It was the old Daniel, the one from a few days ago or even the one who was so determined to rescue me. In that look, nothing mattered but me. "I'll be okay."

They ushered him away before he had a chance to speak. I sat down at the metal table and sighed. I was alone, and yet I wasn't. The classic mirror was in front of me. Everyone knew it was a one-way window, but I could only imagine what my two special agents were saying about me now.

The door opened behind me, and a new person came in.

This time a woman. “Hello, Emma. I’m Special Agent Madeline Knight.”

“Hello.”

“They thought you might be more comfortable talking to a woman. Is that all right?”

I met her gaze. “I’ll be comfortable talking to anyone who isn’t Agent Phillips.”

She was trying very hard not to smile. “All right. I need to tell you that this will be recorded.”

“Do I need to speak to a lawyer?”

Sitting down across from me, she set the file she held down on the table. “You’re not under arrest, and this is an informational interview, so I personally don’t think so. But if you want to speak to one at any time, that is your right.”

The answer was good enough for me. “What do you want to know?”

“Anything you can tell us about Simon Derine, the Riders, and how you came to be their prisoner.”

Despite the nerves, I felt a bit of pleasure in knowing they had vastly underestimated me and were about to see it. “All right. The story can come later. First, Simon Derine’s phone number is 406-555-7230. It’s been disconnected for a while, and I don’t have his new one. I can list every phone number for every person in his organization. I imagine most of them are dead, but you can probably do more with them than I can.

“He has twenty-seven safe houses across various northern states. Twenty-six, if you don’t count the one where I was hiding. Not all of them have addresses, but I can pinpoint the locations on maps if necessary. I know every transaction that has taken place between the Riders and various gun and drug dealers for the last three years.”

Agent Knight stared at me. Her mouth had dropped open in shock. “You can recite all of that information?”

I smiled, half gratified and half still nervous. Reciting all that information had the potential to get me killed. But I could do it. "I told the agents I had perfect recall. And the reason Simon wants me dead is because I found his records. He knows I know. Not everything, I didn't get a chance to look further back, which is why all of this might not be useful. But yes, I can tell you. Names, dates, whatever."

She stood. "I'll be right back."

While she was gone, I tried to relax. When they'd seen the wall, they'd thought I was crazy. It was why I hadn't told anyone at Resting Warrior about it. I knew how it looked. But no matter how worthless the information might be now, I wasn't going to write everything down for anyone to find.

A few minutes later, Agent Knight came in, followed by a slim man with a camera on a tripod. "Can I get you anything, Ms. Derine? Coffee? Water?"

"Water would be nice."

She reappeared with a bottle a few minutes later. The change in tone was immediate. Before, she hadn't been unkind, but knowing I was suddenly a gold mine of information made me a person of value in her eyes.

I tried to push the thought aside, but I couldn't quite manage it, because it was always the same. I was always a resource. Never an individual. Daniel was the only one who really treated me like a person. The rest of the people at Resting Warrior too.

"If it's all right," Agent Knight said, "let's start at the beginning."

Sighing, I took a sip of the water and watched the blinking light on the camera. This was going to take a while.

My mind was a puddle, and I wasn't even finished.

They really did want *everything*.

When it came time for everyone to go home for the day, they didn't want to leave. But I was exhausted. Still, when Daniel asked if I wanted to find something to eat, I said yes.

Now we were wandering in a place called Pike Place Market among approximately a thousand people just like us. Tourists and locals. There were amazing smells and sounds, but it was all overwhelming. I couldn't focus on any of it.

It seemed a shame to come all the way to Seattle and just eat pizza, but it was all I could manage. Daniel, too, was quiet, leaving me to my thoughts until we finished eating and we went down and walked by the waterfront. The sun was finally setting, and the way the light spilled across the water was beautiful.

"Now that we're away from the watchful eyes of Agent Phillips," he said. "Why didn't you tell me who you were?"

I'd already told the story once, but he deserved to hear it now. "I never knew who my father was. My mother knew, but she never let me reach out. She passed when I was eighteen, of cancer."

"I'm sorry."

"Thanks." I leaned against the railing and sighed. "I found his information and contacted him. Honestly, it was like a dream. He wanted to be in my life. He gave me a home and paid for college. The perfect picture of a parent, and I never understood why my mother would keep me from such a kind man."

Daniel leaned on the railing next to me, and I was distracted by his build—and the way the shirt he was wearing showed off that build.

"Having the memory I do, school was easy. Not always fun, but easy. Thank goodness, because I'm not smart."

He opened his mouth to say something, but I smiled and continued. "I'm not saying I'm stupid, because I'm not. But people always think just because I have perfect recall, I'm some sort of genius, and I'm not. I stared at the wall of evidence for six months and couldn't put together anything about where Simon is or what he's doing."

"You can't blame yourself for that. You may have perfect recall, but you don't know if you had all the necessary pieces."

"I know, but it's still frustrating to feel like you should be able to figure something out and know someone smarter might be able to do it while you sit there and spin your wheels." I looked out at the water. "Anyway, I went to school for computer science, and when I graduated, Simon hired me at his company. I *thought* he ran a construction company."

Daniel blew out a breath. "Smart. Owning property or being in and around abandoned or run-down houses wouldn't seem strange for someone in construction."

"Right. Exactly. One day, I had a question about something, and I went into his office, figuring the answer would be in a file. That's when I found everything. All the real records were on paper. At first, I didn't understand because all the hard copies were different from what I'd seen online.

"As soon as I understood what it was, I started looking at every piece of paper I could get my hands on so I could do this. Come to the authorities and tell them everything. All the stuff Simon had me doing was simply surface level. Things to make the company seem legit. And I couldn't believe the man I'd known for five years could do that. But there wasn't any denying it."

A cool breeze came off the water, and I shivered, scooting a little closer to Daniel and his warmth. He didn't move away.

"He caught me. I wasn't fast enough, and then I was in the cage. Everything else I told you was true. He was planning to kill me and still is. When you rescued me, I ran to one of the locations I'd memorized as one of Simon's safe houses. But to answer your question, I didn't tell you because I was—" I took a breath. "I *am* afraid."

"Of what?" The words were soft, and I didn't dare look at him.

"Of him finding me, of what you would think of me. And at the time, I didn't *know* you like I do now. For obvious reasons, I find it hard to trust people. But I'm sorry. You didn't deserve to be lied to."

"Thank you for telling me."

"Is that forgiveness?" I wished the hope weren't so obvious in my voice.

He was looking at me, and I was looking at the water. "I don't know if you need my forgiveness, Emma. You didn't owe me anything then, and you don't owe me anything now. But if you want my forgiveness, you have it."

Orange and pink streaked over the water, creating a blazing sunset. Back on the ranch, it would have covered the sky and felt like it was almost an aurora above us. The awkwardness I'd sensed between us was gone, and I…

I knew the risk, but I couldn't stop it now. There'd been too many moments between us, and I had to try. At least once to see if I was alone or if he was here with me.

Daniel was still looking at me. I turned and met his stare. He didn't move and neither did I. So I rose on my toes and kissed him.

He went still with shock before relaxing and kissing me back. *Fuck* yes. Heat rolled over me along with a longing so strong it stole breath I didn't have. This was a *kiss*. I'd been kissed before, but nothing like this. Daniel's mouth was hungry on mine, and being pressed up against the body I'd been staring at for weeks sent tingles down my spine.

Then he stiffened, and dread spiraled through me.

Gently, Daniel pulled away. I could already see the regret

in his eyes, and I didn't think I'd be able to breathe ever again. I thought—

It didn't matter what I thought. I was wrong. It was all me projecting my dreams on to him, and nothing more. "I'm sorry. I'll go back to the hotel."

"Emma, wait." He caught me by the shoulders and held me still. "Don't apologize. You didn't do anything I didn't want."

But he'd still pulled away, so I wasn't going to give myself the dignity of hope.

"Please believe me when I say it's nothing to do with you and everything to do with me."

When I didn't respond, he tilted my face up to him with one finger, and what I saw there made me go still. There was hunger in his eyes. Dark, pure hunger that matched his kiss. And along with it, devastation. The kind of grief that never left you alone. That look made me want to wrap him up and never let him go, if he'd let me.

"I told you I'd dreamed about you," he said quietly. "I did. I still do. And it's more than you being in a cage, Emma. You're beautiful, and I don't care what you say about yourself. You're smart and funny, and I can see how kind your heart is. I won't lie to you and tell you I haven't had to stop myself from kissing you half a dozen times in the past two weeks."

"You didn't have to stop yourself."

A sad smile appeared on his mouth. "Yes, I did. For so many reasons. None of them you."

"Then tell me why?"

He hesitated for a moment but sighed. "First, I'm too old for you."

I raised an eyebrow. "How old are you?"

"Thirty-seven."

That didn't bother me in the slightest. "Is that all?"

"No. I want to do you the same favor and tell you everything, but it might be…a lot for tonight. But I will tell you once we get back to the ranch if you want to hear it. But the short answer is I'm too broken for you to waste your life on, Emma. Too old and too broken to tie down someone like you."

Staring at him, I didn't agree. Nothing about Daniel told me he was broken. If anything, he seemed like one of the most complete people I'd ever met. The people around him loved and respected him, he did work that made a difference, and he was mind-bogglingly attractive. There wasn't anything I could think of that would make me find any of those things untrue.

"I can decide who I spend my time on."

"You can, but you won't want to."

"I'll be the judge."

He pulled me into his arms, and I let him. Pure warmth. It called back hazy, delirious memories of him carrying me when he saved my life. Both times, he'd had to. These arms meant safety, and I wasn't sure Daniel understood how rare that was or what it meant.

More than anything, I wanted him to know he would never be a waste of anyone's life. One way or another, I was going to show him. In the meantime, I relaxed into his embrace and took the only version of Daniel Clark he would allow me to have.

Chapter 11

Daniel

Through the window into the room where Emma was reciting information into the camera, I could see she was fading. Though they were being as kind to her as they could, the questions were grueling. Every detail of everything she'd seen, heard, and remembered.

Her memory was incredible, and shame washed over me at the possibility I'd briefly considered of her not being of sound mind simply because she'd put blank pieces of paper on the walls. I knew better than to think things were so simple. They never were.

Emma's shoulders were beginning to fold in, and she looked smaller. All I wanted to do was push into the room, pick her up, and pull her out of there. And hold her close while I did it. Take her to dinner, make sure she was all right before reenacting the kiss I'd had to pull away from.

Just because all the things I told her were true didn't mean I didn't *want* her. And god, that kiss destroyed me. It made me question everything I believed about myself. It unlocked the brutal truth I'd known but had avoided facing for years.

I was lonely.

Caring for people in the way I did at Resting Warrior was gratifying, but it wasn't enough. I wanted to care for someone who was mine. Love them, spoil them, make sure they were safe, and just have someone in my life with whom I could spend time.

So, the fact that all I wanted to do with Emma right now was protect her and keep her close wasn't lost on me. She was so much younger and it should have bothered me, but it didn't. It didn't change anything. I was too broken for her to spend what could be a brilliant life on, and I still…

I needed to see Rayne. I already knew what she would say, because she'd said it before, but my resolve to stay alone and protect others had never wavered like it was now. My decisions had cost people their lives, simply because I'd allowed myself to trust the wrong person.

Wasn't that worth penance?

But my resolve was softening. And I was becoming lost. The reasons I'd chosen this life hadn't disappeared. Nor would they disappear. So, what did I do? Because the woman in front of me was a temptation I wasn't going to be able to resist forever. Especially since my denial of the kiss didn't remotely take once I'd told her I wanted to kiss her.

I wasn't going to pretend it wasn't amazing. Nor would I pretend it wasn't replaying in my mind every fucking second. But for now, I needed to focus on Emma and getting her out of here whole and safe.

Agents Phillips and Jones entered the little room where I stood, and my mood shifted. Phillips continued to be a dick, but Jones was at least friendly about it.

"How much longer?" I asked, glancing at my watch. It was almost five, and she was fading more by the second.

"We're almost done," Phillips said, not taking his eyes off her through the one-way window. "If you're willing to stay after the official end of day, we can be completely finished."

"Give her a break," I said. "And I'll ask."

Jones nodded and left.

"You might also want to talk to Noah Scott and Kate Tilbeck. They may not know the ins and outs, but if you need more witness statements, they can corroborate parts of Emma's account and give a few more insights."

"You gave us their information?"

"I did."

"Then we'll be in touch." His arms were crossed, everything about him hard and unyielding. My insight into people, which everyone claimed I had, told me there was more to this for him than a normal investigation. It didn't excuse his behavior, though.

Jones peeked his head inside the room where Emma was, and she sagged in relief, immediately leaving the room. "Let me go talk to her."

Phillips stopped me with a hand on my shoulder. "If you're helping her hide something about Simon Derine, we will find out."

I shrugged his hand off my shoulder. "You heard what I had to say. If you really think I would be protecting someone who put a gun to my friend's head? You don't know me at all."

"You're right," he said, eyes hard. "I *don't* know you, and I've seen stranger things."

Shaking my head, I pushed out of the room. Arguing with him wasn't going to change his mind, and I wasn't going to stay and listen to accusations like that. He was reaching, and it was his job to do so. But his attitude got under my skin. Him being in the same room with me wasn't a good idea.

The small break room where Emma and I had been given free rein to sit during breaks was where I found her. "How are you holding up?" I asked and couldn't help but laugh. I'd asked right as she'd started to down a cup of coffee, and she didn't stop until she'd finished.

She looked at me and refilled the cup. "I'm ready to be done."

"I know. You're almost there. They say if we push a little further tonight we won't have to come back tomorrow. Can you make it?"

The heavy sigh and slump of her shoulders had me reaching for her, and I barely redirected my hands into my pockets in time.

"Yeah. The coffee helps. I'll be glad to go back to the ranch, though. Seattle seems nice, but I think I'd like to see it under better circumstances."

"I'll make sure they have us on a plane tonight. Hang in there."

Emma smiled slightly. "Knowing it's almost over helps. It's weird too, because it's not like this is hard work. I'm not running a marathon or anything. I'm just talking."

"Talking about things that have caused you trauma and remembering the exact details of hundreds of documents? It's still draining."

"Yeah. Guess I better go back in and finish this."

"You can do it."

She smiled, but it didn't reach her eyes—not the way I knew it could—and she topped off her coffee before she went back. Thankfully, Jones was the only one in the observation room when I went back in. "She's going to keep going, but we both want to be back on a flight tonight."

"You're sure? We'll be happy to keep you at the hotel."

"Very sure." The hotel they put us up in was nice, but it wasn't home. "This has been hard for her. Phillips hasn't made it any easier."

Jones chuckled. "I know his bedside manner isn't great, but he's a good agent."

That remained to be seen. "Just please get us on that flight and make sure Phillips isn't the one driving us to the airport."

"You got it."

I sat down after he left, watching Emma do more than anyone had imagined she could.

~

We were on the last flight into Missoula, arriving just before midnight. My truck was waiting for us in the moonlit parking lot. I wasn't looking forward to the drive, but I was looking forward to sleeping in my own bed.

Neither of us said much while we were on the plane or getting into the truck once we landed. Emma was exhausted. If she wanted to talk to me, she would, but I thought she mostly needed to process the experience.

It wasn't long into the drive before she was asleep, leaning against the window. The moonlight coming through the window allowed me to see her, and when I could do so safely, I looked at her.

I needed to stop lying to myself. The instincts and draw I felt toward Emma weren't entirely to do with saving her or protecting her anymore. It started out that way, seeing her in the cage and the dreams. Seeing her sick. But it had stopped being just about those things a while ago. Beautiful, kind, vibrant, and funny. Those were the words I could use to describe the woman sleeping next to me.

Now that I'd realized I *was* lonely, the knowledge was

eating away under my skin like acid. My thoughts immediately turned to my usual excuses. I needed to stay strong and stay away to make sure I didn't hurt anyone else. She didn't deserve to be with someone like me.

But for the first time, a smaller voice inside me was asking if those words were true. And even if they were true, hadn't I already paid enough?

I didn't have an answer to those questions, and by the time I pulled in to Resting Warrior, my head was aching with running around in the same thought circles. No matter what, I couldn't release myself from my commitment until I knew for sure. Which meant that Emma and I could be nothing more than friends.

My heart sank with the thought, and I closed my eyes as I pulled up to her cabin. That was the truth, then. I wanted to let everything go, regardless of the consequences. But I couldn't.

She didn't stir as I walked around the truck, and she barely moved when I opened the door and lifted her out. Here, in this moment, I could focus on the luxury of holding her when I wasn't actively trying to save her life.

Emma fit in my arms like she was meant to be there, the same way she'd melted into me yesterday during our kiss. Those brief moments felt like coming home. Like waking up refreshed with the entire world before you, knowing happiness waited.

I laid her on her bed and retreated, trying to memorize the feeling of this moment, knowing it could be all I'd ever have.

Chapter 12

Emma

“You’re sure?”

“Yes,” Kate said, laughing. “Of course.”

It was the second time I’d asked, because I couldn’t quite wrap my head around the fact that the bags on the floor of my cabin right now were *all* for me. All filled with clothes that were my size.

The clothes I’d been wearing were all borrowed, which was fine. I didn’t have money, and I wasn’t going to steal again. But Kate had gone and bought me all of this.

I would find a way to pay them back. Daniel for helping with the grocery store and Kate for the clothes. I would.

“Thank you.”

“Girl, I promise, it’s not a problem,” she said with a smile and glanced at her phone. “I have to run and meet a client, but I’ll see you at family dinner later this week, okay?”

“Okay.”

I sat on the couch in my cabin and stared at the

clothes. It was too much. All of it. I liked it here at Resting Warrior, but I felt very out of place. They didn't really know what to do with me, and I didn't really know what to do either.

With the investigation and Simon wanting me dead, it wasn't safe for me to go into town and get a job. Yet I didn't want to sit around and do nothing. That was all I'd done for the last six months, and I was restless.

I came across Mara a few days ago, and she seemed willing to let me help her, and no one disagreed. So that was what I did. I helped with whatever she happened to be doing, which was usually some kind of simple repair or gardening.

That was where I had been heading before Kate stopped by with the clothes. I couldn't look at the clothes right now—I was already overwhelmed, and the kindness in the gesture could be enough to make me cry.

Instead, I locked the cabin door behind me and headed down the road past the next three cabins to where Mara and I had been slowly working on some decorative flower beds.

She didn't talk much, but that was fine with me. I liked the company, regardless, and the simplicity of working with things like dirt and plants.

"Hi, Mara."

"Hello." Her voice was quiet. She was already kneeling in the dirt, digging a new row for some kind of bulb.

I looked over what she'd already done and moved to mirror it on the other side. "Sorry I'm late. Kate stopped by to give me something."

A soft laugh took me by surprise. "You're not late. You can't really be late since you're a guest. But I'm happy for the company."

"Me too. And…" I sighed. "I know I don't really work here. I'm just not sure what to do with myself. If I'm ever getting in your way, please tell me. I don't want to make things harder for you."

She smiled. "Thank you. But you're not bothering me. I won't be working long, though. I have an appointment in town."

"Oh, okay. Just let me know."

We fell into silence, and I busied myself planting rows of the flowers, watching what Mara did and following. I asked questions when I had them, but it was uncomplicated, and it was a relief to have my hands doing something so I wasn't stuck with my own thoughts.

They'd been going like crazy since we'd returned from Seattle a few days ago. Or rather, since I'd woken up in bed in my cabin after we got back, not remembering how I got inside. Which meant Daniel had carried me in from the truck.

I sighed, wishing I *had* been awake for that. Just once, I would like to be conscious and healthy when he picked me up and held me so I could have that memory since he seemed determined not to give me any others.

And yet…

Shaking my head, I knew I couldn't puzzle it out any more than I had the last few days. Daniel was everywhere. Working at the lodge, I saw him. He seemed to be out walking a fair amount, and every time I was around him, I swore I had to be imagining the way he looked at me. With the same hunger he'd had in those brief moments of vulnerability while we were near the water.

But he didn't make any moves, and he kept his distance more than he had before.

I hadn't changed my mind. Daniel was—

He was everything I'd always wanted. Strong, kind, and honest. Ludicrously hot. Not to mention, he'd saved my life. I didn't care about the rest of it. Yes, he was older, but not so much older anyone would really raise an eyebrow. Would they? Maybe. I hoped not, but it wasn't a guarantee.

And for what he said?

Daniel hadn't told me yet what he meant about being too broken for me to waste time on, but I didn't believe it. If I wasn't too broken to love, then neither was he. I couldn't imagine something he could have done or had happen to him that would render him anything other than the good man I knew he was.

The sun was getting higher in the sky when Mara finally put down the spade she had in her hand and stretched, arching her back. "You don't have to worry about anything," she said. I nearly missed her voice because it was so quiet. "I'll come back to it this afternoon."

"I hope you have fun."

She winced, and I saw her deciding whether to say anything. I was grateful she did. "Probably not. I mean, therapy is always good, and Dr. Rayne is nice, but fun isn't the word I'd use."

Dr. Rayne again. So many people had mentioned her at this point, I half expected her to materialize. "That's true. Well, in that case, I hope you have a productive session."

"Thanks."

She left without saying anything else, but that was par for the course with Mara. She talked more than anyone made me think she would, but she was still quiet, and that was fine with me. I'd spent six months in a cabin, mostly silent. I understood.

I stood and brushed the dirt off my jeans. Seemed like it was around lunchtime, so I walked toward the main lodge. For the last few days, Daniel and I had eaten together, just talking and laughing and dancing around the things neither of us was saying.

My cabin was on the way, so I stopped in, quickly looking

through the bags Kate had brought for something that wasn't dirty jeans and a T-shirt which only fit okay. Nothing too fancy, but a pretty blue shirt and a clean, well-fitting pair of jeans suddenly made me feel like a person again.

Before Simon, my life hadn't been easy, but I'd had friends. I'd gone on some dates and actually done things normal people did. After graduation, I didn't. I was too busy working for him and trying to make him proud because I was making up for lost time.

Whole lot of good it did me.

I smelled the pizza as soon as I walked into the lodge. Daniel was already sitting at the table, two boxes open beside him, pepperoni and cheese. Usually we had sandwiches.

He smiled. "I've been craving…pizza since Seattle. So, I went into town and got us some."

"Us?" I couldn't help the smile that came to my own face.

"I shouldn't have assumed you'd come by, but I'm glad you did."

"I don't know. Lunch is kind of our thing now, right?"

"Right."

I served myself and sat across from him, trying not to stare and trying not to think about the pause he had taken before he'd told me what he was craving.

Daniel was handsome, and he was the first man in my life who truly gave a shit about me. I wasn't going to give up until he provided me with a real reason not to give us a shot. We both wanted it.

But first, I had to ask, "Is there anything I can do?"

He looked at me, surprised. "What do you mean?"

"I've been helping Mara around the ranch, and I want to be useful if I can. I'm not paying to be here, and I can't get a job…" I sighed and took a bite of pizza. "I don't want you all to feel like I'm taking advantage of your hospitality. If there's something I can do to earn my stay here, I want to do it."

Daniel reached across the table and took my hand where it rested. It was the most natural motion he could make, and it froze us both in place. He hadn't intended to do it, but I didn't want him to let go. "We're happy to have you here," he finally said, staring at our connected hands. "I hope you know you don't have to do anything to earn that."

My heart skipped a beat. "I do know."

We hung in silence together for another minute, and finally, I gently squeezed his hand. "Let me put it this way. I spent six months in Simon's cabin, trying to figure out where he went so I could keep myself alive. Now I'm not trying to solve anything, but it's all that's in my head. I need something to do, or I'm going to go crazy."

He squeezed my hand back, neither of us wanting to let go and holding on as long as we could. "I'll think about it," he promised.

I hoped that putting me to work wasn't the only thing he would think about.

Chapter 13

Emma

I had no idea what to expect walking into what Resting Warrior called *family dinner*. All I knew was I was to be at the lodge at six and be prepared for a lot of food and people.

The latter was true, and I wasn't even inside yet. Trucks and cars lined up outside the lodge, more than I'd seen in the time I'd been here.

Suddenly, I was nervous. I'd met a few people here and there, but not this many all at once. Daniel—ever the gentleman, even if he was determined for us to only be friends—had come to get me from my cabin and brought me here. I looked over at him.

He gave me a smile. "Just family dinner, that's all."

This was one giant family. I could hear the hum of conversation even outside the door. But it wasn't like a smaller group would help me feel more at ease. I had no idea what a *family dinner* should be like. Hell, I had no idea what a *family* really was.

He opened the door for me, and we walked in. The room was filled with people, and I only knew a few of them. Noah, Liam, and some other men were gathered by the fireplace and bar, while Kate and all the other women were in the kitchen and at the table, drinking wine and laughing. I didn't see Mara, and more importantly, I had no idea where to go.

"Emma!" Kate saw me, and her eyes lit up. "I'm happy you're here. I get to introduce you to everyone and induct you into the girls' club."

I smiled, but my chest was still tight with nerves. "There's a club?"

A short, curvy woman with colorful streaks in her hair grinned. "There's definitely a club, and while you're here, you don't have a choice but to join. I'm Lena." She extended a hand, and I shook it. "I belong to that one."

She pointed to the giant in the corner of the room. He had a glass in one hand and eyes that were only for the woman in front of me. I'd seen him around and knew his name was Jude. But we'd never directly spoken.

Now she was looking at him, and her cheeks tinged pink under his gaze. I glanced down at her fingers and spied a ring. "He's your fiancé?"

"Yes, he is." Her voice was breathy with awe, like she could hardly believe it.

Jude downed the drink he was holding and stepped around Liam to come straight for her. "Excuse me, ladies. I need to borrow Lena for a minute."

"A minute?" A redhead sitting at the table laughed. "We'll see you in fifteen."

He was kissing her before the door fully closed, and my heart did a little flip. What would it be like to have someone so entirely focused on you they needed to have you despite being in a room full of their friends?

My eyes strayed to Daniel where he sat by the fire, and he was looking at me too. This was dangerous territory.

"Are they like that all the time?"

"All the time," the redhead said. "Took them three years to finally get together. Now that they are? They can't keep their hands off each other, and it's kind of adorable."

"Like you and Harlan weren't exactly the same?" another woman asked. I tried not to do a double take when I looked at her. Her arms were covered in visible scars, and not the kind some people gave to themselves. They looked like someone had taken a blowtorch to her skin. "I'm Evelyn, and that one—" she pointed at the redhead "—is Grace. Don't let her fool you. She and her husband were just as bad as them."

"We were *not*," Grace said.

"Were too."

She rolled her eyes. "Fine. But we can all agree none of us are as bad as Grant and Cori, right?"

"Hey," a small blonde with teal highlights in her hair pouted in mock sadness. "We're not so bad."

"As if you don't love every second," Evelyn said with a laugh.

Cori blushed and drank deeply from the wine in her hand. "Can't argue with that."

"Can I get you something to drink, Emma?" Kate asked.

I blinked. "What is there?"

"Anything from the bar. Wine, whiskey, we've got a bunch of soda and, of course, water."

Wine? I could do wine. It might help the nerves swimming in my gut. "White wine, please."

"You got it."

I followed her over to the bar as she went. "Kate?"

"Yeah?"

"Does everyone here—" I paused, lowering my voice. "Does everyone here know who I am? Why I'm here?"

She made a face. "Yeah, they do. None of them will say anything or ask you about it. But we were all worried about the woman who disappeared."

"Really?"

She placed a hand on my shoulder. "It's not every day you end up in a cage next to someone. We were all rescued, so when you disappeared? Everyone wanted to make sure you were okay."

Tears pricked at my eyes, and I blinked them back. They were all strangers. Why would any of them care about me?

Kate saw and turned me toward the bar, where she poured my wine. "And I know it's weird to have a bunch of strangers know something so intimate about you. It wasn't shared as gossip, and none of the people in this room will ever judge you for what happened or think less of you. They'll also never ask you to share anything beyond what you're comfortable with."

Quickly swiping at my eyes, I smiled. "That sounds nice."

I glanced around the room and felt my heart settle. I understood why it was called family dinner now. All these people…none of them were related, but they *were* a family. It felt like a family. The comfort and safety of it, and it was everything I'd ever wanted.

A fierce longing sprung up in my chest. *Here.* I wanted to belong here, more than I'd ever wanted to belong anywhere. Everywhere else, I'd never felt anything close to the comfort I felt in this room, and I wasn't even a part of this group.

I wanted to belong with Daniel, and I wanted a place in this world where people loved and protected one another. And just like that, yearning turned to determination. I could belong here, and I would. I was going to fight for my place here—and fight for Daniel.

Kate dragged me back to the table. "Okay, real introductions. Everyone, this is Emma. Emma, you already met everyone, but now you're a part of the gang."

"It's nice to meet you guys."

"I haven't seen you come by Deja Brew." Evelyn looked at me. "Make sure you do, and Lena and I will take care of you, for sure."

"Sounds good," I laughed. It was only because of my memories driving through town that I remembered Deja Brew was one of the coffee shops. "I'm not sure how far I'm allowed to go, given everything. But I'll try."

She shrugged. "Ask Daniel if you're nervous. He'll come with you."

He probably would. "I bother him enough without dragging him into town for coffee."

Grace glanced behind me subtly, and one by one, they all followed suit. Where I was sitting, Daniel and the rest of the men were behind me. Cori finally laughed and looked at me with a smirk. "I don't think anything you do would bother him."

I was turning bright red, but I ignored it. "Why do you say that?"

"Because." Lena sat down next to me, eyes sparkling. I hadn't heard them come back inside. "They're very used to watching a man want someone from a distance, and Daniel has that look all over his face."

Deflating, I took a long sip of my wine. When I set the glass down, they were all looking at me. "What?"

"Okay." Kate glanced at the men before refocusing on me. "You don't have to say anything, but we know that look. And everything you want to tell us about what's already happened between you? We want to know."

Nothing had changed. I still felt safe and secure here. But would they disapprove? They didn't seem to. More, would Daniel be upset if I said anything?

"You guys would be fine with it?"

Grace frowned. "Fine with what?"

"With—" I swallowed. "With me and Daniel."

Lena leaned in. "This might sound rude, but it's not meant to be. Why the hell wouldn't we be fine with it?"

I kept my voice low. "The age difference. At least, that's what he said."

"Oh boy." Grace chuckled. "Remind me to tell you my whole story when the boys aren't here and we can get hammered, cry, and be completely irresponsible."

Evelyn laughed. "Agreed. It's been too long. But no." She focused her gaze on me. "No one here gives a rat's ass about it. You're an adult, and Daniel is one of the most honorable men out there. He probably doesn't want to take advantage of you. But if you want him and he wants you? Who cares?"

The rest of what he'd said—about him being broken—wasn't mine to share. But this helped. If no one in this group took issue with us before we even started, then it made everything easier. And gave me ammunition in the fight Daniel didn't even know we were having yet.

"Thank you."

"No problem," Grace sipped from her own glass. "And Emma, I've known Daniel for a while, and I've never seen him with anyone. Hell, I've never even heard him say he was interested in dating or love. If you've managed to crack that shell? It's both a good sign and a damn miracle. As far as I'm concerned, take a hammer to him until he cracks the rest of the way."

We all laughed, and suddenly I felt him behind me like a magnet, pulling me to face him. "How's everyone doing?"

"Good." Evelyn grinned. "Food will be ready in a few

minutes. And don't forget, next time it's the men's turn to cook."

Jude put his hands on Lena's shoulders. "We haven't forgotten. Promise."

She reached up and grabbed his hand, leaning back into him. The simple gesture and the way he bent down and kissed the top of her head made me *ache* inside. That was what I wanted.

"Good. In that case…" Evelyn was grinning even wider. "Let's eat."

A sharp knock on the door made everyone freeze. Noah looked around. "Did we miss someone?"

"Anyone else who might be here knows to come in," Daniel said. He strode to the door and opened it. I read the shock in his body before I heard him speak. "Agent Phillips. Agent Jones. Surprised to see you here."

Dread spiraled down through me. Why were they here? Through the door, I heard one of them say something, though I couldn't quite make out the words.

Turning, Daniel looked at me. "Emma? They'd like to speak to you."

"Is it mandatory?"

His mouth quirked into a smile. I loved the amusement I saw there, like we were sharing a secret. "No, it's not."

Sighing, I stood and went to the door. "Stay with me, please."

"Always."

My heart flipped and my stomach dropped. He didn't really mean the word in the way I heard it, but I savored it anyway. The two FBI agents stood on the porch in the sunset light. "This couldn't have been a phone call?"

"I suppose it could have been," Jones laughed. "But we need to ask you something, and we thought in person would be better."

Phillips looked over at Daniel. "You don't need to be here for this."

"Actually, he does," I snapped. "Because I asked him to be. If you have a problem with it, go sit in your car and give us a call I can put on speaker where you won't know the difference."

My own anger shocked me, and it equally shocked Phillips, who suddenly looked at me like I was a new person. And in his eyes, it was clear that wasn't necessarily a good thing.

Finally, Agent Jones cleared his throat to break the tension, and I was intentionally not looking at Daniel, because I could feel him looking at me. "The information you gave us was very helpful, Miss Derine. We have a very credible lead on your father's location, but—"

"That man is not my father," I said. "Please don't refer to him as such."

Jones nodded, starting again slowly. "We have a good idea of where Simon is hiding, and we wanted to know if you'd help us in catching him."

"His network is big," Phillips said. "Bigger than we thought, and we already knew it was large. This is important. Taking him down would be a huge win and would have an impact on getting a *lot* of illegal guns and drugs off the streets. You need to help us do this."

I glared at him. His insistence was getting old. I understood the good I could do, but bullying me into the choice he wanted me to make wasn't the way to do it.

"Is it dangerous?" Daniel's voice was calm and even. It brought me back from the panicked place my mind was working toward.

"It could be," Jones acknowledged. "But we'd be with you the whole time, and we will do everything in our power to make sure you're safe. After your part in the case is finished, you'd be eligible for witness protection. There, you'll be completely safe. We'll take care of everything."

The whole world went red. "No way in hell," I spat.

"No one's ever been lost in witness protection." Jones held out his hands like he was explaining. "You would be safe, I promise."

"You need to listen." My voice was raw. "I don't give a shit if it's safe or not. I'm not disappearing into the system like that. Did you forget I have perfect recall? I know what kind of information I gave you, and I know there were dirty cops on those lists. If he can get to them, it's not a far stretch to getting to other people who are supposed to be good. And telling me that's my only option is the last way to get me to help you. You can't force me to go."

Phillips stepped forward, and Daniel was there, his body blocking the path between the agent and me. But I saw the man wasn't trying to get physical; he was trying to be intimidating. His voice was as near to a growl as I'd ever heard. "No, we can't force you. But you and your perfect recall need to think about it. Your life was and is in danger already, and as long as Simon is out there, it will continue to be. You might as well do some good for the world either way and take the offer to protect yourself before you overstay your welcome here, bringing more trouble to these people."

Daniel went deathly still. "You are out of line."

"Am I?" he asked. "You said yourself Simon wants revenge on you and your employees. You really think harboring his daughter, whom he wants dead, is going to make him feel less inclined to torch this place to the ground?"

"He already tried that," Daniel said. "And failed. He's welcome to try again."

I stared at the agent, and he stared back. It was clear what he thought of me. He thought if I didn't put my own life on the line to catch Simon, I was a bad person. And he was going to make sure I knew it.

"I'll think about it," I said, directing the words only to Agent Jones. "And I'll do it without assholes breathing down my neck."

Before I could question anything, I went back inside, leaving Daniel to get them the hell out of here.

Chapter 14

Daniel

"You need to convince her," Phillips said as soon as the door closed behind her. "She needs to do this, and she listens to you."

I looked at him and tried to see what was driving this fervor. Nothing came up, but I shook my head. Emma hadn't reacted badly to helping; she'd reacted badly to Phillips's attitude and the mention of WITSEC. And for whatever reason, she was far more afraid of going into witness protection than she was of Simon finding her.

"I'm not going to do that. She can make her own decisions, and she will do it without you gaslighting her until she does what you want."

He stared me down and shrugged. "She's going to help us one way or another. It's easier if she says yes now."

"She's right. You can't force her to help."

"Unfortunately, no," the man admitted. "I can't *force* someone into doing the right thing. But Simon wants her. So whether or not she decides to help, her name is one of the few things that will draw him out, and we can get permission to use it, regardless of Miss Derine's opinion."

I shoved my hands into my pockets before the anger currently burning in my chest made me hit this man. I didn't want to get arrested for assaulting an FBI agent. "We'll be in touch," I said. "Now, respectfully, leave Resting Warrior property."

Jones looked ashamed as he left, and Phillips looked angry. Must be awful to have someone like that for a partner. I felt sorry for the man.

I waited until they drove away before I went back inside, where everyone was intentionally and joyfully ignoring the FBI-shaped elephant in the room. They were all in the process of serving themselves mashed potatoes and gravy and healthy portions of Evelyn's pot roast—a dish that was coveted at family dinner.

No one said anything about it, not even Emma, though she locked eyes with me when she sat down. Anger simmered below the surface, and I didn't fucking blame her.

The entire rest of dinner, I couldn't focus. Instead, I watched Emma to make sure she was okay. She was smiling and laughing, and I loved that she was comfortable enough to do so. But I could tell it was only on the surface. Beneath everything, she was as distracted as I was, and I needed to hear what she was thinking.

I craved listening to her in a way I hadn't with anyone in a long time. Our lunches every day this week were the highlight of my waking hours, and each day that passed made me realize how much I wanted her, and it killed me.

Rayne had said exactly what I'd expected, which was I was punishing myself too harshly for something that happened too long ago. And if I did deserve to do penance

—which she didn't believe I did—then I had done more than enough.

It felt like I'd blinked through family dinner. Everyone was standing and gathering their things. Noah and Kate were collecting the dishes, and Grace was going to help them. But I couldn't wait through it. "I'll do the dishes," I said. "You guys can leave them."

"Are you sure?" Grace asked. "There's a lot of them."

"I don't mind. Need to clear my head anyway."

She smiled. "Next time it's your turn, we'll make sure to swap."

All the dishes were piled in the sink, but I didn't move from my seat until everyone had gone. Everyone but Emma, who was still sitting in her chair. I knew we would talk, but the dishes still needed to get done.

Rolling up my sleeves, I got to work.

Emma stepped up beside me, drying while I washed, and we fell into a quiet, easy rhythm. But the tension between us was so thick I could feel it, as if the small physical space between us had weight and substance. I sensed every inch.

The last dish passed from my hand to hers, and I leaned on the sink. "Can I ask you something?"

A soft laugh spilled from her lips. "I've been waiting for it."

"Why did you react so strongly to witness protection? Not because I disagree, I just want to understand. More than being used as bait, that's what made you angry."

She put down the dish and dried her hands, tossing the towel on the counter. "Because I can't take it."

I waited as she paced across the space, arms crossed. "When I was growing up, I only ever had my mother. She was amazing, and I miss her so much—" Her breath hiccupped, and I gripped the counter where I held it in order to stop myself from going to her. She needed to get this out.

"Then I *thought* I had my father. I never had a chance to belong anywhere and find my place because of him. Now I'm here, and I want *this*." She pointed to the room. "The feeling when everyone is in here and talking and laughing and knowing, no matter what, you have one another's backs. Kate told me everyone here knew about me and was concerned when I was missing. They're *strangers*, and they cared about me. I've never had that. And I'm not going to lose it, Daniel. I can't. If they take me away and hide me somewhere I don't know anyone, it will break me, and I don't know how to handle it."

She felt at home here.

The thought warmed me so much I almost smiled. Almost, because smiling at that admission wouldn't win me any favors. "I would never force you to do anything you don't want, and I'll admit I don't like the idea of witness protection, but I do want you safe."

"I can be safe here."

"Simon knows about this place. I wasn't lying. He tried to burn down the ranch the night we rescued you, and with your memory, I don't doubt you remember him saying he would kill all of us for messing around in his business."

She sighed. "Yes, I remember."

"He might have bigger problems right now, but the threat to the ranch and to you isn't something we can just ignore. You can't live with a sword hanging over your head for the rest of your life."

"So, I should banish myself to some backwater town where I *hope* he doesn't find me while they put me in a database he can probably gain access to?"

I looked at her and raised an eyebrow. "Is that what I said?"

"It's so frustrating." Her voice rose, echoing off the ceiling. "I want him taken down as much as anyone else, but I don't want to be blackmailed into doing it. I don't want to live my entire life looking over my shoulder. But I'm just one person, and even my memory doesn't make me a match for this. I'm not a character in a TV show. My 'perfect recall' doesn't come with a side dish of genius and the ability to turn into a badass at will."

I chuckled, and she smiled a little. "I want you safe," I told her. "In whatever way is best to ensure that. I don't know if WITSEC is it, or if we're able to protect you here, but I do know you need to talk to Agent Jones."

"Only him."

"I agree. He would be the one. After you went inside, Agent Phillips made it clear they'll be using your name as bait whether you're physically helping them or not. You need to be aware of their plan either way, in case it backfires."

Emma whirled from her pacing and stared at me, mouth agape. "Can they do that?"

I shrugged. "I hesitate to say it, but I'm not sure there's much Agent Phillips *wouldn't* do to catch Simon. He seems… particularly dedicated to the cause."

"Yeah."

The silence hung between us, growing tighter until it felt like there was a line tugging me toward her. I didn't move, but she looked at me like she felt it too. I saw determination in her eyes, and it had everything to do with her situation and nothing to do with me.

But I could tell the moment it changed. The hunger I felt in my gut was mirrored in her gaze, and I wasn't able to do anything but stare. She was so incredibly beautiful. Both sides of her called to me. The frightened woman who needed protecting, and the fiery one who was angry at the unfairness of her situation. Every part of her only made me want her more.

Seeing her fit in seamlessly with my family was a bonus.

The thread between us snapped.

She crossed the space to me, and my arms were held out before I registered making the decision. As she wrapped herself around me, I held on to her. All softness and warmth and temptation. I needed to step back and set our boundaries in place once more, but I didn't.

I was *tired* of living my life alone, and I was tired of having held on to so much for so long. It was so tempting to simply let the burden roll off my back and run free. Yet it was also terrifying. Who was I without this?

The code I lived my life by was all I'd had for years. Abandoning it felt like diving off a cliff, with no guarantee of safe water at the bottom.

But I didn't pull away. Instead, I pulled her closer. My lips brushed her temple, and I rested them there. I leaned back against the counter and let our legs slowly tangle. I couldn't have said how long we stood there, breathing in each other's air and slowly syncing our pulses, but I didn't release my hold.

And no matter my fear, I needed to come to terms with the fact that this was where I wanted to be. Emma was here, and I didn't want to let her go.

Chapter 15

Emma

My body relaxed, easing into the embrace more and more the longer Daniel held me. And I couldn't remember a time I'd felt more safe. After everything I'd been through and everything I'd survived, I needed this.

It was different from merely being rescued or him making sure I was healthy. This was everything. He'd been keeping my soul safe too, been on my side even when I hadn't expected him to be, and wasn't making choices for me.

Every action he'd taken so far had been to protect me, even if it was from himself, even if I didn't agree with him. And right now, like this, I couldn't stop my imagination from running its course. What would it be like if I twisted my face up and kissed him again, and how would it be if he kissed me back? I couldn't stop my brain from traveling down that line of thought to something I'd never experienced but always wanted.

But it was more than mere sex and pleasure that drew me to Daniel. It was this life. The good he did and the steadiness of the ranch. He helped people instead of using them, even at the cost of himself. In the short time I'd known him, never had I seen him put himself first. He was always an afterthought.

I wanted to be the one who put him first and made sure he was taken care of in the same way he took care of everyone else. Everything we could possibly have was so close, and I wanted to try. Nothing was certain—I knew that more than anyone—but after all that I'd been through, I also knew you had to try. Life was too short and too brutal not to take a chance on the things you wanted.

And I'd never wanted anyone like this before. Wholly and completely.

"Can I ask you something?" My voice was muffled by his shirt, but he held me tighter instinctively and a part of me soared.

"You can ask me anything, Emma. I'll never lie to you."

I didn't want to, but I needed to see his face when I asked this question, so I pulled away from him. Our arms were still around each other, and it was comfortable. My heart pounded in my chest and my mouth was dry with nerves, but I needed to know. "Do you like me? I mean—" I cleared my throat. "Are you attracted to me?"

Daniel froze. This close, I felt the tension in his body, but he didn't let me go. And he couldn't deny it if it was true, not now that he'd said he wouldn't lie.

Shock was on his face too, and the rawness there did nothing to diminish how handsome he was. His throat worked as he swallowed, and he sighed, closing his eyes. "Yes. I am."

Pulling away fully, I looked at him. "Then what's the deal?"

"I—"

"I know." I waved a hand. "You told me your reasons in Seattle, but I don't buy it, Daniel. The reasons you gave me aren't things you get to decide for me. I'm perfectly capable of deciding if someone is too old for me, and I can decide if you're too broken—which I doubt—for me to spend my time on. But I can't do that if you don't tell me the truth."

He leaned against the counter, and he suddenly looked *tired*. Like the weight he held on his shoulders but didn't let anyone see suddenly became visible. The change was visceral and brutal. "You don't need to listen to that," he said. "It's my baggage, and I'll be carrying it forever."

"But you don't have to."

"Emma."

"Daniel." I crossed my arms and stared him down. "You know a fucking lot about me. Things I wouldn't just walk up and tell someone. Everyone here knows I was a prisoner, but they don't know the details. *You* do. You're holding my secrets with me, and I trust you with them. Let me do the same for you. I know you think you can do it alone, but I see the way it's eating at you. Right now? You sank in on yourself like you suddenly had one of those two-ton weights from the cartoons drop on you. Even if you don't…" I took a breath, and the words burned in my throat. "Even if you don't change your mind and don't want me, please let me help you. You deserve to have someone help hold your pain just like everyone else."

The look in his eyes was strange. A mixture of that same pain and the hunger I'd only seen directed toward me. That, and indecision. But the indecision didn't last long.

"SEALs do a lot of different things," he said, looking at the floor. "And more often than not, despite being in the Navy, they don't involve water."

I smiled, sitting down at the table close to him and listening.

"I'll tell you what I can, but not everything can be shared. Not because I'm holding back, but because it's still classified."

"I understand."

He glanced at me, his brief smile grateful. But the look in his eyes had shifted to pure grief. "I can't tell you where we were, but my unit was going after some bad people. While we were there, we became aware that they were holding hostages. A lot of them. And they were like you. People in cages. Starving and dirty. I still don't know what they meant to do with them. But whether they were meant to be sold or something else, we wanted to get them out.

"It changed the plan, but my unit and I were fine with that. Civilians came first. The people we were tracking, we'd found them once, and we could find them again."

Daniel paused and crossed the room to the bar. I didn't speak or ask any questions. This was hard for him, and I wasn't going to stop him from doing whatever he needed to get through it.

He poured a small drink and knocked it back before turning to face me once more. "There was an informant. We'd been using him for years, and not once had his information been wrong. He told us where the hostages were, how many there were, and how to get to them."

Dread pooled in my stomach, and as he spoke, it became entirely justified.

"He wasn't on our side. After all that time, he was working for *them*. Feeding us the information they wanted us to have and giving us just enough to hang ourselves. They might have had other plans for those prisoners, but when we arrived, they unquestionably turned them into a trap for us.

"We went in, and I'll never forget the sight of them in

those cages. I dreamed—dream—about them the same way I dream about you. Your face changes to theirs and vice versa. I can still hear the screams. Because as soon as we went in, it was an ambush. Shots and explosions."

"Oh god, Daniel."

He kept talking, not acknowledging that I'd spoken, like he was trapped in the memory. "I got lucky. Pinned under some rubble, but nothing broken. They couldn't see me in the dust and debris. Everyone else…everyone else was gone. My entire team. Every single one of the people in those cages. Just dead like it was nothing, and that's on me."

Daniel looked at me then. "It's on *me*, Emma. I'm the one who made the call and trusted him, even though the information, looking back, was too specific and detailed. Even though it was the easiest infiltration we'd ever had, with no resistance. It should have dawned on me it was a trap. Nearly forty people dead. Because of me.

"So yes, I'm broken. I clearly don't have the best judgment, and especially since you're actively in danger, I need to keep a clear head so I can keep you alive. I already thought you might be dead, and my dreams wouldn't fucking leave me alone. I *can't* have your face be one more life on my conscience, Emma. I can't do it."

He was halfway back across the room, chest heaving and eyes wild like he was back in that place with the shooting and the explosions, and I wanted to wrap my arms around him. But I didn't.

"And that's why you won't be with me?" I asked softly. "Because you're afraid of what might happen?"

"*Yes.*"

I stood up slowly, sensing he was still partly in the past. "Should I have known Simon was some kind of drug kingpin?"

"What?" Daniel blinked, the jump in topic throwing him

and breaking him out of the hold his memories had on him. "No, of course not."

"The person who claimed to be my father integrated himself into my life, made me feel loved, paid for my school, gave me a job, and basically saved me after my mother died. He did all those things, and I was convinced I was in an amazing, wonderful place—until it fell apart in an hour. If I shouldn't have been able to tell he was one of the worst people on this planet, then why would you think you should have been able to do the same?"

Daniel stared at me, his expression unmoving.

"You said you'd been working with him for years and it was all perfect. He did that, not you. You had absolutely no reason not to trust him, and so you did what made sense in the moment. You made the decision with the information you had at the time, just like everyone does every single day."

I took one step toward him and then another. He still didn't move, looking at me like I was both his end and his salvation. Once again, I *felt* the hunger he wouldn't admit.

"I know it doesn't make it easier, or the fact that so many people died better, but you don't bear the responsibility for something you had *no reason to know* any more than I do. And yes, I'll be struggling with it forever, just like you will. I've decided to talk to Dr. Rayne while I'm here."

Daniel suddenly unfroze from the pose he'd taken, running both hands through his hair. "That's great. I'm glad."

"I'm not done," I said gently. "Bad things happen. I know that more than anyone. But it doesn't—it *can't* mean you stop living your life. I know I'm in danger, and I know Simon wants me dead. There's a reason I stayed in the cabin trying to figure it out before I had to leave or die. And yes, I'm scared. But you pulled me out of it and reminded me there was something before Simon, and there will be something after him. *You* make me feel safe. All the anxiety I've lived with? It's gone with you around."

"Emma—" He sounded resigned, but I wasn't going to let him stop this. Not yet.

I crossed the rest of the distance between us and touched him. Pressed my hands to his chest and looked him in the eye. "Don't, Daniel. Please. Don't try to make excuses to get out of something that makes sense. And I'm telling you now, what you're clinging to doesn't make sense. Even taking me out of the equation. Living in the past with this for the rest of your life, it doesn't make sense. And there's another reason I don't want to go into WITSEC. It's because even if this is new and I don't completely know what I'm doing, you've shown me I can have a life. And I'm finding I can have one here. More than that, I want to keep it."

I watched my words sink in, and he caught me by the shoulders. I wasn't sure if he wanted to pull me closer or push me away. God, I was close enough to twist up and kiss him, but if we were going to do this, he had to make the move.

"Please think about it, because I don't need to. Neither of us knows the future, but I'm finished holding myself back because I'm afraid of something going wrong or because of pain and anxiety. I've learned enough to know you can be careful all you want and it doesn't change anything. I want you, Daniel. I want to give whatever this is between us a go. I don't care about our ages, and I don't think you're broken. The things you say are barriers aren't to me, and I'm not giving up on what could be between us."

With that, I turned and left the lodge, hauling in the night air like I'd just finished running a triathlon or something. My legs were shaking with adrenaline for the second time tonight.

Standing up like I had, first to Agent Phillips and now to

Daniel, wasn't the way I normally spoke. I was content to fade into the background and live my life quietly. Or I had been until I realized all it did was get you locked in a cage. Whether that cage was in the real world, made of metal, or a cage in your mind that held you back from what you really wanted, it didn't matter. A cage was still a cage.

Daniel had broken me out of one cage. Like hell was I going to put myself in another one on purpose. If I could, I would keep him from locking himself away too.

I hadn't made the conscious decision to see the therapist they suggested until it came out of my mouth, but it was a good idea. The things I said were true. I didn't deserve to beat myself up for things I couldn't have known, and I still felt guilty for it. Tomorrow, I would make an appointment and see how I liked it. One appointment couldn't hurt.

Looking up, I watched the stars finally appearing as I walked back to my cabin in the nearly eerie Montana silence.

Everything in me wanted to turn around and go back to Daniel and beg him to tell me what he was thinking and whether what I'd said had any effect. But I couldn't. He needed time. I knew it like I knew my own name.

I blew out a breath as I jogged up the steps to my cabin and unlocked the door. It wasn't late, and I wasn't about to sleep. My mind was too busy for that.

The bags Kate brought me still hadn't been fully unpacked, so I grabbed them and brought them to my bedroom, determined to put the clothes away and at least do something useful while my brain was running in circles.

But go figure, the first thing to drop out of one of the bags was a bra. It was pretty and simple, with a little lace trim. And it did nothing to stem the tide of thoughts and fantasies of Daniel realizing I was right, deciding to give us a chance, and showing up at my door. I would deal with the nerves of that situation if it happened.

In the meantime, I grabbed the clothes and put them away, hoping I would be able to keep myself busy enough not to go mad.

Chapter 16

Daniel

I wasn't sure how long I stood there after Emma left the lodge without looking back. But I was aware I stared at the door for far too long, hoping she'd return just so I could see the fire in her eyes and the conviction when she spoke. Because everything she said was true, and still, my soul ached with tension and hesitation.

Fuck sleeping. That wasn't going to happen.

I poured myself one more drink and downed it before heading out the back door to the gym. Most of us kept spare clothes there, and I changed quickly into a pair of shorts so I could do…something.

We had machines, but I didn't really feel like running or biking, and given the thoughts in my head regarding Emma, I didn't want to punch a bag. The violence didn't sit right with me.

I headed for the weights and stacked a bar with a low number I didn't need to be spotted for. Pushing it, I went until my arms burned before I released it. It felt good, so I went further, grabbing a jump rope and forcing my heart rate higher.

The door opened and Jude came in, taking one look at me and raising an eyebrow. It wasn't unheard of for any of us to hit the gym this late at night, but it was far more common when something was bothering us. I hadn't expected anyone to come here now, least of all him.

"Why aren't you at home with Lena?"

"She left a dish here she needs tomorrow at Deja Brew for an order. I told her I would come and get it. The gate was still open and your truck was still out front, but you weren't in the lodge, so I wondered if something was up. Clearly, I was right. And I imagine it starts with an *E*?"

I let the rope stop and put it back on its hook. The teasing grated on my nerves, but I also deserved it. I'd dished out plenty of advice to Jude that I specifically wasn't taking myself. I was well aware of the hypocrisy.

The truth was something I owed him, at least. "I guess the tables are turned, huh?"

"Only if you wait three years," he said with a smirk.

Lying back on the bench, I did another set, not letting myself think, simply speaking. "I want her, but there are too many things wrong with it. I'm too old for her, which she says isn't an issue, but I don't know if I agree. She's in a life-threatening situation, which I have a history of misjudging. And again, she's in a life-threatening situation and therefore might not be thinking clearly."

"Do you have any reason to believe she's not thinking clearly?" His voice was closer.

I gritted my teeth and pushed again, my arms nearing the point of failure. "No."

"Then what's the problem?"

"I think you need to get your hearing checked," I said with a groan, letting the bar rest.

"And I think you need to, with love and respect, get your head out of your ass."

I looked at him. "Jude, she's fifteen years younger than me."

"And?"

"And—" I opened my mouth, looking for the reason to give him, but nothing came. Other than the outward appearances, which might make some people uncomfortable, there was nothing *wrong* with it.

Jude smirked and pushed one of the punching bags so it was swinging. "Not so long ago, you told me the same thing," he said. "Not in the same words, but essentially that my head had been in my ass, and you were one hundred percent correct."

I sighed. "Your point?"

"Are you making choices for Emma?"

Fuck. That wasn't the way I'd been thinking about it, but I was. By telling her it wasn't good for *her* to be with me, I was robbing her of the choices she wanted to make. If I didn't want to be with her, that had to be a reason for me, not using her as an excuse.

"I learned the hard way, that's not the way to go. It's my biggest regret now."

"Making choices for her?"

"That, and waiting so long. Every second with Lena is a fucking miracle. But the time we have now doesn't make up for the time we *could* have had if I hadn't been afraid of what she'd think of what I really wanted—or if I'd been willing to tell her why I was trying to protect her instead of staying away, *knowing* she was waiting for me to make a move."

Jude had his happy ending, and everyone was ecstatic for

them. He was right. It had been a long time coming. "I'm not sure this is the same."

"It is." Jude pushed the bag again, throwing a couple of idle punches. "In a different way. With Lena and me, everyone was waiting for us to get together. With you, everyone is simply waiting for you to be happy."

"I am happy." The words were an automatic reflex. And for a long time, they'd been true. Only recently had things finally begun to surface and eat at me. Being surrounded by happy couples emphasized my solitude, and once you saw it, you couldn't go back to ignoring it.

"Are you?"

I let the words hang in the silence. That was the real question. The one I had to answer by myself before I could decide anything about Emma. She deserved that. I refused to use her as a crutch for my own pain, and I wasn't going to saddle her with half measures if I wasn't sure.

The leader part of my brain kicked in. The piece of me that made it easy for me to coordinate teams and run a place like Resting Warrior. I could lay out data and see the best course. But I was man enough to admit I hadn't done it for myself because I hadn't wanted to and I wasn't ready.

Was I ready now? I didn't know. But for Emma's sake, I needed to figure it out. Right now.

Was I happy?

I had a good job and good friends. A good family. Day-to-day, my life was pleasant. I enjoyed what I did and that I was able to help both people and animals who needed it. But did it equate to happiness? On a surface level, yes. Because I wasn't *unhappy*.

But that wasn't the same thing.

And that was what that scared me the most. So much, I hadn't ever truly wanted to put words to it. I wasn't happy. Not on the primal, instinctual level I craved. I was existing.

But the memories I was plagued by and the mistakes I was paying for were stopping me from reaching for that happiness.

Would it ever not feel wrong to be happy when I'd been the cause of so much death?

You made the decision with the information you had at the time, just like everyone does every single day.

I shook my head. It never ceased to amaze me. You could be in therapy for years and do the work, and yet sometimes it still took hearing someone else say exactly what you needed in the exact right way for it to sink in.

"No," I finally said aloud. "I'm not."

"Will Emma make you happy?"

I let my head fall into my hands. "Yes. But how do I get past the feeling she's wasting herself on me?"

"I don't know, but that feeling has nothing to do with her."

Looking up, I told him with my expression I needed to hear more.

"Correct me if I'm wrong, but Emma isn't the one who's said you're not worthy of a relationship. It's all you. You're the one who's put yourself in the category of 'not worth it.' It's not something Emma can fix, and if you don't work on it yourself, with Rayne, or another therapist, then it has the potential to become a self-fulfilling prophecy."

"Fuck."

He chuckled. "The truth is a bitch, isn't it?"

"I would say you have no idea, but you know well."

"I do." Punching the bag one more time, he stepped forward and clapped me on the shoulder. "Just think about it. No one here would mind seeing you happy, Daniel. Emma seems nice, and I'm sure that will only continue as we get to know her more. I'm going home."

"Have a good night."

His smile told me he planned to, and the spark of jealousy it brought forward only made all of this worse. It was the kind of smile that came from knowing he was going home to fall into the arms of the love of his life.

Which was what I could be doing and still chose not to.

I didn't know if Emma was the love of my life, but she was the first woman to reach me this way. I couldn't stop thinking about her, no matter how hard I tried. And my thoughts turned toward what might have happened after our kiss, though I'd tried to resist that too, out of respect for her.

Since the mission, I hadn't been with anyone. I was abstaining from being in a relationship, and that, in my mind, included sex. Even before, I'd never been a one-night–stand kind of guy. I wasn't built for it. When I was with someone, I wanted to be with them and give them all of me for however long we were together.

That was frightening too. Because I knew myself, and allowing myself to let go enough to be with Emma was more significant than simply something light and easy. Which meant, if it didn't last, it would hurt.

It felt more shameful to be avoiding potential emotional anguish than to be afraid of physical pain. But sometimes I felt like my entire life was pain, and I shouldn't blame myself for not wanting more.

Now I was alone in the gym, but I didn't go back to working out. I again let the puzzle pieces fall out before me in my mind.

Was the situation with Simon fucked up? Yes.

The man had put a gun to Noah's head and promised vengeance on all of us and the ranch. That threat wasn't something we could ignore.

But was the whole situation enough to stop me from being happy? When I reframed the question in my mind, it sounded a lot simpler than I'd been making it. Jude didn't think my objections held weight, and when I allowed myself to see the whole picture, I didn't either.

It was true that Emma was younger than me. That fact wasn't something I could ignore. But she'd also gone through more shit in her life than people double her age. For me to negate her ability to make choices about what she wanted wasn't okay.

We both wanted each other, and it was clear everyone at family dinner had seen the tension that always seemed to float in the air between us. Fuck.

I stood and retrieved my shirt before jogging back through the lodge to my truck. The shift in me was clear. I wasn't completely sold, but I saw where the path was heading, and working myself to death in the gym wasn't going to help.

But I hoped a shower would, so I drove back to my house.

~

The shower helped, and yet it didn't. Now I was pacing back and forth in my house. A house I'd made smaller than those of the others who lived on the property on purpose. Because I knew I was always going to be alone here. I never intended to have anyone else live in it, and looking around, that was brutally apparent.

Jude's words and my own resolved thoughts were banging around in my head. I knew if I didn't take the advice he'd given, I would regret it. Furthermore, it *was* hypocritical of me to dole out advice and then not listen when it was aimed in my direction.

All the worries I had were still there, but being in my house alone was slowly eating away at me. Everything I'd been avoiding for years was now starkly visible. The biggest truth being that family dinners took the edge off the loneliness I felt, but they weren't enough.

The one final hurdle was Emma's place here. If I went to her now, was I taking advantage of her? She didn't have anywhere else to go. If I did this—

I stopped my pacing just as I halted the negative line of thinking in my head. If I did this with Emma and she changed her mind, I would help her go anywhere she wanted. I would step back and make sure she was happy and protected.

But the truth was, she'd been on my mind a lot longer than my catching her in the parking lot. Maybe this was always meant to happen, and maybe it wasn't. But something had to change, and it looked like that thing had to be me.

Would the world end if I allowed myself some happiness?

No.

No, it wouldn't.

I blew out a breath and grabbed my keys.

Who was I kidding? This decision had been made a long time ago, and I'd been holding back out of some misplaced sense of martyrdom and out of protection for Emma. I would protect her from the people who wanted to hurt her. But I would also protect her ability to choose what she wanted. She'd made it abundantly clear she wanted me.

I didn't know how to do this anymore, and I needed to tell her before we fell into bed together. But I was done resisting. At this point, the only person I was hurting was myself.

The lights in her cabin were on.

I climbed the steps, and I didn't even knock on the door before she opened it. She was standing in front of me, dressed in what looked like pajamas. Clothes that were small, exposing skin, and something I would have tried to look away from before. I didn't now.

It was a relief to let myself look at her as the woman she was and not merely someone I was trying to protect. Every perfect inch of her, and the desire I'd been pressing into the deepest parts of myself came racing forward.

And when I met her gaze, I didn't see a woman looking at a broken man. All I saw was desire.

She knew.

Reaching out, she grabbed my shirt and pulled me inside.

Chapter 17

Emma

Daniel's mouth came down on mine before the door was even closed behind him, and oh *god*, it was like those moments in Seattle before he'd pulled away. He was entirely focused on me, arms coming hard around me and holding me to him like I was the only thing on earth that mattered.

Now that he'd made the decision, it was final. I felt it in the way his hands moved and the way he traced my lips with his tongue. My body was on fire, stomach all aflutter with nerves.

"You thought about it." It wasn't a question.

"I did a lot of thinking," he said. "Not all of it was easy. But where you are concerned, everything is always easy, Emma. You have never been the problem. It's all me. I need you to know that. *You* were never the thing stopping me."

It felt good to hear those words, even if I'd already known them. "Thank you."

He guided us to the couch and pulled us down. I twisted so I sat over his lap and smiled. "I do have a bed, you know."

"I'm *very* aware."

I felt exactly how aware he was beneath me, and his hands on my hips sliding lower were tense, straining to not fully hold on to me. "We need to talk first."

Kissing him, I finally gave myself permission to do what I'd wanted to all this time. I touched him, stroking over his shoulders and running my hands through his hair. Feeling the muscles under his clothes in more detail. "Daniel, if you came all the way over here and didn't plan on taking me to bed—"

His hands fell to my ass, and he dragged my body against his, pressing us together exactly where I needed, and we both groaned. "No. I want more than anything right now to take you to bed, Emma. But I need to tell you something first."

"Have you committed murder in the last couple of hours?"

Daniel laughed. "No."

"Then I don't care."

"Please," he said quietly. "I just need you to know."

The look on his face was serious, but it didn't feel like he was about to get up and walk away. "Okay."

Slowly, he slid a hand up my back until it rested behind my neck. He pulled me closer and kissed my cheek. My jaw. Down to my neck. "Everything I told you about what happened… I haven't been with anyone since. So, I am… very out of practice."

A flush raced up my cheeks, and my breath went short. "We'll fumble together, then. I've never done this at all."

His head came up, and shock covered his features, along with a small bit of awe. "And you're sure? You want to do this with me?"

Nodding, I kissed him again. "I've never put much stock

in virginity. I just never found the right person. You are the right person."

I saw the hunger I craved seconds before his lips met mine. This time with pure, clear intention. He turned us on the couch, spilling me onto my back so he was above me. I wanted to linger in this moment as much as I wanted to move forward faster. We had too many clothes on, and yet I wanted to memorize every second as we removed them.

"I tried not to think of you like this," he groaned against my lips. "Tried not to want you. And it didn't work. Especially since Seattle."

"I want you thinking about me. Because I can't stop thinking about you." I pulled at his shirt, and he helped me get it up and over his head before he tossed it aside.

His body…

I took my time and stared. Muscles from this kind of rural life, and a dusting of hair across his chest that matched the sandy blond on his head. All this skin, and right now, it was mine. I ran my fingers down his chest and stomach, watching as those same muscles tightened under my touch.

"I guess you've already seen me," I said quietly.

"It's not the same," Daniel said. "I wasn't thinking about you like *this* while you were bleeding. And at the same time, that glimpse has been tormenting me for weeks."

Moving enough so I could lift the edge of my camisole, I tugged it up and over my head. It joined Daniel's shirt on the floor. Not sure what he was going to do, I'd only put on items to sleep. And they didn't include a bra. Hell, I was already in bed when I'd heard his truck pull up and realized he'd decided.

Daniel stared down at me, eyes roving over my skin. That brought another blush to the forefront. I'd been kissed before, but I'd never been naked with anyone, and we weren't even all the way there.

He moved suddenly, standing up and leaning back down to haul me into his arms. I squeaked in surprise before relaxing into his hold. "Where are we going?"

"The two of us need time to explore, and I can think of a better place to do that than the couch."

The bedroom was dim, only lit by a single lamp, and immediately, everything became more intense. He set me down on the bed and knelt in front of me, nearly tall enough to be even with me while on his knees. Smiling, he stroked his hands down my arms. "You are so beautiful, and I want to explore every part of you."

I shivered, goose bumps rolling over my skin. "I'd like that."

In my head, I'd thought we'd move quickly, tearing each other's clothes off and going at it like animals. But this was better. This was *Daniel.* He was careful and kind and deliberate, and I knew just from experiencing the one kiss that he could go hard and fast. But not before either of us was ready for it. I wanted to savor him.

And I wanted to let him savor me.

Hands on my shoulders, he pulled me forward and pressed a kiss to my collarbone. Soft, gentle touches, smoothing his thumbs over my skin. Only Daniel's mouth moved. Over to my shoulder and back to the center of my chest, slowly down between my breasts.

He eased me back on the bed, standing to follow me. "Is this all right?"

"Yes." My voice was breathy and thin because all I could think about were his lips on my skin and the way they were drifting closer to my nipples. They hardened under his breath before he closed his lips over one, and my whole body bowed off the bed. Heat and pleasure raced through me, and I wasn't sure how a simple touch like that could feel so *good.*

Daniel swirled his tongue around the peak, drawing it farther into his mouth before releasing me and moving to my other breast and repeating his action, creating shivers all down my spine.

"I don't think you're out of practice at all," I managed.

The soft chuckle brushed the underside of my breast, and it was the single hottest thing I'd ever felt. "I told you I *tried* not to think of you like this. I didn't say I was successful."

"What did you think about?"

His only response was to drag his tongue down my stomach and circle my belly button before continuing down to the waistband of my shorts. "So many things, Emma. More than we have time for tonight."

"Fuck."

He laughed again before hooking his fingers in my shorts and drawing them down my legs. Daniel glanced up at me as he did it, mischief in his gaze. The only thing left between us was a barely there white thong that had been in the bags Kate had given me.

"But tasting you was—no, *is*—at the top of my list."

I was already wet between my legs and had been since he'd kissed me like his life depended on it. His words only made me wetter.

Virgin I was, but I wasn't entirely unfamiliar with pleasure. I'd thought about him too, in this very bed, pretending my fingers were him and sighing his name into the darkness. The way he was looking at me now paled in comparison to any fantasy.

Letting him settle between my legs was effortless. Butterflies flew like a tornado in my stomach, but delicious tension curled through me, swirling with the anticipation of him removing the final barrier.

He didn't.

I felt the softest pressure on the wet fabric, and Daniel made a sound of pure hunger. Again, he licked me through the fabric, using the friction of the material to his advantage.

"Oh my god."

"You're all right?"

I managed a single choked laugh. "All right? I think I'm flying or maybe dead? I don't know."

"Not dead," he whispered the words into my thigh. "Never that. I'm not nearly finished with you yet."

He slid his palms up the outsides of my hips, and now he did take off the thong, barely lifting himself enough to remove it before he was between my legs again. This time, he devoured me. Lips and tongue and grazing teeth.

Nothing I'd ever imagined was close to what this felt like. A storm of sensation that was all pleasure and perfection. I grabbed the sheets, needing to hold on to something —anything.

Daniel lifted his head, and the soft light showed his face shining with my arousal, which only turned me on more. "You taste amazing."

I wasn't sure I believed him, but the way he went back to tasting me was convincing. He slowed down, using his hand to reach up and touch me everywhere while he used his mouth.

Closing my eyes, I relaxed into the feel of it, trying not to feel self-conscious about this. That wasn't an emotion I'd expected, to worry about whether I was doing enough or tasted good or if I needed to be *better* at something.

I found Daniel's hands with mine and held on. He moved his tongue, and my hips jerked. A spike of molten heat crashed through me. "Oh my god."

He repeated the tiny motion, finding the place that had made me gasp, and he didn't release it. Only the same movement over and over, driving the thread of pleasure higher.

Delicious and dangerous, I wanted all of it and more. But I had enough nerves firing wildly in my gut. I didn't think I would tip over the edge with him down there. I needed *him*.

"Daniel," I gasped. "Come here."

In seconds, he was over me, eyes blazing, searching for the thing he assumed was wrong. "I'm fine. Everything is perfect."

"Good."

He began to sink back down, and I caught him, shaking my head. "I don't think I can, from that. It's not you. *Believe me*, it's amazing. I'm just not…used to it with someone else."

The unexpected embarrassment hit me hard. Why should I be embarrassed about it? But the shame made me blush, and I looked away from him.

"Look at me," Daniel said gently. "Please."

I did. In the low light, his dark eyes were even darker.

"We've both been through hell and back, and we've made it here. There's nothing to be afraid of in this room, and I'm just as out of my depth as you."

Raising one eyebrow, I looked at him. "Hardly."

A slow, sensual smile spread across his lips that made everything in me tighten. "I'm taking my time because I need to. If we dive into this too fast, I'm going to last about as long as when I was in high school."

I laughed with him, but nerves still gripped me.

"Let's agree on one thing," he said. "No embarrassment. Not here where we're figuring it out. Not everything is about an orgasm." Leaning down, he kissed me gently. "Though I would love for you to have one before the night is over, I won't be disappointed either way. It takes time to learn each other."

I knew that, and I knew sex wasn't as easy or simple as people often made it out to be. Still, I wanted our intimate moments to be effortless. "Okay."

Daniel closed his eyes and laughed. "Speaking of embarrassment. I was in such a hurry to get here, I didn't think to grab a condom. There are some at the lodge, though."

I grabbed his shoulders, holding him close. "I have a birth control implant. Got it in college. And I obviously don't have anything to worry about as far as infections, and neither do you. Real sexy talk."

"Real sexy." His smile *was* sexy. "Are you sure?"

"Yes. Don't leave."

For long moments, he searched my face, and I saw the moment when he decided to stay. He kissed me hard then pulled away, standing briefly to shed his jeans. And…wow.

Even if I had something to compare it to, I didn't think I'd be able to. Daniel was beautiful. That was the only word to describe him. Everything from his face down to the hardness standing out from his body was perfect, and he was looking at me the same way.

Somehow, the distance between us evaporated, and I couldn't remember how. He was kissing me and I was kissing him, and I wasn't sure who started it but it didn't matter because any awkwardness had melted away. The same chemistry that had zinged between us for weeks was coming back in full force.

When his hands and lips were on me like this and I was wrapped up in him, I felt no nerves. Only the fiery burn of want and a fierce need to have him closer.

"We'll go slow," he whispered between kissing me. The tiny sips of breath we needed, so we didn't have to come apart.

Our bodies were lined up, and I felt him there at my entrance. Everything was still sensitive and swollen, and just the brush of him there made me shiver with pleasure.

Slowly, he pushed in. He dropped his forehead against mine, and I clung to him through the sudden fullness. It felt both good and strange at once, and I wanted more and didn't know how to ask.

A little more, and it burned. A gasp escaped me, and Daniel kissed me, stealing my breath as he eased past the tightest part of my body. Another movement and he was suddenly through, easing deep and settling inside like he was meant to be there.

I suddenly found it impossible to breathe. I was so full, and everything in my body felt *alive.* My clit was even more sensitive—I felt as if I'd come at the slightest breath now, when I'd been so far away before. I was squeezing down on him out of instinct, and Daniel groaned. "Keep doing that and you'll be the death of me."

"No death, remember? We're not finished with each other."

"No," he said, looking down at me, bracing his arms on either side of my head. "We're not."

I still couldn't fully catch my breath, and I tried to touch him everywhere. My hands moved over his shoulders and hair, pulling him toward me and pushing him away. I wasn't sure what I needed except for *more.*

"Are you all right?" he asked.

"*Yes.*"

He moved, and it ached and felt impossibly good at the same time. "Oh god."

"I know." His lips found mine, the gentle movement of us together the background to his words. "If I hurt you—"

"You won't, Daniel."

"*If I do,* I expect you to tell me." His voice held no room for argument.

Nodding, I finally pulled him all the way closer so our bodies were touching everywhere. "I don't hurt."

And I didn't. Yes, I felt some discomfort because my body wasn't used to this, and it might feel achy tomorrow, like a bruise, but it didn't hurt. And beneath all that was the potential for it to be so much more.

"Don't hold back," I whispered.

A smooth, rolling movement of his body made me gasp. "I'm not," Daniel said. "But I'm also not someone who's going to pin you to the bed and jackhammer you into oblivion. You've been in my dreams for months, Emma. I want to take my time."

My eyes closed, a wave of deep arousal and pleasure flowing between his movement and his words. A shift happened between us, flipping off the uncertainty and the doubt. And we took our time.

Daniel kissed me like the world was burning and it was the last thing he wanted to do in this life. And when he wasn't kissing me, he slipped his hand between our bodies, teasing me along with the slow, thorough movement of being taken.

It felt *good.* The sensation built in me in a suddenly familiar way until I was gasping under his mouth. The orgasm peaked, a small burst of light behind my eyes and a shaking sigh as I shuddered around him.

My orgasm drove his, the thrust of hips harder and the low sound of his groan vibrating against my neck. We came to stillness together, breathing in each other's air, and I savored the feeling of Daniel relaxing. Allowing me to take some of his weight.

I smiled, though he couldn't see it. To me, this was perfect. It wasn't the explosion of passion and exquisitely choreographed sex you seemed to think would happen when two people who wanted each other finally came together. This was better.

Every time, I would want the reality of the two of us together over a glossy illusion. And the truth of our reality was that we were two people with struggles. We needed to learn our way with each other, and I needed to learn the way this worked altogether.

"Stay here," Daniel whispered, kissing my cheek as he eased himself from my body and stood, disappearing into the darkness of the rest of the cabin. I heard a door open and running water before he returned, washcloth in hand.

That was a different kind of intimacy. He cleaned me up, and I was flushed pink. He'd just been inside me, and yet I felt embarrassed by this act. I wasn't sure why. But I let him do it and watched as he tossed the washcloth into the laundry basket before he returned to me.

"Do you want me to go?"

I snorted. "Yeah, no chance in hell."

We hadn't used the blankets, and he helped me under them before pulling me against his body and kissing me thoroughly. "I was already cracking on my own, but Jude pointed out I was ignoring the same advice I'd given him not too long ago. Not only that, but I was invalidating your choices."

Raising an eyebrow, I let myself smile. "So, you don't want to be here?" My comment was meant to be teasing. I could tell how much he wanted to be here, but his eyes went serious.

"That's not what I meant."

"I know." Reaching out a hand, I touched his chest. "I know. I'm sorry. I was teasing. I'm—" One breath in and another out. "You know I'm new at this, and I'm not sure what to say. But there's nowhere else I want to be, and nowhere else I want you to be."

"Good," he finally said, slipping a hand behind my neck and pressing his lips to my forehead. "Because I don't think I could keep myself away now."

I sighed, leaning into him, and we let comfort and warmth carry us away.

Chapter 18

Daniel

I woke first.

Emma was curled into my side defensively, but her face was relaxed. Trying not to wake her, I moved, stroking slowly down her arm. Her body eased under the touch, releasing the pose of someone under attack, and my heart swelled.

While I wasn't sure I deserved the unconscious trust she gave me, having it was precious, and I savored it just as much as I did the knowledge she'd shared her body with me.

I couldn't keep the smile off my face. Now that I was here, this felt like the easiest thing in the world, and I wondered how I'd managed to hold back for so long. We fit together. My body fit in hers so perfectly, and *god*, she felt amazing. But it was more than that. We understood each other in ways others couldn't. She'd pointed it out last night, and it was the truth.

The next time I saw Jude, I needed to tell him thank you for pulling my head out of my ass.

That didn't mean this was going to be easy—I doubted that. Emma's situation was still precarious and everyone at the ranch could still be in danger, but I felt settled. Settled and…happy.

I hadn't noticed the normal weight on my shoulders when I woke. My baggage was still with me, but it was currently stowed away where I could take a break from dragging it around with me. And only after feeling that weight lift from my shoulders did I realize how heavy it had been.

Beside me, Emma stirred, stretching and startling when she felt me beside her. The same shock turned into a smile when she remembered, and she cuddled closer without even opening her eyes. "Good morning."

"Morning."

"Thought I was dreaming for a second."

I laughed softly. "I knew I wasn't. This is much happier than my dreams of you have been."

She opened her eyes then. "Well, hopefully your dreams will be better now."

"I certainly hope so." I stroked my knuckles down her cheek.

Emma blushed before rolling onto her back and staring at me, eyes sparkling. "Is it weird that I'm relieved? Because I am. Instead of looking at you and trying not to want you, I know I can have you."

"No, it's not weird. I'm right there with you."

We stared at each other for a second before we both burst into laughter. I couldn't keep my hands off her then, kissing her. It felt impossible. Like a miracle.

"I asked them if it would be weird," Emma whispered. "All the girls, and they said no."

"I knew it," I said. "I thought you might have been talking about me, but I didn't want to be that asshole."

She pressed herself up against me. "Pretty sure everyone knew, regardless."

"You're right." A thought occurred to me. "Lucas and Evie's wedding is soon. They gave me a plus-one, and I didn't use it. Come with me?"

For a moment, I saw nerves in her eyes. She bit her lip, and I suddenly found the tiny pout of her lower lip the most fascinating thing in the world. "That's like… Wow. It's at the end of the week, right? You can't just throw me in there. Catering and seating will be all messed up. I don't want to be an imposition."

Knowing what I did about the ceremony, I doubted it would be a problem, but I loved that she was sensitive enough to care. "Will you let me ask? I won't force them to say yes, but you're here, and now with…this, I'd like you to be there. With me."

Emma's pupils dilated, realizing the double meaning behind the words. I wanted her with me not only because we were trying this, but because it would be a statement of us being together to my friends, soon to be her friends. "If it's too much, it's okay."

"No." Her answer was quick. "No, you can ask, but I don't want them to change everything just for me. That's not fair to Evelyn."

Which was exactly why she wouldn't care if I asked to bring Emma. But there were other considerations too. "Let's assume Evie says yes, and you come to the wedding. I know it's not something either of us wants to think about, but it's very public. If your—" I stopped to correct myself. Simon might have given DNA to Emma, but he wasn't her father. "If Simon is watching you in any way, it could be dangerous."

"Why would you think he'd be watching? I mean, I know there's a chance. But there haven't been any signs."

Sighing, I scrubbed a hand over my face. "I don't know how quickly Phillips intends to enact his plans if you say no. They want to use your name, and if it's floating out there at all and Simon tracks you down, it's not a huge leap to think he'd observe the wedding."

She cursed. "I really don't like him. But call the FBI. Tell them, regardless, they have to wait until *after* the wedding to make my name public. I want one thing that's normal, and if Evelyn is okay with it, then I want to dance with you. Just once, I don't want Simon to dictate what happens in my life."

Sitting up, she turned away briefly, and I got to see her bare skin in the morning light. Emma was thin—a natural side effect of being imprisoned and then on rationed food for the better part of a year. But there wasn't a single part of her I didn't find beautiful, and I reached out to trace my fingers down her spine.

"My entire adult life, Daniel, he's been there. And even the good memories don't mean anything now. He's a part of everything. Even you."

She looked over her shoulder at me, her face soft. "Don't get me wrong. I'm not upset about meeting you, and we both know I would be dead without you several times over. But that doesn't change the fact that the only reason we met in the first place is because Simon is a stain of a human being. Even the good memories are tainted by him.

"I just… I'd like just one thing that has nothing to do with Simon. And the wedding could be that one thing. Or if not, maybe we can find something else?"

"We will," I promised. It was a simple promise to make, because I already wanted to do everything with her. All the things I'd thought about and shoved aside because of my own stubbornness and reservations. They were all possible.

"Okay."

She was fidgeting with her hands, and I snaked an arm around her waist, yanking her back across the bed. Now that I was allowed to touch her, it was all I wanted to do. "This will end," I told her. "It will. Whether through the FBI or not. Men like Simon can't stand to remain in the shadows forever. He'll show himself and be dealt with. And then you'll be free."

A pang of anxiety clanged through me. Once she was free to do as she pleased and wasn't being hunted, would she leave? I needed to be prepared for that. But it wasn't something to worry about right now.

"I've been thinking about it," Emma said. "How quickly it happened and then everything after. It was like the person I'd come to know never existed, and I don't understand."

"Which part?"

She made a small sound of frustration. "Why even bother trying to form a relationship with me? Why pay for school and give me a job when he could toss me aside so easily? What kind of monster is able to put their child in a cage and promise to murder her without a second thought?" She went quiet for a second. "I've wondered if my mother knew."

"She didn't want you talking to Simon?"

Emma shook her head. "No. But she never hid who he was. She had a picture of the two of them together, and they looked happy. But she always told me he wasn't a part of our lives and that was the way it was meant to be. She forbade me to contact him, always saying nothing good would come of chasing the past, and she was right."

"You couldn't have known," I said, noting the similarity in what she'd said to me before.

"No, I couldn't have. But I'll never forget him looking at me while I was in that cage and just…saying it. 'When we get to North Dakota, we'll get rid of her. No one will ever look for her, and the grave will be easy to hide.' Just like that, like he was listing groceries to be bought."

The anger burning in my gut made me want to rage and go out right this second and join the FBI in order to hunt the fucker down. But Emma didn't need more anger. Instead, I pulled her closer. "I'm sorry."

"I'm going to call Dr. Rayne and see if she can see me. You were right, I need to talk to someone about it, and everyone speaks so highly of her. I can't lay it all on you."

I kissed her hair. "You can lay anything you want on me, Emma. But I'm not a therapist, and she'll be able to help you more than I can. At least in that area."

Flipping us over so my body hovered above hers, I enjoyed the sight of her hair all spread out on the pillows. She needed a distraction, and I was more than happy to give her one. "There are other areas I can help you with."

Emma grinned. "Oh really?"

"Really." I dropped a kiss directly between her breasts. "I only got the barest taste of you last night, and I want more. Care to try again?"

The shade of pink that rose to her skin made me harder than I already was. "Don't you have work to do?"

"Nothing that can't wait a while."

"Then I think I'd like that."

I smirked, my only answer to sink down between her legs—my new favorite place to be.

Chapter 19

Emma

I walked down the sidewalk in Garnet Bend, feeling like eyes were searching for me around every corner. Daniel was down the street at Deja Brew, and I was holding the coffee Lena had made me to my chest like it was a shield.

Dr. Rayne had an opening, and I was going to her office now. When I'd said I was going to do the whole therapy thing, I hadn't really meant *today*, but no time like the present, right?

There. The office was only a couple blocks away, and already, I felt more comfortable. The building looked more like a house than a real office. Somewhat out of place on the main street. I remembered that from driving through, but I had no context for it at the time. Now I did, and the cute house made sense.

"Miss Derine."

The voice sent tingles across my skin, and I turned to

find Agent Phillips on the sidewalk behind me. "What do you want?"

"Just to talk."

His tone didn't sound as overbearing as usual, but I wasn't in the mood to deal with him right now. I doubted I was going to want to deal with him after the session either, but that was a future-me problem. "Well, you're going to have to wait. I have an appointment, and I won't be late because you want to be rude to me again."

I caught the brief shock on his face before he covered. "I'll wait."

He probably would too. I rolled my eyes before pushing through the door into the little house. Inside, it looked surprisingly like an office with a small reception desk that was currently empty.

But the door behind it was open, and a woman stepped into sight. She smiled. "You must be Emma."

"That's me." I shifted my coffee to one hand so I could shake hers. "Thank you for seeing me so fast. I honestly didn't expect it."

"I had a cancellation, so it was perfect. Come on in."

Her office was cozy. Not quite the "lie back on the couch in a stuffy library" vibe I'd expected. Instead, it was more neutral with a healthy number of plants in the sunny windows and two big, comfy chairs for us to sit.

Rayne herself surprised me. She was younger than what I thought of as a "therapist," with long brown hair curling around her shoulders and wearing an outfit that was both cute and professional. I recognized her own touches, while at the same time noticing no extremes that could push someone to form an opinion about her on sight. It was smart.

"Now, if you're at Resting Warrior, I think I can make a couple of assumptions," she said. "First, the people there care for you, and you've seen some kind of trouble."

I took a sip of the coffee before sitting in the chair. "The first, maybe. Or we're getting there. The second? Yeah, you could say that."

She crossed her legs and grabbed a notepad. "Why don't you tell me about it and why you're here? And you can see if you feel like I might be the right person to help you."

Where did I even start with something like this? "Well, before I get into all of it, I need to tell you there's an asshole of an FBI agent lurking outside waiting to talk to me after we're finished. So, if you happen to see someone who looks like he has a stick up his ass, that's him."

Rayne blinked once and then burst out laughing. "Okay, noted. This sounds like it's going to be interesting."

I shrugged. "I'll explain all of it in detail, but the summary is my biological father is the leader of a huge network that runs illegal guns and drugs. He kept me locked in a cage for a month with the intention of murdering me and, as far as I know, is still going to kill me on sight."

She'd started to write something on the paper but looked up at me, eyebrows rising. "I see why you made an appointment. Can you start at the beginning?"

"You can't say anything to anyone, right? Not even the FBI?"

"Correct. Nothing you say to me leaves these walls. I'm duty bound to keep all information confidential without a direct court order. Given the FBI outside, is that likely?"

"Probably not. And even if it were, there's not much they don't already know." But hearing her say this was entirely confidential made me feel better anyway.

"All right. I'm ready whenever you are."

I took one more sip of my coffee and started at the beginning.

"And that's where we are now." I glanced at the clock. "I think we're out of time."

Rayne waved a hand. "I don't have another appointment. We can take a few minutes."

She'd listened with rapt attention to the whole story. The *whole* thing, including everything after the cage. Including Seattle and Daniel. She didn't bat an eye at our relationship, and I guessed she already had an idea of that part from Daniel. Since he had been struggling with it, he'd likely talked to her about it.

"What would your goal with therapy be, Emma? There's no right answer, but depending on what *you* want, we can tackle things in different ways."

"I—" Stopping, I thought about it. "I know there's no wrong answer, but is it okay if I say I don't know? I'm still in the middle of it, so part of me doesn't know where to place this. It's not in the past since it's still happening to me. I've just been *going* this whole time, and only in the last few days do I feel like I've slowed down."

Rayne nodded. "It's totally fine not to know. Many people don't, especially when they've had experiences on the same level. Deep, formative things."

"Yeah."

Formative was certainly one word for it. Life-changing was another.

"Do you think you'll be here for a while? And by here, I mean Resting Warrior and Garnet Bend."

"Yes." My answer was instant. "At the very least, I want to be. I'm going to try however I can to stay."

Setting her pad aside, she leaned forward on her knees. "How about this, then? If you feel comfortable continuing with me for a few sessions to get more of an idea of how I work and whether we're a good fit, we'll make an appointment for next week. In the meantime, let the question of what you'd like to work on just rest on the back burner. Sometimes what comes from therapy and speaking things out loud takes time to unfold in our minds. It might come to you. And if it doesn't, that's fine too."

I nodded. "I'd like that." Nothing had happened to make me think Rayne and I wouldn't work well together. She was a warm and comforting presence, and I understood why Resting Warrior worked with her, after just the one session.

We made plans for the next week, and she smiled at me. "Great. And please feel free to call me if something happens. If you're triggered or anything else. There's no reason for you to go through anything alone."

She handed me a small card with the time of my next appointment and her phone number. "Thank you." Even this was good. I felt a comfortable certainty, knowing I had somewhere to be.

"I'll walk you out," she said. "I want to see if your FBI friend is still outside."

"I'm sure he is," I grumbled. "Waiting to try to force me to do what he wants."

"He won't if I have anything to say about it." There was a fire in Rayne's eyes as she held the door open for me.

And there he was, leaning against the outside wall, eyes closed. "You seriously waited out here the whole time?" I asked him. "You know where I live, Agent Phillips. You could have called me instead."

He looked over. "Your friend, Mr. Clark, didn't seem too interested in having us back on the ranch property, so I'm trying to respect his wishes."

"So you stalked me in town."

"Stalking is harsh. I saw you walking down the sidewalk by chance." His eyes flicked behind me to where Rayne stood in the doorway and back again. Immediately, he looked at her again, in a full double take.

Rayne stepped outside. "Emma told me there was an FBI agent lurking outside my office. I needed to see for myself."

He held out his hand. "Agent—"

"Phillips. Yes, I heard. I'll thank you not to stand outside my door like the angel of doom, intimidating my clients. Please and thank you."

Phillips's jaw tightened. "Of course. I'm sorry for the inconvenience."

Rayne touched my shoulder briefly. "I'll see you next week."

I looked at Agent Phillips, evaluating exactly how much he wanted to talk to me against how much I wanted to go back to the ranch and relax after word-vomiting my whole life story. "I'm meeting Daniel at Deja Brew. You have exactly that long to talk to me about whatever you want to talk to me about, and then I expect you to walk away."

It felt like strength, but the way my hand was shaking told me otherwise. This was borrowed strength from the force of Rayne's dismissal and the knowledge Daniel was waiting for me. The real me wanted to curl up into a ball on the sidewalk to make myself completely fucking invisible.

He sighed like I was the one putting *him* out. "Fine."

We began to walk.

"What I'm going to say isn't new," he admitted. "I'm here to get you to help us. I know you don't want to, and I know your…unique perspective on Simon's network makes you skeptical about whether we can protect you. But we can."

I snorted but said nothing. We were already a block from the office. One block to go.

"You don't have many options here, Miss Derine. Like it or not, you're one of the only people who can draw out a monster like Simon. You need to think about that before you dismiss us entirely. People are *dying* because of that man, and you would have been one of them. Can you really live with yourself if you do nothing while he keeps murdering people? And believe me, he doesn't have to touch them himself for it to be murder. Every gun and every batch of drugs he ships contributes.

"You could be the one who stops it, or you could be the person who stands by and does nothing. It's your choice, but in my opinion, it's your moral obligation to help stop him. But if you still say no, we've already petitioned a judge to use your name without you present. Simon Derine will be stopped, one way or another."

We now stood in front of the coffee shop, and I looked at him. "I guess what I said to Dr. Rayne was true."

He waited, expectant.

"You're an asshole, and, more than that, you have a stick up your ass." My entire body was shaking like a leaf. So much that what was left of my coffee was spilling out of the hole in the lid. "Only someone like you could put the entire responsibility of catching someone like Simon on me. You said it yourself. He wants me dead. And I'm not going to hand myself over to be slaughtered because the FBI hasn't been able to do their job with the mountain of information I've already given you."

The door opened, and Daniel was suddenly by my side, arm around my shoulders. He was steady while I wasn't. "There's a wedding in a couple of days," I told Agent Phillips. "If the judge says yes, be a decent person for *once* and wait to start using me as bait until after it's over. I'd like one normal night."

He flinched at the implication he wasn't a decent person, but he could disappear and I wouldn't care at this moment.

Daniel guided me away from Agent Phillips and toward

his truck. He pressed me up against the door and lined his body up with mine, holding me upright. "Are you okay?"

"I will be," I said. "I think. *God*, he sucks."

A laugh burst out of Daniel, loud and free. "Yes, he does. What did he want?"

"The same. With a healthy dose of blaming everything Simon's ever done on me because I'm not helping to stop him."

I swallowed. Logically, I knew I was only one person, and the responsibility didn't lie with me, but I still felt a twinge in my gut where Agent Phillips's words had struck their target. Simon was a horrible human being, and all the things the FBI agent said were true. Was blood on my hands if I didn't do what they wanted?

It wasn't my fault I'd been born Simon's daughter, and I'd never asked for what had happened to me. Was it truly my moral duty to stop him when all I was trying to do was survive him?

"Hey," Daniel said gently, tucking a strand of hair behind my ear. "You still in there?"

"Yeah. Just thinking."

"Want to think at home?"

The glow of the word *home* was like being lit from within. "Yes, please."

He helped me into the truck and got in on his side. "I spoke to Evie while you were at your appointment. It's no trouble, and she's thrilled you'll be coming to the wedding."

"Really?"

Daniel reached across the truck seat and took my hand, smoothing his thumb over the back of it. "Really."

I hadn't expected her to say yes. I had a sense of how much planning weddings took, and how much it could throw off the entire day if even one person was added.

Unexpected tears blurred the road in front of us. I

should have known it would be fine. If there was one thing I'd seen at the ranch, it was the family. They took care of their own and welcomed those who needed a home. For however long I was here, I was under the same protection, and the thought was beautiful.

Overwhelming, but beautiful.

"Oh, crap."

"What?" Daniel looked over in alarm. "Do we need to turn around?"

I squeezed his hand. "No, nothing like that. But now that I'm going to a wedding? I have nothing to wear."

Chapter 20

Emma

My borrowed dress fit better than I thought possible.

Given what Agent Phillips was doing, no one felt it was safe enough to take me dress shopping. So I ended up at Kate's house, trying on some of her clothes since we were similar in size.

The one I'd borrowed was a deep violet. The dress had one shoulder and gathered below my breasts before it flowed gracefully down to the floor. I'd never worn anything this beautiful in my entire life.

Only one thing came close—when I'd saved money to buy a prom dress from the thrift store. But this was so much better. And when Kate winked and told me she knew Daniel was going to love it, I almost fell through the floor.

Now I was waiting for him on my porch. We were driving to the wedding together, and after… Well, after, I hoped we were continuing what had been some very fun nights exploring each other.

His truck turned into view, and butterflies rose in my stomach. It was just a wedding. But for some reason, this moment felt significant. After everything, I was going to pay attention to the instinct.

The truck stopped, and he got out. Daniel in a tuxedo was *magnificent*. Watching him walk around the truck toward me was like watching one of those overly stylized perfume ads that only featured beautiful people and made no sense.

It also made me want to pull him inside and take off the same tuxedo as quickly as possible.

"Emma," he said, stopping at the bottom of the steps. Then he shook his head and took a step back. "You look incredible."

"I can say the same about you."

Climbing the steps one by one, he stopped on the one below me so our faces were even and kissed me. *Kissed* me. Heat built under my skin, and I pulled away with a gasp. "If you want us to make it to the wedding, you can't kiss me like that."

"I'm only ever going to kiss you like this," he murmured. "I swear I could drown in you."

I gripped his arms and looked at him, unable to respond to a statement so fierce. I understood exactly what he meant, and yet it was too big.

"I think the tuxedo is my second favorite look."

An eyebrow quirked. "Second?"

"Second," I told him. "Because I already know what's *under* the tuxedo, and it doesn't matter how many clothes you put on, nothing will ever compare to when you take them off."

He grinned. "A man could get used to compliments like that."

"Better get used to them, then."

Taking my hand, he helped me down the stairs and back

up into the truck, taking a healthy handful of my ass as he did so. "Naughty."

"It's the dress," he said with a shrug. "My self-control is nothing in comparison."

"If I'd known all it would take to get you to lose control was a pretty dress, I'd have made Kate lend me one *way* sooner."

Daniel smiled, and as he liked to do while we were driving, he took my hand. This time, he lifted mine so he could kiss the back of it.

"Any word?"

He shook his head.

We hadn't heard anything from Agent Phillips in a few days, not since my encounter with him outside my therapy appointment. No sign of whether he'd decided to abide by my request to keep my name private until after tonight.

But I was determined not to spend the entire night worrying about it. This was going to be fun. I was going to dance with Daniel, and Simon wasn't going to ruin it.

The venue was actually Grace's home, a few miles down the road from Resting Warrior. A ranch named Ruby Round. It no longer had any animals, and the barn had been turned into a space where she and Harlan could host parties or, in this case, host a wedding. I was told Grace and Harlan's wedding had been here as well.

We pulled up to lovely house, the ranch just as green and beautiful as Resting Warrior. We were a little early, as Daniel was in the groom's party. But not so early it would be awkward.

Daniel helped me out of the truck, and I loved the possessive hand on my back as we headed around the house to the barn, which was decorated with fabric and flowers. Lena was in a pretty pink dress, directing Jude to adjust a last-minute decoration, and she beamed when she saw me.

"Hi! Daniel, I know Lucas wants to see you in the house. I'll make sure Emma gets to her seat."

"All right." He turned and looked down at me. "You'll be okay?"

"Yeah."

There was a second's hesitation before he leaned down and brushed his lips across mine. But I didn't need to hesitate. He was looking at me to see if it was all right since this would be the first kiss in front of people we knew. And yes, it was fine. It was more than fine.

I held on to him longer than was strictly necessary, and he smiled at me when he released me. "See you soon."

Lena looped her arm through mine and walked me into the barn. "Seems like everything worked out?"

"It's working out for now," I said with a laugh. "I should thank Jude. He said something to Daniel to change his mind. Or at least to make him realize he was overthinking it."

The inside of the barn was light and airy, all the windows open for an uncharacteristically mild summer day. It also looked absolutely magical. The theme of pink and white continued throughout the space, with deeper shades mixed in as accents. And lots of flowers sprinkled around in the same color scheme.

"This is beautiful," I told her.

"Thank you. I want everything to be perfect for Evie. She deserves it."

I'd picked up bits and pieces of Evelyn and Lucas's story, and when I was at Kate's house, she'd finally told me the rest of it. What she knew, anyway. She hadn't been here for it. But the story of Evelyn's stalker of an ex-fiancé who'd been so obsessed with her he'd scarred her *twice* tugged on my heartstrings.

I knew exactly what it felt like to have someone who was supposed to love you more than anything turn on you and do harm. For both Evelyn and Lucas, this wedding had been a long time coming.

"Yeah, she does. And I'm grateful she let me come. I know last-minute changes can throw things off."

Lena led me up to the front of the barn to the second row of seats. "Honey, it was no trouble at all. We have plenty of space, and like we already told you, all of us are way more excited to see Daniel with someone than we'd ever tell him to his face. I hoped he would ask you, but Jude told me I couldn't just put you on the guest list without asking Daniel. Otherwise, I would have."

I laughed, but the gesture struck me. "You guys are all so nice, and you just met me."

Lena put her hand on my arm and then pulled it away. "Sorry, I should ask first. I'm a touchy-feely person, and I forget. Is it okay if I give you a hug?"

"Yeah, that's fine."

She hugged me and squeezed me tight. "We all end up here for a reason, and we all have stories. We're not nice for any other reason than you're a person and you deserve kindness. And beyond that, we understand."

I didn't have time to respond. She pulled away and smiled. "I need to go check on the bride, but things will start in just a few minutes, and I'll see you at the reception."

Lena nearly skipped away, and I had to sit down, suddenly worried my legs wouldn't fully hold me. People were filtering in, and I just sat there in the middle of it all with my thoughts. They weren't being kind out of obligation, and frankly, I'd forgotten what that was like.

Lena had already wanted to invite me here, and she'd never know how much it meant to me. I blinked away the tears misting my eyes and listened to the soft music coming through the speakers. People I didn't recognize sat around me, and I couldn't help the nerves forming in my stomach.

Out of habit, I searched for faces I might know who could cause me harm. Any of Simon's men that I'd encountered or Simon himself, but of course, I saw none of them. Everyone seemed happy and friendly.

No sign of my favorite FBI agents either, thankfully.

From the side of the barn, Lucas came in with the officiant. The music swelled, and we all turned to watch as Liam came down the aisle alone with a pillow and the rings, completely hamming it up as the adult ring bearer. Laughter rang out, and a spike of yearning wove through me.

This was beautiful—a community that could laugh together in the midst of both sadness and beauty.

Next, Lena came down the aisle with Jude. There weren't any official roles, I'd been told. Everyone was too close for there to be titles like best man and maid of honor. Not when their chosen family was so tangled. The other pairings followed. Grace and Harlan, Cori and Grant, Noah and Kate.

They all stood together at the front, and when the music changed again, everyone stood. Lucas looked at the back of the church, and the emotion on his face as he saw his bride was so pure, I choked up with him. Such love and awe. I couldn't imagine someone looking at me like that.

Turning, I watched Evelyn walking down the aisle, escorted by Daniel. He was perfect, as the leader of the group, to stand in for a role traditionally held by the father.

The expression on Evelyn's face matched Lucas's.

Her dress was incredible and made more so by its strapless design. The scars she'd suffered were on full display, and it was beautiful. They were both a part of her and a testament to the fact that she'd survived the impossible.

The only scar I had from what had happened to me was the one healing on my side, but I still hoped I could be as brave as she was one day.

Her hands overflowed with calla lilies, and she also had one in her hair. Lucas couldn't take his eyes off her. Even when she was finally in front of him, he was swiping at his eyes while he had the biggest smile on his face.

"Please be seated."

As I sat, I caught Daniel's eye. He was staring at me, the hunger and intensity he used to hide now on full display. My stomach did a flip-flop, and I could only stare back. Again, I felt the vastness of these feelings and didn't know what to do with them. I put my hand to my heart, hoping he understood.

The ceremony itself was short and simple. Lucas and Evelyn exchanged vows and rings, and everyone was poised, waiting for the pronouncement of husband and wife, when Lucas held out a hand. "I have more to say."

Evelyn startled. "Really?"

I saw his hand squeeze hers. "Really."

From the pocket of his tuxedo, Lucas pulled a piece of paper and unfolded it. "I wrote it down because I don't want to get sidetracked in the middle."

He still held one of her hands. "I will never forget the first time I saw you. Jumpier than a brand-new foal and terrified of your own shadow. Before you ever saw me, I looked at you, and I knew you were going to change my life."

"Lucas." His name was so quiet only those of us in the first couple of rows could hear it.

"And I know it was chance that brought us together, but every day, I say thank you to whichever person forgot to take down that flyer. So many days it could have been thrown away, and I might never have met you and lost you before I ever had the chance to know you." He took a second, and it felt like the entire building held its breath. Even if everyone here didn't know the whole story, they knew enough.

"So when I tell you I vow to love you forever, through

everything, no matter what, I do it knowing we've already survived what might be the worst. We've already overcome so much just by finding each other, and now I can fully breathe, knowing you're finally my wife."

The piece of paper disappeared, and he took her other hand again. "I love you."

Evelyn was truly crying, and so was I. So was half the room. Lucas kissed her, and no one thought twice as the officiant pronounced them married without ever giving permission for the kiss. It wasn't a normal wedding kiss. It was the all-consuming kiss of two people who loved each other more than life itself and had already proven it.

The entire barn burst into cheers when they came apart, and they weren't remotely aware of it. Lucas brushed away her tears and said something to her too soft to hear over the applause. Finally, they retreated up the aisle, smiles on their faces, still practically unaware of the crowd that had assembled for them.

After the bridal party left, everyone else did too. An absolutely *massive* tent had been set up for the reception a little way from the barn, and a bar with cocktails was available while the wedding party took pictures.

Everyone I knew was in the wedding party, so I grabbed myself a drink and stood to the side, watching everyone's faces. Across the room, I saw Dr. Rayne. She saw me and smiled but didn't approach me, which I appreciated. She was nice, but I wasn't sure how I felt about talking to my new therapist at a wedding three days after meeting her.

A hand touched my back and I jumped, nearly spilling the remnants of my drink.

"Whoa," Daniel said, holding me against him. "Sorry. I didn't mean to startle you like that."

"It's okay." My heart was pounding in my ears. "Just wasn't expecting it."

"They're doing photos with just Evie and Lucas now. I wanted to come check on you."

I smiled. "I'm fine. Just people watching. You don't have to worry."

"Or maybe I wanted to come find you just to have the excuse to have you in my arms."

"I like that reason better." As I twisted to face him, he kept his arms around me. "And you're really okay being here with me? In the open?"

His smirk teased me, calling up heat that had nowhere to go while we were in public. "Should I not be?"

"No, just checking." A blush heated my cheeks. "Everyone knows you, and you were worried about the age difference—"

Daniel slipped a hand behind my neck, tilting my face up so he could kiss me. Truly kiss me. More than the light kiss in front of Lena and Jude, and more than I ever expected him to do in a room full of people.

"If I made you think I wanted us to be a secret, or I was ashamed to be with you in front of others, I will get on my knees right now and ask your forgiveness."

"No," I whispered. "It's just new. And, you know, new things can be nerve-racking."

He smiled. "I don't do things in halves. If I'm with you, I'm with you. I'm never going to treat you like my dirty little secret."

"So, you weren't worried?"

"I was. But it was misplaced. The worry I had about derailing your life was more about taking away your choices. And the worries I had about how it would seem to everyone else—" he shrugged "—well, it's not anyone else's business."

"Good," I said with a smile. "Because I want to dance with you."

He looked over my shoulder before dropping another

brief kiss on my lips. "We will. Absolutely. I'll be right back. We need to do the entrance."

People's eyes followed Daniel, and then they landed on me, making me want to squirm. I felt the reality of what he'd just said. People would wonder, and they would question. And between the two of us, if they were going to cast blame, they would throw it at Daniel's feet and not mine.

But it truly wasn't any of their business. If the rest of the Resting Warrior family was okay with it, everyone else should be too.

Still, I felt subtle glances as Daniel came in with the bridal party. So I downed what was left of my drink and smiled and clapped like I didn't have any other cares in the world.

Because right now, I didn't. Whatever was happening beyond the walls of this tent could take a fucking break for the evening.

Daniel came back to me. "Let's go."

"Where are we going?"

"To sit."

But he was guiding me toward the head table. "Daniel, I'm not in the bridal party."

"Ask Evie if she cares. Because she's the one who made sure there was a place for you."

Sure enough, I glanced at the bride, and she lifted her glass to me. We were at the very end of the head table, which I was grateful for. Not the center of attention, just the two of us in our own little bubble. This was all surreal.

The food was delicious, and the cake was out of this world—which surprised no one, given Lena had made it. And when I was full and nearly drowsy, Daniel held out a hand. "Dance with me?"

"You'll have to hold on to me, or I might fall over."

He laughed, but there was no humor in his whispered words. "Where did you get the idea I was letting you go?"

We spun together into the dancers, and I stared up at him. "You can't just say things like that to a girl. She'll get ideas."

"I like it when you have ideas."

The way he led me around the dance floor was confident and smooth. It was easy to follow him and not get lost. Also true to his word, he didn't let me go. "Would you be offended if I told you I didn't expect you to be as good of a dancer as you are?"

"No. Most people would probably say that. I'm very out of practice, regardless."

"You said you were out of practice at something else, yet you're pretty good at that too," I pointed out.

Daniel threw back his head and laughed before pulling me straight against his body so absolutely nothing separated us. "Fair point."

"Okay, everyone, the happy couple has to get on the road. Let's go see them off!" Lena's voice came through the speaker system.

It was dark now, and the entire wedding was given sparklers for Evelyn and Lucas to run through while the photographer took pictures. After another picture in which he dipped her back and kissed her against the backdrop of the glow, they were bundled into the car and gone. It was so beautiful, my chest ached.

I wanted that. The way he looked at her, and the knowledge they were together, no matter what.

As if he'd been reading my mind, Daniel stepped up behind me and wrapped me in his arms. "Want to stay?"

Shaking my head, I leaned back into him. "No, that's okay." In my head, I'd come up with plenty of other fun things we could be doing. Dancing was an option, but horizontal dancing was another, and we hadn't had nearly enough practice.

"Couldn't agree more."

He turned with me in his arms, toward his truck, and the *Crack!* ricocheted out of nowhere. Daniel jerked and fell, taking me with him down to the ground.

Screams broke out, and sudden panic erupted as all the guests started running and taking cover behind the vehicles and the house.

Oh my god. Oh my god. That was a gunshot. "Daniel." I frantically rolled over. "Daniel?"

Blood was seeping through his shirt over his right shoulder. The bullet wouldn't have hit anything vital on the outside of his arm. The anatomy charts I'd studied in health class were vivid and clear in my mind. But there was still a lot of blood, and it was obvious it wasn't a small wound. I wished I had more skill than just remembering things.

I didn't have anything to use to stop the bleeding. It might not have hit anything life-threatening, but blood loss was still a real possibility.

"Get to cover," Daniel groaned, pushing me away from him. "*Now*, Emma."

Cold fear seeped through the panic. The shot had been meant for me. I came up to Daniel's shoulder. If he'd delayed turning us around even for a second, the bullet might have gone through my head. And I was still out in the open.

"Jude!" I called, scrambling across the ground until I was behind the corner of the truck. No part of me wanted to leave Daniel, but I couldn't help him if I was dead.

The big man was already at Daniel's side, along with Liam. They were carrying him over to where I hid. Liam pointed at Lena. "Call nine-one-one. Get an ambulance here."

"Emma, here." Jude handed me his suit jacket. "Keep pressure."

"Will he be okay?"

"I'll be fine," Daniel grunted out. "Find the shooter. Get everyone to safety."

They sprang into action, and I covered the bleeding wound, pressing down on it with my limited strength. He grunted in pain. "I'm sorry," I told him. "Oh god, Daniel, I'm sorry. It was meant for me."

"Thank fuck it didn't hit you, then."

"You're going to be okay." My heart was in my throat. "You're going to be okay."

"I will." One hand came up and touched my arm. "Don't cry, sweetheart. I'm okay."

I hadn't realized I was, but sure enough, tears were streaming down my face.

Noah hit his knees beside us. "Ambulance is on the way. Lucky you took that where you did. Could have been a lot worse."

"I know." Daniel grunted. "Noah, you have to get people out of here."

"We are," he said. "*You* need to stop giving orders. We've got this, and you were just shot."

Daniel's hand was gripping mine. "Keep her safe."

And he passed out.

"Is he going to be okay?" My voice was hysterical. I knew the shot was a flesh wound, but he was still bleeding on the ground in front of me. *For* me.

"I think so. We just have to get him to the hospital. When the ambulance gets here, make sure you stay covered, but go with him."

"Okay."

Leaning down, I kissed Daniel's forehead, praying to a God I wasn't sure I believed in that he would be all right.

Chapter 21

Emma

Daniel would be fine.

A whirlwind ride in the ambulance and Daniel was rushed away through the emergency room. It was a clean wound that didn't hit anything vital. Mostly cosmetic.

But they'd had to check to make sure, so he was sedated now, sleeping while I sat by his side.

The others were here too, coming in and out to check on me. They decided one of them would always be outside, just in case, but they didn't try to make me leave. I wouldn't have gone anyway. This was the safest place for me to be. Simon wouldn't risk himself to come into somewhere so public or with so many cameras.

If he tried again, it would be from a distance.

It was Simon—whether it was him in person or someone he sent. He was the only one who had the motive to shoot straight at me.

A figure in the doorway startled me. My heart pounded

in my ears until I realized it was the police chief, Charlie. "Hello, Emma."

"Hi." I tried not to sound hesitant. But it wasn't like we were on the best of terms.

"I know it's late, but if you're up to it, I'd like to hear what happened while it's fresh in your mind."

"Yeah." That made sense. I gestured to the other chair in the room. "I'm afraid I don't have a lot of details that will help you."

I outlined exactly what had happened from when we'd stepped outside the reception tent to the time we got to the hospital. I hadn't seen anything, and other than the gunshot, I hadn't heard anything. There hadn't been a second shot.

"Maybe the guys out there have something more? Daniel told them to look for the shooter."

"Not yet, unfortunately. Given this was a targeted shooting, I'm going to leave an officer here. And I'll be back tomorrow to talk to Daniel."

I nodded, and he stood. "Can you do something for me?"

"If I can."

Taking a deep breath, I straightened my shoulders. "I want to talk to the FBI. I know they're still here, and I'm not stupid. If they're in town, you know about it. Tell them I want to talk to them."

The police chief studied me for what seemed like forever. "I can do that."

"Thank you."

I heard him speaking to Jude outside in low tones before he retreated, and I was left completely alone. The chair wasn't comfortable, but I was fine being uncomfortable—I was alive.

Once again, Daniel had saved my life. This time, it

wasn't even on purpose. But I was starting to wonder if he was some sort of guardian angel sent to keep me safe.

Either way, I wasn't leaving his side.

Pulling the chair close to his bed, I held his hand and laid my head beside him, getting as comfortable as I could for the wait.

"Emma?"

I jerked awake at the sound of Jude's voice. "Yeah?"

"You have some…visitors."

One look toward the door told me the visitors were the two suits I'd summoned last night.

No longer was I afraid and shaking, barely able to put a sentence together in front of them. This time, I had the questions, and they were going to answer them.

I pushed away from the bed and shut Daniel's door behind me before I turned on them. "Was this because of you?"

"We didn't shoot him," Agent Jones said. "So no, this wasn't us."

"You think this is a time to get cute with me?" I asked. "I'm aware at least one of you doesn't have the best opinion of me, and I couldn't give less of a shit right now."

Jude was behind me, and probably others too. I hadn't looked. But it was fine. They deserved to know what had happened to get their friend shot just as much as anyone.

I focused on Agent Phillips. "I asked you to wait. And you didn't, did you?"

To their credit, both agents looked sheepish. Once again, Agent Jones spoke. "We're truly sorry for the trouble. This wasn't what we'd anticipated."

"I wasn't talking to you." I looked at his partner. "You used my name?"

"We did."

"And it was really so urgent you couldn't have done as I asked and waited until after the wedding?"

His face went dark. "We'd already used it when I saw you in town. I told you we'd already asked the judge for permission."

I noted he kept saying *we* instead of *I*. "And so you decided it was better for me *not* to know you'd already put a target on my back? Are you kidding me?"

"Whoa." Agent Phillips held out a hand. "We only used your name. Put it out there like you had a presence. We didn't attach a location to it or do anything to indicate you were here. We simply wanted him to surface."

"And he did do that, didn't he?"

My whole body shook with rage, but the image of Daniel bleeding and unconscious kept me focused. I nearly felt sick about what I was about to do, but this couldn't happen again.

"You're getting your wish, Agent Phillips. You want me to help? Fine, I'll help. I don't want another close call. Because the next bullet might be the one that kills me. Or kills Daniel. I'm not going to let that happen. So congratulations, asshole, you win."

Phillips, who'd been mostly silent, looked grimly satisfied. "Good. We'll need a day to set it up, but we'll be in touch with the details."

He started to turn away, and I couldn't stop the words that flew out of my mouth. "If the shot had hit its mark, would you be sorry?"

"Excuse me?"

"If I were lying on a slab in the morgue right now instead of calling you out, would you be sorry? Knowing this was entirely because you're up on your high horse with no grace for people who have gone through things you can't even imagine."

Agent Phillips's face twisted into fury. "You have *no idea* what I've been through."

"And you know *every bit* of what I've been through. How dare you tell me to my face you think I'm weak for trying to protect myself and then put me in danger because you're desperate. You might want to rethink 'Fidelity, Bravery, Integrity.'"

Shock registered on his face, and Agent Jones caught him by the shoulder and forcibly turned him down the hallway before he could say anything else. "We'll be in touch, Miss Derine. Thank you for your cooperation."

As soon as they turned the corner, the borrowed strength left my body. I sagged against the wall, shaking and trying to catch my breath.

That was when I saw just how many people were behind me. All the Resting Warrior gang, minus Evelyn and Lucas, of course, and the police officer standing guard. And all of them were staring at me with varying degrees of shock and awe.

"Sorry," I said quietly. "I'm not normally that forceful."

Lena burst out laughing. "Girl, do not apologize for a single second of your performance. That was a piece of art."

"They used your name?" Jude asked. "Without permission?"

"With a judge's permission. Not that it makes it better. But this has to stop sometime. Next time, it might not just be me and Daniel—it could be any of you. Maybe Agent Phillips is right and I am a coward, when I'm one of the ones who can stop him. But…" I sighed. "Either way, it's done."

"We'll help," Noah said, pulling Kate in front of him and

holding her close. "For obvious reasons, we want Simon gone too."

"Thanks." I touched the handle to Daniel's door and turned back. "Please don't tell him. He needs to hear I'm helping them from me."

Jude inclined his head. "Of course."

I left the door open and was rewarded by Daniel smiling, even though his eyes were closed. "I thought I heard you talking."

"You heard right. Are you okay? Do I need to call the doctor?"

He winced but shifted himself up in bed. "Only if they're going to send me home. I've been shot enough times to know this is all right, and I'd rather be on the ranch than here at the hospital."

"See?" I teased. "And you gave me a hard time about not coming to the hospital when I collapsed."

He reached out with his left hand to grab mine. "I'm not suffering from an infection that has me on the brink of death, Emma. It's a glorified scratch."

"Hardly."

"You'd be surprised," Noah said, leaning in at the door. "Getting shot somewhere like the shoulder can be kind of like a nasty scratch. It's painful when you move it wrong, but otherwise doesn't really get in the way. Especially a shot like that."

Daniel grinned at me. "See?"

"People here to see you, if you're up for it," Noah said.

"Sure. But only if someone can ask Dr. Gold to get my discharge started."

Outside, I saw Grace turn and leave, presumably to track down Dr. Gold.

Everyone came in and I went to make room, but Daniel

didn't let go of my hand, keeping me close. "Do Lucas and Evie know?"

"We called them," Jude said, sitting in a chair across the room. "They wanted to come back, and I told them not to."

"Good," Daniel said. "They deserve their honeymoon, and I'm not going to mess it up for a scratch."

"It's not a scratch," I grumbled under my breath.

Kate said something that had everyone laughing, and Daniel tugged me down so he could whisper in my ear. "Trust me, you want it to be a scratch. Because if I'm put on bed rest with no sex? We'll both go mad."

My face flushed red, but I didn't say anything. He just looked at me, eyes full of heat, and if anyone else in the room noticed the way he was staring at me, they didn't say anything.

"Seems like a lot of people are bothering my patient," Dr. Gold said, walking in.

"You know us, Dr. Gold. We're always bothering someone," Noah said.

"Yes, I do know that," she sighed. "Everyone knows that." But the way she said it wasn't unkind. More exasperated than anything else. "Give us some breathing room, and I promise you can play sardines once I'm finished."

They filed out, and once again, Daniel's hand stopped me before I could leave. "She stays."

Dr. Gold looked at me and smiled. "Ah, my wayward infection patient. Next time, you need to come to the hospital."

"I had my reasons."

"I know. But you were still lucky. Regardless, I'm glad to see you alive. You too, Daniel."

"What's the prognosis?" He sounded a little sarcastic, and I squeezed his hand.

"It's a graze, but we can barely call it that. It's deep and likely going to scar. But on the whole, you got lucky with the placement. It's going to be a pain in the ass for a while. No lifting with that arm until you're fully healed. And if anything you do tweaks it, don't repeat that action for at least two weeks. I mean it, Daniel. If you see any signs of an infection—" she glanced at me "—or sense something else is wrong, of course come in."

"But other than that, I can go home?"

The doctor rolled her eyes. "I've learned my lesson with you guys. You'd rather be home than here ninety percent of the time, and I trust you not to ignore your symptoms. Give me a few minutes. I'll write you a prescription for pain medicine, and we'll get you out of here."

"Thanks, Dr. Gold."

She smirked. "Thank me by not getting shot again."

We were briefly alone, and Daniel looked at me. "You're still in your dress."

"I didn't leave."

"You could have. I'm fine."

I glared at him. "If it had been me, you wouldn't have moved. You probably wouldn't have slept. You saved me again. Even if it wasn't on purpose this time."

"Did they—"

"All clear?" Grant knocked on the doorframe.

Daniel sighed. "No heavy lifting, but other than that, all clear."

"Excellent."

The rest of it I didn't want to talk about while we were in the hospital. While he was here, I still felt vulnerable. Like he could still slip away from me even though he was mostly fine.

It took a while to get everything settled, but all through it, Daniel kept me by his side. He didn't let me go even for a second, and the rest of them saw. No one said anything or even gave a look like it was strange.

I wasn't sure why I was waiting for that to happen, but I was. Yet it dawned on me I didn't feel out of place here. I felt…included.

"All right," Daniel finally said, when he was dressed with his arm in a sling. The shirt was still bloody, and I hated the sight of it. "Everyone get the hell out of here. I'm fine. Feel free to check on me tomorrow. Today, Emma and I are going home."

Jude clapped him on the good shoulder. "Call us if you need us."

"I will."

They left, and I held out my hands. "Keys?"

He laughed and pulled me to his side. "I'm not so injured I can't drive my own truck." Harlan had driven Daniel's truck over from Ruby Round at some point in the night. I had a drowsy memory of him dropping the keys in the bag with Daniel's things.

I looked at him. "You don't have to pretend with me, you know. It's okay to be in pain, even if it isn't serious. You've seen me in more than enough pain."

"I know." The words were soft. Metal clanked together, and he took the keys out of his pocket. "Thank you."

"This means I get to see your house. Hope you hid the porn." I smirked at him, and he broke out into a grin.

"You're all the porn I need."

A snorted laugh made its way out of me. "Good to know."

"Let's just get out of here."

I couldn't agree more.

Chapter 22

Daniel

The wind blew Emma's hair wildly around her as she drove, and all I could do was look at her. She was so beautiful, and the pain in my shoulder was a visceral reminder of how quickly someone could disappear.

Only a second. That was how close it had come.

And I couldn't shake the feeling that I should have known something was wrong. Why didn't I feel the eyes on me? Was I so out of practice I couldn't sense the changes in the air anymore?

Or was it simply because I wasn't the target?

Either way, I didn't want Emma out of my sight. After last night, dancing with her in my arms and seeing the tears on her face, something flipped in me. I went from wanting her and finding joy and relief in being together to *needing* her more than I needed to breathe.

I was barely holding myself back from sliding across the

seat of the truck and touching her now. Which would only distract her from driving and get us both killed.

"You're staring at me," she said, looking over quickly before her eyes were back on the road.

"You're right. I am staring at you."

"Do I have something on me?"

I smothered my smile. "There doesn't have to be anything wrong with you for me to stare, Emma. I was never allowed to before, and now I can. All I want to do is look at you."

She pressed her lips together, and her hands tightened on the steering wheel. A beautiful contradiction. She'd been the one to tell me what she wanted, and yet sometimes she was shy.

It wasn't unexpected. With what she'd gone through, her own father only giving her value until he needed her gone, I was happy she wasn't doubting herself more than she already did.

"Where is your house?" We were turning into the ranch. "I don't know where I'm going."

"Past the lodge and take a right," I said. "Keep going straight, and you'll see it."

A couple miles down the dirt road, my house came into view. Looking at it how she must see it, I wished it were bigger and a little nicer. I liked my house, and it suited my bachelor ways. But this wasn't a place you brought someone home to.

And I did want her to feel at home.

Emma jumped down from the truck and sprinted around to my side, opening the door just like I'd done for her. She was smiling. "If I could lift you, I'd help you down."

"I would love to see that."

Still, I held her hand as I stepped down.

I had the prescription from Dr. Gold, but I wasn't going to take it yet. No chance was I was going to sleep while this woman was in my house and could be in my arms. I needed to feel her, and as strong as she was, I could sense the underlying anxiety in Emma. She needed me just as much as I needed her.

Taking the keys from her, I unlocked the door and ushered her inside.

"This is nice."

"Not as nice as it should be."

"What does that mean?"

I tossed the keys and pills on the entry table and turned, pinning Emma against the door with my body and my good arm. "I mean I wish I had something nicer than a bachelor's shack to bring you to. But this will have to do, because I can't keep my hands off you."

"Daniel—" Emma gasped before I kissed her. "You're hurt."

"Not badly enough to make me stop."

Her small moan drove every thought from my head aside from the ones of her skin and the other sounds I already knew she could make.

"Are you sure?"

"Yes." The word was muffled since my lips were already pressed to her neck. "I am sure. I need to feel you and tell my subconscious we're both still here and still safe."

"Are we?"

I pulled back, and her big, beautiful eyes repeated the question. One blue eye and one brown. So unique, and yet they fit her perfectly.

"What if they followed the ambulance? What if they followed us here and shoot through the windows?"

"Every building on the ranch is built with bulletproof

glass. And given what happened not only with Evelyn, but with Simon and the fire, no one is getting on this property without us knowing. I promise."

"Okay." She melted against my body as I walked us to the bedroom. It was a clumsy walk, bumping into walls because neither of us was willing to come apart enough to walk in a straight line.

My shoulder ached, and every time it got bumped, the pain was sharp, but I'd had worse, and I didn't care. I needed my hands on this woman more than I needed to be without pain. The pain reminded me he'd missed.

What if I'd turned the other direction? The shot might have been far closer to my heart and all this might have been different.

Getting out of my clothes was the easy part. I dropped the sling to the floor, and Emma opened her mouth in protest. "I'm not taking the sling to bed," I said with a laugh. "Don't worry, I won't lift you. Come here."

She did. I pushed the one shoulder her dress had off and watched the fabric fall in a wave, pooling around her feet, still in the heels she'd worn for the wedding. And the underwear.

It had been long enough since I'd done this with anyone that I'd forgotten the way underwear could send heat swirling through your mind and your body all at once.

"Fuck."

The word slipped out, and immediately, she was looking at me. "Do you need the pills?"

Tilting her face to mine, I kissed her. *Consumed* her. "I only need you, sweetheart. That was because you're so fucking beautiful, I can't breathe."

"Daniel."

I wrapped my one good arm around her and held her tight. "You can let it go now, Emma. I'm sorry I scared you."

Her eyes were glassy. "I knew you were okay."

"Knowing it and feeling it aren't the same. We both know that."

Up on her tiptoes, she put her arms around my neck. "I'm just glad we're both here."

"Me too, sweetheart."

With my good arm, I gripped her waist and reversed our positions, bringing her down onto the bed with me. Sprawled over me, her cheeks suddenly pink, she was looking at the center of my chest like she was embarrassed. "What's wrong?"

"Nothing. Nothing at all. But I'd like to try—" She pulled away from me until she was on her knees on the floor. Her flush was even more intense. "I've never done it."

"Nor do you have to," I told her.

"But I want to. I just don't want you to be disappointed."

I reached out and touched her cheek. "Emma, nothing you could ever do would disappoint me."

The relief in her eyes was clear, and gone were any signs of hesitation. She reached for me and bowed her head, taking me between her lips, and I swore I'd died and gone to heaven.

What I didn't tell her—and what I could no longer say because her mouth had robbed me of the power of speech—was that it had been so long since anyone's mouth had been near my cock, I could barely remember it.

Even if there hadn't been a gap in my experience, it was perfect. All warmth and heat—I was lost in the power of her mouth and the sweet, eager sensation of her wanting to care for me.

I needed her in so many ways, and most of all, I needed to hold her. This was so beautiful, but I needed to see her and hear her. "Emma."

She looked up.

"Come here, sweetheart. Please."

I saw uneasiness in her eyes as I dragged her into my lap, my erection so, so close to where I wanted it to be. "You are very much *not* bad at that." I told her quietly and felt her body relax. "I just need you to be here with me right now and not kneeling in front of me. Is that okay?"

"Yes," she breathed. "But I do want to try that again sometime."

"I'm not going to turn down the offer," I laughed. "But after last night—"

"I know."

She stood for a second, shoving the gorgeous underwear off her hips before coming back to me, and neither of us made an effort to move to a different position. We came together, sliding against each other like we'd been doing this every day for years and not only a few days.

"No matter what," she said. "I'm taking care of you this time."

She backed up her words, rocking her hips and using her own momentum to drive us together. I held her with my good arm, and I used my bad arm to bring her mouth to mine.

Slow, easy movement with waves of pleasure from both of us. She gasped into my mouth as I thrust upward. We could take care of each other.

I shuddered at the true reality of how close we'd come, again, to disaster. I suddenly understood Lucas's words during the wedding so much more. I understood Jude's desperation and devastation with Lena's close call, and I understood Noah's urge to protect Kate at all costs. Grant's sacrifice of his body to keep Cori alive.

There was nothing I wouldn't do to protect this woman. This brilliant, beautiful, and kind woman. I didn't want to let her go. Ever.

My thoughts stuttered to a stop even as our bodies kept moving, pleasure spiraling through me and driving us faster.

I didn't know when it started. Whether it was seeing her in my dreams and hearing her call to me, or the moment I caught her when she fell. Maybe it was the quiet lunches and conversations. But I was falling in love with Emma Derine, and no part of me was afraid.

Keeping my hand around her waist, I spun us to the bed so I was over her, her legs around my hips. She laughed, pure joy on her face. And with my next rolling thrust, the laugh turned to a moan. I could live forever on the sound of her voice like this—breathless and wanting.

My mouth roamed her skin, tasting her nipples through the lace of her bra and drawing kisses along her neck. She held me close, and I wondered if it was possible to be addicted to someone. That was the way I felt right now.

Maybe it was the endorphins in my body from the injury or maybe it was just her, but the only thing I wanted was the taste of her on my tongue.

"Daniel…" Her breath was short, and I didn't stop. I kept my rhythm steady, exactly as it was, grinding my hips down into her clit, making sure Emma had every chance at pleasure.

"I've got you," I told her. The words came from the deepest of places. Where my instincts dwelled. Together, right now, we were both creatures of instinct, acting as our base selves and no more. Our most desperate needs were on display for the other. "I'll always have you. Whatever you need," I leaned down and whispered in her ear. "If you need safety or pleasure, comfort or love, you'll find it here. With me. In my arms, with me buried inside you. We belong to each other."

Emma shuddered, fingers clawing at my shoulders and the back of my neck to bring me closer. The pain was nothing in comparison to feeling her come, squeezing me like her body depended on it for life. I had no way to hold back, my climax barreling through me with the force of a train.

I kissed her, hard and deep, sealing this moment between us. It felt sacred and precious—not something I ever wanted to lose.

We caught our breath together, finally slipping apart and rearranging ourselves on my bed. "Well." Emma finally broke the silence, voice rough as if she'd been screaming. "That was incredible."

"You're incredible." I kissed her hair and savored the way she snuggled closer.

We lay for a while, simply breathing, before she finally stirred. "Last night, the police chief came to your room. He listened to my story, and actually said he would be back to listen to yours today, but I'm sure he knows how to find you."

I laughed. "You bet he does. I'm sure the last thing he wants to do is talk to me. Resting Warrior and the police department are on tenuous terms at the moment. We bring more trouble than he likes."

Emma sat up and smirked at me, eyes sparkling. "Maybe he should learn to like trouble."

"Maybe. But Garnet Bend was a lot more peaceful before Resting Warrior and all our demons showed up."

She swallowed. "Speaking of demons, I told him I wanted to talk to the FBI. And they came this morning before you woke up. When you said you heard me talking? I was talking to them. Or rather, yelling at them. I didn't want to tell you until we were here and comfortable."

My gut tightened. If someone delayed telling you something, it was never good news. "Why?"

"Because the bullet was meant for me, and we both know it."

"And what did they say?" I kept myself in check, not wanting to react until I knew everything. But I wasn't optimistic.

"When I ran into Agent Phillips outside of Dr. Rayne's office and he said he'd petitioned the judge? It had already been signed off on. My name was already out there. They claim they didn't attach any location to my name, just floated it in order to draw Simon out. But it doesn't matter whether they did or didn't. This is still on them."

I cursed, pushing myself up to sitting and hissing when pain flared in my shoulder.

"You need your meds." Emma didn't wait to go retrieve them, and I didn't argue. For one, the sight of her walking through my house in nothing but a bra was incredible, and also because she was right. The pain was pulsing through my shoulder now, and I knew not to push it.

I heard the faint sounds of cupboards opening and my kitchen sink turning on before she came back with a glass of water and the pill bottle. I let my eyes rove up and down her form, body reacting. If I weren't about to be seriously medicated, I'd pin her to the bed and make her moan all over again.

"I'm not used to bedside service in my own house."

"Just this once." But she was grinning.

I downed the pills in one go. "Seriously. I'm not sure what they did was legal, regardless of the judge."

She sat with me again. "Either way, it's already done. Cat's out of the bag. So I told them I'd help them. Because I'm not having this happen again. The next time, they might not miss."

"Emma." She was looking down at her hands, fidgeting. I knew how badly she didn't want to be involved. "You don't have to do this because of me."

"I know. But if I help, maybe it will be over sooner."

"That would be nice," I acknowledged. "And you know I'll do whatever I can to help keep you safe."

"I know."

In that same deep place where my words to her had come from, I felt the tension in the air. This situation was tightening. Something was about to snap, and I needed to make sure *all* of us were safe when it did.

As much as I was pissed at the FBI for endangering Emma and causing me injury, I was still glad they were the ones with the operational burden on their shoulders. All of us at Resting Warrior were willing to do what we needed to in order to protect our own, but we were outmatched here. Outmatched, outgunned, and in the dark.

There were too few of us, too many of them, and in spite of Emma's fucking incredible memory, we didn't know enough about Simon's operation or where any of them would strike from.

The longer I spent in Emma's presence, the more my deepest soul told me I wanted this to be forever. But that didn't change the truth of my original apprehensions—you didn't make lifelong decisions with a situation like this hanging over your head.

For both of us, I wanted clear skies above us before we made that kind of commitment. But I already knew how I felt, and I didn't think it was likely to change.

I held out my good arm, and she lay down with me, bringing up the blanket from the foot of the bed. "I'm probably going to be asleep soon. One of the things I hate the most about pain medication."

"It's fine," she whispered. "I'm just going to snoop through your house for that porn you claim not to have."

"I don't have anything to hide. Snoop to your heart's content. But until I am actually asleep?" I hauled her onto my chest and kissed her.

The feeling of her skin, the scratch of lace on mine, the taste of her lips. It could be the pain medication kicking in early, or it could just be her. But this was heaven. It was the only place I wanted to be.

Chapter 23

Emma

I didn't like this van. It smelled weird, was cramped, and had the unfortunate presence of my two least favorite FBI agents.

"So you're saying getting Daniel shot was worth it?"

Agent Phillips's jaw tightened. "No, I don't believe that is what I said, Miss Derine. I said we were able to track Riders' activity attached to your name back to them. It's not much, but it's something."

Daniel cleared his throat from where he was standing just outside the open back doors of the van. "I don't like this. The operation is just the two of you? If the FBI is truly so desperate to catch the Riders, why aren't they providing more operational support?"

Agent Jones grinned. "A fair question. But this is still just data gathering. We can't do much until we know where Simon is, and more importantly, where he's moved his resources. His operation can continue without him, so we need everything. If we can take him and get that information, believe me, you'll see all the organizational support you can dream of."

That clearly wasn't the answer Daniel was looking for. "In that case, I'm going with you."

"No," Phillips said.

"Liam, Noah, Jude, and I will be joining you, then. Unless you have a reason for telling us no beyond dislike?"

Phillips slammed his fist onto the tiny desk in front of him and pushed out of the van. "I'm getting tired of this, Mr. Clark. My like or dislike of you has nothing to do with this. Nor does your inflated sense of importance. Believe me, I would love more support, and I've asked. But as Agent Jones just said, the order is a no from the top. I know who you all are—I've looked into Resting Warrior—and I appreciate your service as SEALs and the work you do now. But I can't *imagine* why I'd say no to four *civilians* on a dangerous operation."

"I thought you said it wasn't dangerous?" I asked.

"Everything has its risks. It's as safe as it can be."

Liam was smirking and hid it behind his hand. We were cornering the special agent, and he had nowhere to go. And a little part of me loved that, given the shit he'd put us through.

"Either it's too dangerous for Emma to go with only the two of you as escorts, or it's safe enough for civilians to tag along. Which is it?"

"*For fuck's sake.*" Phillips walked away. We were in a town to the west of Garnet Bend, along the shore of Flathead Lake. There was a coffee shop down the street, and it seemed like that was where he was headed to cool off.

"Thoughts, Special Agent Jones?" Daniel asked.

"He's not wrong. We're not supposed to bring along unauthorized civilians. But I don't see the harm. You guys clearly know how to handle yourselves, and I understand why you want to be here. On the surface, this seems more dangerous than it is. I'll talk to him. Besides, this is just an observation task. I don't imagine there will be much danger."

"What good will it do to ask?" I asked. "He'll just say no."

"He can't," he said. "I'm his superior. If I say you can be here, you can. But I need to make this clear. You will not do anything but *watch*. Got it?"

"Got it," Daniel said through his teeth. Clearly, he didn't agree with that, but he also wasn't going to say anything that would keep him from coming with us.

Jumping out of the van, Agent Jones headed in the same direction as his partner. "You'll have to stay with this van, though. Like I said. Observation only."

I went to the back and sat on the bumper. At least the air was fresher here. They'd told me all about what was supposed to happen. This time, they'd provided additional information about me when they released it to the public. I'd supposedly left Resting Warrior and moved to this town, working in my given field at a little computer shop on the other side of town. They'd leaked an IP address and a couple of other details, essentially sending up a flare for Simon. *Come get her! She's right here!*

The idea was that someone would come for me, and they would intercept him—or her, I supposed—before the FBI pulled me out. Jones would be in a van across the street, and Phillips, Daniel, and the others would be here. A five-minute drive away, with a straight shot across town through some side streets. I already had the map memorized.

Phillips said they'd made it clear it was a *rumor* about where I might be and not solid information, so Simon's people wouldn't be able to take a shot from afar like they had at the wedding.

Still, nerves swam in my gut.

Jude stood the farthest away, watching, but he was looking at me. "Don't worry, Emma. We'll be around whether we're in the van or not. We need these guys gone. And we protect our family."

Now my gut swam for an entirely different reason. Did they consider me part of the family because I was staying on the ranch? Because I was with Daniel? Or because they saw something deeper?

I knew what I felt, but it terrified me almost as much as coming face-to-face with Simon again.

Daniel winced, and I went to him. "Is it okay?"

"It's fine."

"I'm sure we can track down some ibuprofen. Since you won't take the real meds."

He smiled down at me, but there was an edge to it. "Like hell am I going to be impaired while you're doing something like this. If I had my way, you wouldn't be going in at all. They'd just watch and see if the person showed up. But I'm not running the show."

I swallowed. "I'm sure it will be fine."

"Here." Daniel stepped close and laid his hand on my neck. "I'm going to put this on you."

In his hand was a small, clear, round sticker that looked like a Band-Aid. It had a little hard circle in the center. "What is it?"

"A tracker."

Pulling my shirt away from my skin, he placed the sticker right over my shoulder blade. "You really don't trust them, do you?"

He shook his head. "It's not that. It's that I know now not to take any chances. Nothing is guaranteed, and I will do anything, no matter how small, to make sure you come back to me."

We stared at each other, smiling like idiots, until Liam

cleared his throat.

"Earth to the lovebirds."

Daniel ignored him completely, pulling me down off the tail of the van and kissing me like the world depended on it. "It's not too late to change your mind," he whispered against my lips. "We can go home. I'll cook you dinner, stare at you in this *stunning* color, and whatever happens after that…"

"I have to do this," I said. "I'm not going to be the thing that kills you, and I'm quite a fan of being alive myself."

Daniel sighed. "Well, I'm still going to stare at you in this color. For a few more minutes."

The shirt I wore was a vibrant blue, and he hadn't been able to take his eyes off me all day. But I wasn't sure if it was the color or the worry we both shared. Either way, I made a note in my head to buy more things in this shade.

"All right," Agent Jones said. I jumped, having not noticed them coming back. "Mr. Clark, you and your friends are permitted to stay here with Agent Phillips. You'll be able to hear and see everything, and there's no danger of you affecting the surveillance."

Phillips didn't look particularly happy about it, but since he wasn't in charge, it didn't matter.

"Can you go over it one more time?" I asked.

He nodded. "Phillips, get the earpiece."

Phillips brushed by me, and I moved closer to Daniel.

"You're going to walk across town to the intersection of Barnes and Trinity. The store you're headed for is Cole Computers and More. We've already informed the owner what's going on, and he's taking a long afternoon break. The door is open, and there's a sign on the door that reads 'By Appointment Only.' That should stop the casual shoppers and give you a reason to send them away if you need to. Obviously, Simon and his men won't be deterred by a sign. But that's why I'll be outside. As soon as you see someone you recognize, head into the back alley where Phillips can pick you up. We'll take care of the rest.

"Your transmitter." He pointed to the little earpiece Phillips was holding out to me. "It's voice-activated. So we'll hear whatever you say."

The plan sounded simple enough, but I was uneasy. Not just because I didn't *really* want to do this, but it seemed too simple.

"You've done things like this before?"

"Yes."

I glanced over at Phillips, and he nodded. "More or less."

Despite the man being a dick, his confirmation made me feel better.

"Guess I better get going, then?"

Jones checked his watch. "Yes."

"Okay." Turning to Daniel, I hugged him. "I'll see you soon."

"Yes, you will." He kissed my head and climbed into the van behind me.

Taking a deep breath, I crossed the street in the direction I was meant to go. This morning, I'd looked at a map, so I knew the layout of the town.

"Testing, you can hear me?"

"Loud and clear," Jones said.

Phillips added. "Yes. But don't talk unless you have to."

"Okay, Grumpy."

I thought I heard Daniel laughing, but it was faint.

The path to my destination wasn't far, and I walked slowly. This wasn't meant to be some kind of sprint. I was meant to blend in. On my way to my new boring computer job. Simon was the only person whose attention I wanted to attract.

God, it was hot. It was still early enough in the season that the weather could be nice. There was a breeze off the lake from across the street, but it felt like the sun was beating down on me.

I had some cash, so I stopped in at a coffee shop on the way, grabbing an iced drink to keep me going. My nerves were building the longer the silence lasted.

Finally, I reached the cross section of streets. "Okay, I'm here. Going into the store."

No answer. That was fine. They were listening and waiting. Everything was exactly the way Jones said it would be. The little shop was dim, quiet, and empty, with the appointment sign on the door. It was almost like a look into the past. A lot of computers I hadn't seen since I was a kid, dusty shelves, and older technology. The owner must work on computers that had long outlived their technological lifespan.

Standing behind the counter, I waited. There wasn't much to do, other than get on the guy's computer and mess around on the internet.

That was where my memory could actually come in handy. I remembered everything, including what I'd found that led to Simon locking me up in the first place. Since they'd basically told him I was here, there was no point in hiding it. Odds were Simon would have wiped anything to do with himself, but I wanted to try anyway.

The main page to the cover business was still intact, but it looked dead. My log-in and the admin log-in were gone. I knew enough to get around it, but there wasn't anything left. What little had been there online to begin with was completely blank.

I was disappointed, but at the same time, that wasn't unexpected.

It had been an hour, and I hadn't had any contact from either Phillips or Jones, and no one passing by on the street had even glanced inside. We hadn't said how long this was going to take, but at the same time, I wanted at least to hear someone's voice.

"Okay, guys. I know you're trying to focus, but can you say something? Please? I'm starting to get nervous."

Nothing.

Okay, maybe it shorted out and wasn't working. That wasn't good, but it was something I could fix. The van was across the street—I could see it from where I stood. Maybe I could sneak out and ask Agent Jones if he could fix it. I wasn't going to do any of this while they couldn't hear me.

I slipped out of the store and looked both ways before crossing the street. No one was in the driver's seat of the van. Where was Agent Jones? Low panic built in my gut. It didn't feel right. "Can anyone hear me?"

Retreating across the street and back into the store, I jumped when Agent Jones was standing behind the counter, and then I breathed out a sigh of relief.

He winced. "Sorry I startled you. I wanted to check in on you without giving anything away. The earpiece isn't working."

"Yeah," I said. "I realized."

"We'll try this again tomorrow, once we figure out what's wrong with it. Or, if you want, we can just go without."

I blinked. Of course I didn't want to do that. Being alone without them to hear me put my life in danger. Why would he even suggest that? My gut churned, and I suddenly felt alert. Adrenaline ran through me, and I breathed in and out, trying to get a hold of the sudden panic and think through whether my anxiety was real.

"No, I'd like to be done. I want to be able to hear you guys."

He smiled. "Fair enough."

I looked outside, back in the direction of the other van. "It's a nice day. I think I'll walk back to the others."

He laughed. "Don't be silly. It's hot as balls out here. I already called them. They're out back."

"Oh. Okay."

I moved toward the back of the store and the alley. True to Agent Jones's word, the van was in the back. But no one was in the driver's seat of that vehicle either.

Why would Agent Jones pull all the way around to the back of the store, risking someone seeing him get out of the van, when everyone was already back here? That didn't make sense.

Phillips didn't like me, but I imagined he could check on me without taking my head off.

I glanced down at the license plate on the van and just managed to disguise my whole body freezing as a stumble. It wasn't the same. This wasn't the van Phillips and Daniel were in.

"Are you all right?" Jones asked.

"I'm fine."

The front of the van was facing me, the back facing the end of the alley farther down.

My memory kicked in. The street ahead of me led back toward the *right* van. I could circle the block and use the alleys to get back to them. The entire map was in my head. I could do it.

When I glanced back, Agent Jones was smiling, and I didn't trust that smile.

We circled the back of the van, and Agent Jones knocked on the door. The second he turned his back, I ran.

Agent Jones cursed behind me, and the van doors opened. I didn't slow down. The heavy sound of his boots echoed down the alley behind me, and I put on as much speed as I could.

Get around the corner. Half a block. Get to people. All I

needed was people. Then I could make my way to where I needed to go.

Skidding around the corner, I slammed into a wall. Not a wall, a body. Someone huge. I tried to spin off him and couldn't.

"Don't let her go!"

With terrifying clarity, I realized this was what he wanted. The van wasn't the trap. *This* was the trap.

Pain shattered through my skull, and the world went black.

Chapter 24

Daniel

After the first comment about Phillips being Grumpy, we didn't hear anything.

It had been too long. Not long enough to cause a full alarm, but long enough. Something was wrong. Every instinct I had screamed it.

I was here with the asshole who wouldn't tell me shit if he thought things were fine, but restless energy slithered under my skin. Emma's transmitter was voice-activated. We should have heard something by now, even if it was her talking by accident.

We hadn't even heard her cough or breathe.

"I need some air."

Not waiting for permission, I slipped out the back of the van and took out my phone. So far, I'd resisted looking at it, not wanting to let Phillips know I'd interfered in that way. But I needed to know she was fine and less than a mile away.

My woman had spent six months alone in a cabin. If anyone could spend this long in silence, it was her.

The app opened, and my stomach plummeted. The tracker wasn't here. It was speeding away from us to the east. She was gone, and no one knew.

Fuck.

Fuck.

I should have listened to my instincts earlier than this and checked, regardless of what Phillips thought. She was still within reach, but at a speed that fast? Soon, she could be gone forever.

It was only years of training and missions that kept my mind in check. Already, my heart was pounding, and adrenaline was spiking through my system with the need to run and scream and panic. But I couldn't do that. Emma needed me to be the leader and the man I was and get her back before her father had a chance to kill her.

And I needed to be that person myself because I needed her. In my life and in my bed. I could no longer pretend Emma wasn't the best thing to ever happen to me, pulling me out of years of drowning in my own sorrow with no end in sight.

"Jude, Liam, Noah, can you come out here for a second?" I leaned my head into the van. "Sorry, Phillips. Ranch business. It'll only be a minute."

He looked at me, giving me the distinct impression he didn't give a shit what I did. If I drove off back to Resting Warrior right now, he would not care.

Exactly what I wanted. Let him stay distracted enough for me to figure this out. Still, my palms itched with the urge to move.

They hopped out of the van, and I slammed the door harder than was necessary. It felt good.

"What's up?" Jude asked.

I showed him the phone screen, and he swore. "How long?"

"I don't know. But we don't have much time. We don't know where Simon is. And if he gets her? She'll be lucky if he kills her quickly, based on what I know of him."

Liam was glaring toward the van like he could burn a hole through it with his gaze. "This is the FBI's operation," he said. "Could they have set it up?"

"Using her as live bait?" Noah asked. "Not like this. I know Phillips is an ass, but the FBI does take protecting people seriously."

"No," Liam said. "That's not what I'm asking. I don't want to be the one to say it, but is there any possibility these two guys aren't working on the right side?"

My stomach dropped. Phillips had been abrasive and pushy from the beginning, shoving me, Emma, and everyone around us toward the outcome he wanted, no matter who was hurt by it. I currently had a bullet wound on my shoulder because he was so determined to use Emma to catch Simon.

"I don't want to think about it either," I said. "But we have to."

"Let's go talk to him. I have some choice words for him if he has anything to do with this." Noah took a step, and Jude's hand landed on his shoulder.

"Hold on. If he's a part of it, we need to know first. If it's the worst-case scenario, they've been running circles around us because they have more information than we do. We need to find out if they've gone rogue before we say anything. Call the field office."

Liam shook his head. "If they are in on it and they get a call, it'll tip them off."

"What's the better option?" Noah asked, his question carrying only genuine emotion. "Risk them being tipped off by their superiors, or risk them leading us on a wild goose chase because we don't know enough?"

"Neither is a good option," Jude pointed out. "We're doing the best with what we have, and the longer we stand here talking about it, the less time Emma has."

"I'll call them," I said. "They know me. At the very least, I can try to talk to someone who was there when both Emma and I were. While I call, think of options for going after her quickly. Both plans involving the agents and not."

Pulling out my cell phone, I did a quick Google search to find the general number for the field office. It wasn't a number I'd thought I needed to have saved.

"FBI Seattle field office. How may I direct your call?"

"I need to speak to a duty agent. Immediately. This is a matter of life-and-death."

There was a brief pause. "May I have your name, sir?"

"Daniel Clark. I was in your offices three weeks ago. I promise I'm not being funny or making a joke. A woman's life is on the line."

"Hold please."

The vague but pleasant hold music playing in my ear felt like the soundtrack to the end of the world. Every note I might have enjoyed at another time grated across my nerves, and I paced back and forth, unable to keep myself from roaming behind the van like a caged animal.

"This is Special Agent Madeline Knight. I was here when you were with Miss Derine, Mr. Clark. How can I help you?"

"I'm currently in Polson, Montana, with Agent Eric Jones and Agent Cole Phillips. After their badgering, and you all deciding to use her name as bait and getting me shot, she finally agreed to help draw out Simon Derine. But she's gone. I had a tracker on her, and she's been taken. And before I go in there and tell them that, I want assurances that this setup wasn't sanctioned by the FBI."

Dead silence came from the other end of the line.

"Agent Knight?"

She cleared her throat. "Mr. Clark, I understand the severity of the situation right now, and I'm not blowing you off. I need to put you on hold to talk to my superior. It will be no longer than five minutes."

"Thank you."

Once again, the hold music started, but this time, it felt better. It felt…like movement. Not interminable waiting.

"Mr. Clark, my name is Special Agent Joshua Powell. Please tell me what you told Special Agent Knight."

I did tell him. Only this time, I added detail as quickly as I could. "Please. I understand this isn't conventional, and I know I'm a civilian, but Miss Derine's life is in danger. You and I both know he won't hesitate. And if he does, it won't be out of the kindness of his heart."

"No, it won't. And you're correct, the circumstances warrant an ease in protocol, because today's operation is not something we're aware of. The last we heard from Agent Jones, he and Agent Phillips were going to watch and observe, using the information both you and Miss Derine gave us in an attempt to find a more solid location for Simon's whereabouts. I heard nothing else. Not about witness protection or an attempt to use her information as bait—which we never would have approved."

"He said the answer was no operational support for today's activity because you needed more information."

"Yeah, well, it's no operational support because no one over here knows fuck-all about what's happening. It doesn't help you now, but we'll get to the bottom of this. Here's my direct number. Keep me updated, and tell me what we can do. Not much I can from this far away, but if there is something, we'll do it."

"Any idea which of these guys is the mastermind here?"

Agent Powell's voice was dark. "Believe me, I wish I had one. Be careful, Mr. Clark."

The warning wasn't much use now, but it was a relief to know it was one or two rogue agents and not the entire FBI acting against us.

Nerves twisted in my gut. Just days ago, I had been glad the entire thing was resting on the shoulders of the FBI, and now it wasn't. It lay with us once again. Everyone would help, and I was going to take the help so I could save Emma, but I felt sick deep inside too. If they got hurt trying to help me…

It would haunt me forever.

"I'll call you back," I said, hanging up the phone. "It's not them. They don't even know what we're doing here. They're completely in the dark and were told these guys were looking for more information based on our Seattle visit. I have no idea if it's either or both of them. But my money is on—"

"That guy?" Noah nodded at the van. "Yeah. Me too."

"How do we do this?" Liam asked.

Jude pulled out his phone. "I'll call Grant and Harlan. Maybe they can be our eyes from the ranch, and if Emma's heading east, maybe there's a chance for an intercept."

"I don't know how we do it," I said. "I have absolutely no fucking idea, and I can barely think straight as it is." My voice was quiet and even, trying not to send up alarms to Phillips or anyone who might be walking by. But with every minute that passed, Emma was getting farther and farther away from me, and it was becoming harder to hear over the alarm sirens in my head.

"Force Phillips to reach out to Emma," Noah said,

looking at me. He was calm too, but I saw the determination in his gaze. He'd been here too, when Simon had Kate. He knew what was going on in my head and what to do to get me out of it. I needed points of action.

"She's been taken, and her communication transmitter is gone. We don't know how long she's been in motion, but demanding he make contact either forces them to lie or makes one of them realize what the other is doing. I'm not sure we can make more of a plan without their reaction."

I looked down on my phone, the blinking dot moving steadily east. My mind had seen too many bad things, and it was currently filling in all the blanks I didn't know with the worst possibilities of what she could be going through. Nothing about the thoughts was going to help me, but I couldn't seem to banish them from my mind.

Jude stepped back into our circle. "Daniel, let me see your phone."

Without question, I handed it to him. "What are you doing?"

"Sending the tracking signal to Grant and Harlan so they can keep an eye on it from the security office. You're going to want up-to-the-minute information, and I already know you can't have your eyes glued to the screen every second. Not if we want to help her."

"Right." My mind spun the tape through to the end. "Fuck, it's been more than an hour. If he's anywhere in the state—anywhere close, we're going to be way too late."

Too late. I was always too late when I needed to be there. How had I not seen this coming? Why had I not been able to follow the signs? Again.

"Daniel," Liam said quietly, and the tone in his voice made me look at him. "Stop. If you focus on that, it's only going to slow you down. Don't bother trouble before it finds you. Focus on getting to her. Do not worry about being late.

It will delay every thought by three seconds, and that is time you don't have to waste."

The words snapped through me like an order. He was right. The only way to get through this was to act like I didn't feel as if my heart had just been ripped out of my chest.

"Let's do this. I want to know why they thought they could get away with this, and how they managed to do it with everyone watching."

As if I'd summoned him, Agent Jones pulled up in his other van and got out with a grim look on his face. It was an act, but he didn't know we were aware.

It was time for one or both of them to tell the truth.

Chapter 25

Emma

Pain was the first thing to wake me. A sharp, pulsing ache in the back of my skull. I tried to move, and it only got worse, so I stopped.

The last minutes before everything went dark were bright in my mind. It was a trap for me, and Agent Jones was the one to spring it. I had no idea if Agent Phillips was in on it too, but it didn't matter. The people who were supposed to be protecting me hadn't.

I'd never been so grateful that I'd drawn the line about witness protection. I might not have ever made it to that new life, and if I'd let them take me, Daniel wouldn't have even known I was gone. He'd think I was blissfully living in anonymity in whatever small town they dumped me in.

Now, I'd be lucky to get out of being dumped anywhere except a grave.

Focus, Emma.

The rumble and sound told me I was in a vehicle. I

hadn't opened my eyes yet, so I didn't know what kind of vehicle. My money was on the van from the alley, but there was no way to tell yet. How long had I been unconscious?

Again, no solid way to tell. But I wasn't hungry, and I didn't have to use the bathroom, so it couldn't have been too long. That was good. The faster I could get myself together, the more chance I had to survive.

And that was already a long shot.

At the other end of this drive, wherever we were going, Simon was waiting for me. And this time, he was going to put a bullet in my head and bury me in the shallow grave he promised. Who knew? Maybe he'd make it hurt first for talking to the FBI and giving them everything. Because if Agent Jones was a part of this, Simon knew everything.

Shit. He knew everything. Like where I'd been living and who had been helping me. He'd already promised to take revenge on Resting Warrior, and now he had more than one reason to do it.

No wonder he'd known I was at the wedding. They didn't "use my name"; they told him where I was so he could kill me, and when that didn't work…

Slowly, I dared to open my eyes.

My stomach dropped.

Bars marred my vision of the inside of a van. I was in a cage again. Dread slammed down on me like a weight trying to drag me to the bottom of the ocean. Of course he would put me in a cage. He could have put me in handcuffs. Or just tied me up. Hell, he could have injected me with a sedative to make sure I didn't wake up until I got to him, but he put me in a cage. Because he wanted me to see it and know what was coming.

Bastard.

Movement hurt, but I needed to do it. Slowly, ever so slowly, I straightened out my body as much as I could in the cramped little box. The temptation to reach up and touch the place they'd hit me was strong, but I didn't want to know if I was bleeding.

Blood made me panic, and I didn't have any room for panic right now. Though, if I was honest with myself, I wasn't going to be able to hold out against it for long.

The cage was against one wall of the truck and tall enough to sit up in. I wasn't sure if it was the exact cage I'd been held in all that time, but I wouldn't be surprised. Simon had a flair for the dramatic and a way of latching on to revenge. It wouldn't shock me at all if he'd somehow gone back to the hellhole of a house he used as a base and recovered it if the police didn't clear it out entirely.

Moving only as fast as the pain would allow, I tested the walls of the cage. The pounding in my head was getting easier the longer I was upright. It still hurt, but it wasn't making me want to vomit.

Nothing moved.

Not even a wiggle.

Okay.

One deep breath in, and one deep breath out.

I saw nothing else in the van. Nothing I could reach or try to scoot the cage toward in order to help me break free.

All I had right now was my memory—the very thing he wanted to kill me for.

Suddenly I reached up, searching under my shirt for the small sticker on my skin. It was still there, and I hoped it was still working. There was a reason Daniel had put it there. He would be watching, and he would already know I was gone.

Traitorous, dangerous hope filled my chest.

All right, Emma. *Think*. Use the memories you have.

Daniel was coming. I had no doubt of that. If he knew I was gone and could get to me, he was going to try. All I had to do was stay alive long enough to let him.

I started from the beginning, when the two special agents showed up at the ranch, and I went through every interaction. Every word said and every nuance of their expressions. Nothing I remembered pointed to this being a setup. My recollection only revealed the things I already knew to be true. Agent Phillips was an asshole, Agent Jones was charming, and they wanted to take down Simon more than anyone, including me.

Now I knew they were lying.

But even then, the memories were convincing. Agent Jones could make a hell of a career as an actor.

Accessing Simon's old website wouldn't have tipped him off. That trap had clearly already been laid.

Nothing I remembered led me to believe I could have known this would happen. Spinning through the memories again, I couldn't find anything I could use to stall Simon or convince him not to murder his only daughter. The only leverage I had was the fact that I'd already told them everything I knew. I couldn't do any more damage because I'd already done it, and he'd managed to get out of it anyway by turning the agents on the case.

Or maybe he'd already had the agents on his payroll and had used them to find me.

A shiver ran down my spine.

That sounded more like him.

Every layer of Simon that was peeled back was another layer of horror and realization that he had spies everywhere. A network decades old and integrated so deeply, I was starting to wonder if it was even possible to stamp it out.

There were no windows in the van and no way to tell what time it was—only the ambient light that seeped through the cracks.

The longer we drove, the easier it was for the fear to sink in. Breath came shallow in my lungs, and my imagination created no shortage of scenarios for when we got to wherever we were going and I was dragged out in front of the man I thought was meant to love me.

Why didn't I listen to Mom? She told me to stay away from him. She knew. Even if she didn't know the full truth, she'd known out of instinct Simon was bad news.

I should have left well enough alone.

Instead, I focused on the good things within all the bad. I liked to think I would have found my way to Daniel no matter what, but it wasn't true. We were from completely different worlds. Me struggling away in Missoula, trying to make life work without my mom and, without Simon, no way to pay for college. I would have had no reason to come up to this part of the state. No reason to seek out a group of ex-soldiers who helped people.

Even if I'd done everything the same, and Simon had decided not to go after Kate's brother or if I hadn't decided to poke into his office that day, we might never have crossed paths.

Potentially thousands of close-call decisions which could have kept us apart, each one clear in my mind. And of course, there were more than even I could think of.

It hit me in the chest like a blow. Not meeting Daniel—

My breath became shallow, and my heart kicked up into a pounding rhythm in my ears. The visceral fear of never having encountered him or dreamed about him. Never laughing with him or learning his secret smile or seeing the hunger in his eyes before we came together. That fear was far worse than the fear of being driven toward my death.

Would I face the end of Simon's gun willingly? No. But regardless of what happened, I was grateful to have known and loved Daniel.

Loved him.

I brought my knees up to my chest and pressed the heels

of my palms into my eyes to stop the tears. Such a simple thought, and yet it was so real. I loved him. Of course I did.

The truth was, I'd started loving him before we really met. My savior. The one who'd let me out of this fucking cage the first time. I wished I'd pulled him aside before I'd walked away from the van and told him just that—I wished I'd realized.

I didn't have a way to tell him, but in case I didn't get a chance to, I hoped he knew. The last month with him had been the best month of my life. Including all the bad things. I wouldn't trade them for anything.

The van went over a bump, and the cage jostled, throwing me askew, but it jerked back before it could slide.

Turning, I looked closer at the bottom edge of the cage along the van wall. Straps. Two black straps were attached to the bottom to keep the cage from moving. It wasn't much, but it was something.

The bars of the cage were metal, and they weren't polished; they also had sharp edges. The question was if I could find one close enough to the straps to make a difference.

I remembered what I'd said, both to myself and to Daniel. I wanted a life. A life with him and a life with the family I'd found at Resting Warrior. If this was the end for me, I would try to accept it with grace. But until that final second, I would fight like hell to keep the life I'd found.

So I braced myself against the throbbing in my skull, turned, and started feeling along every metal ridge within reach.

Chapter 26

Daniel

I watched Agent Jones get out of the van and walk toward us. "Excuse me, I need to check with Phillips."

But that alone wasn't going to fly. I followed him into the back of the van. "Phillips, I want you to check on her. Hear her talk. It's been too long."

Jones whirled and looked at me. "I let you come along for the ride, Mr. Clark, but I draw the line at you giving orders. We don't break radio silence unless we have to."

"And I'm telling you that Miss Derine wouldn't simply be silent for over an hour. The transmitter is voice-activated. Do you really think she hasn't been within range of a voice this whole time? Or hasn't spoken?"

I needed to hold the line as long as I could to get them to reveal themselves without letting them know I knew. The other guys were behind me, and I knew them well enough to know they were listening at the door I had cracked, touching the handles in case they needed to come in.

But fuck, the line was hard to hold when a ticking clock was flashing in my mind, telling me Emma was speeding away from me and toward danger every second.

Phillips looked at me and then at the back of his partner's head. I read the confusion there and held my breath. "Eric, it's fine. He's right. It's been a little while since we've heard from her. It might be good to verify the transmitter."

"And startle her? Make her act suddenly and irrationally in front of Simon's agents, giving away that it's a trap? No. We hold tight."

Phillips looked at me then back at Jones again, stiffening. "She's inside. They won't see her if they're not in there with her yet, which they're not, because we would have heard, assuming the transmitter's working. Why are you back here at all? You should have eyes on her."

"I don't need a reason to come back and take a breather. When I left her, she was fine, playing on one of the computers. Everybody just needs to calm down."

Phillips's spine straightened. "Let's just check." He reached toward the button that would open the comm channel.

Jones caught his wrist. "No."

"Jones, what the hell is wrong with you?"

"This." I couldn't hold back anymore. Pulling my phone out of my pocket, I turned the screen toward the two of them, showing the tracker I'd put on Emma and how it was moving east at seventy miles per hour. "If you call out to her, Phillips, she won't answer. She's already gone."

Jones moved, and my deepest instincts recognized the movement as him reaching for his gun. And he wasn't turning toward me. He was turning toward Phillips, which was all I needed to know.

"*Gun!*"

The doors of the van flew open at the same time I hurled

myself into Jones, slamming him into the wall and sending his weapon clattering to the floor. It was chaos, and I let myself fade into the only place I could—pure action.

Pain slammed through my shoulder as the hit landed directly where I'd been shot, and for long moments, my arm went dead. I couldn't move it. All I could do was try to turn and protect my body from the onslaught of a man who knew he'd been caught and was now fighting like a caged animal to take me down.

It didn't matter. There were too many of us and only one of him. Still, he'd gotten three hits to my jaw before Jude hauled him off me, pinning him to the floor with a knee in his back.

Phillips was staring down at him, gun drawn, in absolute shock. "You did this?" The tone in his voice was only further confirmation that he hadn't been a part of it, and beneath the pain, the panic, and the fear, a part of myself I'd been trying to ignore ripped free.

"I'm not saying anything."

Phillips holstered his gun and handed Jude the cuffs before turning around and running a hand through his hair. His shoulders heaved, and he turned around with pure fury in his eyes. "You absolute piece of shit. After everything. After *everything*, you're with him? You just handed her over to him like it was nothing? All of this—"

Phillips cut off as the realization of how far he'd accidentally gone down the wrong path caught up with him. "Every time I questioned, and every time I wondered about whether we were doing the right thing… *Every time*, you were right there, your charming ass telling me it was fine and that it was what upstairs wanted." He looked at me. "This asshole showed me signatures. I swear on whatever grave or God matters to you, I am not a part of it."

I smiled grimly. "It only takes one look at you to know.

But thank you. While I was outside, I called the field office and spoke to Agent Powell. He's waiting for an update. Jude, give Phillips the signal information so we can track it here. Liam, I'm going to need some ibuprofen and another bandage. I think I'm bleeding."

Sure enough, I looked down at my shirt and saw blood seeping through it. The wound wasn't nearly healed enough to do what I'd just done. Sex was one thing, giving and taking a beating was another.

Phillips was already on the phone. I stepped out of the van, favoring my shoulder and stepping away to breathe for just a second, because I was spiraling. Once again, I'd believed someone I shouldn't have. Once again, I'd made the assumption someone was operating in good faith, and it was going to cost me.

Because Agent Phillips was prickly and an asshole—not betraying us didn't get him off the hook there—I'd assumed he would be the one on Simon's side. And if I'd taken a step back and looked at the facts, maybe we wouldn't be here. Maybe Emma would still be in my arms. Maybe we would be at home in bed and I would be listening to the sound of her breath and telling her I loved—

Fire raced into me with my breath. I loved her. I loved Emma Derine.

I didn't know what to do with the whirlwind of emotions pouring through me. Relief and pride were the first. Emma was incredible. Beautiful, smart, fierce, and a survivor. She challenged me and accepted me exactly the way I was. She was the only person to crack my walls so thoroughly I knew they'd never be the same.

And it was about time. Those walls needed to come down, and I'd known it. But knowing something was wrong and someone proving it to you were two entirely different things. Emma showed me I didn't need to live a life of penance to make my life meaningful, in spite of my mistakes.

She showed me what it meant to be human and how to embrace the imperfection of it while trying to do better. I loved her, and I didn't want her to go anywhere. From the second I'd locked eyes on her face and those gorgeous, two-colored eyes, something in my soul had shifted and I hadn't looked back.

The second feeling that hit me was dread—and then terror. Because this was too late. I should have been telling her every second, because somewhere deep inside, I'd known this and hadn't let myself realize it.

Phillips dropped out of the van and came to me. "I talked to them, and I owe you an apology, Daniel. I know I've been an ass, I don't deny that, and I can't promise I'll be much different now. But Jones was the one driving this thing, and I hopped on board for my own reasons."

My mouth was opening to ask him what reasons, but he cut me off.

"Those reasons aren't on the table for discussion. But I never lied to you about how much I want Simon Derine. He needs to go down, and I wanted to be a part of it."

"You really knew nothing?"

He threw his arms wide. "Jones outranks me. Or, until five minutes ago, he did. He told me using Emma's name was approved by the judge. He was the one in contact with people at the field office. My contact was basic check-ins and not operational. I'm sure you understand the complexities of hierarchy. It gets so much worse when you're dealing with things that cross state lines, and I don't have a stomach for bureaucracy. Clearly, I was happy to let him handle it.

"It was never my intention to harm Emma. Or you. All I want is Simon."

"Are they going to help?"

He nodded. "They're calling me back. They'll do what they can, but Jones fucked us. I'm hoping you guys have some ideas, because I'm not from Montana, and we don't have the resources we need."

"We're working on it. And," I sighed, shrugging my shoulder and trying to get the muscles to ease for one fucking second. "I owe you an apology, too. You have been an ass, and I let that cloud my judgment. If I hadn't, maybe we wouldn't be here."

His phone rang, and he answered immediately. "Yeah." He listened. "You're going to have to try. Because we're going to lose our best chance at catching Simon Derine *and* our best witness if we don't move. You know what happens if he goes underground again? All that information she gave us is useless. He will burn his entire operation to the ground—her included—before he allows himself to be taken. Make your calls, and we'll work from here."

Liam appeared with the medication and bandage, making me sit down on the back of the van so he could wrap my shoulder, just where Emma had been sitting earlier today. The thought made my stomach bottom out.

Behind me, Agent Jones was slumped against the wall of the van, handcuffed to the vehicle itself, along with several pieces of tape over his mouth. He was glaring daggers at me, and I simply turned away. Right now, he wasn't worth my time.

Liam started to bandage me up, and I stood suddenly, moving away from the entrance. "I'm not letting him hear anything."

"The field office is making calls to law enforcement here and along the route the tracker is taking," Phillips said. "If we can make an intercept, they'll do it. It doesn't solve the problem of us getting to Emma, but it helps."

Jude handed me my phone. The screen was cracked from when I'd dropped it in the fight, but the screen still worked and the phone was still connected to the tracker. I was glad it was live. It helped me breathe. A little.

Visions of explosions went off in my mind. This was on me.

That was all I could think—this was on *me*. I'd trusted the wrong person, and I was going to lose all over again. Only this time, it wasn't going to be faceless captives. It was Emma.

Please. I wasn't sure who the word was for, God or the universe; I was simply begging. I didn't think I could live with myself if for the rest of my life I had nightmares about how I'd let her die.

And I would have those nightmares.

Over and over, her beautiful life being snuffed out in front of my eyes because I wasn't good enough. Wasn't strong enough. My instincts weren't honed, or I hadn't been paying attention.

I recognized the thoughts as a spiral that wasn't true, but I wasn't sure I could pull myself out. The little cursor blinked on the screen. Farther, farther, farther away.

Around me they were talking, but I couldn't listen. All I could do was stare at the screen.

You made the decision with the information you had, like we all do.

Wasn't that what Emma had said?

With every conversation, Emma had been with me. If she'd thought either of them was working with Simon, she would have said something and she never would have agreed to help, regardless of how many bullets the man put into my body.

I wasn't the only victim. I wasn't solely to blame, though every cell in my body was screaming with the guilt. Because making it my fault gave me some control. Knowing I couldn't have prevented this—the man fooled his own partner, for god's sake—made it so much worse. It was like being adrift in a riptide with no help in sight and not enough strength to fight it.

"I'll make the call," Jude said.

"What?"

Noah looked me up and down. "Local rescue helicopter and fire planes and choppers. We're going to call and see if we can get one in the air. It's the only thing fast enough to catch them at that speed."

"Not stealthy," I pointed out. "He'll see us coming."

"He'll already have seen you coming," Phillips said, expression grim. "Simon Derine is a cold, calculating psychopath. There's a reason he's been able to keep an iron grip on the entire northwest while also evading detection. He has people everywhere, as you saw. His resources are layered and nearly infinite.

"All the things Emma gave us? That was good information. But I guarantee it doesn't even scratch the surface of his true network."

"So what makes us think we can catch him at all?" Liam looked at me. "I'm not saying we shouldn't go after Emma. I'm asking what chance do we actually have?"

"One advantage." Phillips checked his phone briefly and tapped out a text. "Both his strength and his weakness. Derine doesn't believe in computers. Not for the hard-core stuff. When he had Emma doing the books and low-tier stuff, it was to keep up appearances, and that's all it ever is. Everything real is a single hard copy, and it's the same for his supplies. So if you find him—and that's a big if—you can get to him. He's slippery, but not invincible."

I moved my shoulder and winced, glancing down at the tracker again. "So getting him to surface last year was pure luck on our part?"

"Luck, and idiocy. No one, at least no one I've ever met, takes on Simon like that."

Noah's jaw went tight enough I thought it might snap. "We didn't think we were going up against a warlord. We thought we were saving a kid from a gang that'd gone too far. If we'd known who Simon was, we still would have done it, but we might have gone about it a bit differently."

I looked at him. "Noah, call Kate. She deserves to know where you are and how you're involved in this. Especially if there's a chance you'll come face-to-face with him again."

He sobered and looked down at the band on his wrist. It looked like a watch but wasn't. It was a dual heartbeat monitor. Both he and Kate wore one after what they'd experienced at Simon's hands. What I wouldn't do to have one of those monitors on Emma's wrist right now for the simple, comforting reassurance her heart was still beating.

I wished I had that.

"Okay," Jude said. "We have a line on the chopper. Are we stopping to get Harlan and Grant?"

Looking over at Agent Phillips, I asked him with a look. "We have equipment at the ranch. Probably not enough, but more than what we have now. I'm assuming there's no way for the FBI to get anything to us?"

"Not in time." His expression bordered on thunderous.

I stared straight ahead. We needed to make the stop. "The guy's ready for us to be there?"

"He is," Jude nodded.

"And he's prepared for whatever this is?" We had a lot of skills, but as far as I knew, none of us could fly a helicopter.

Jude shrugged. "Seems to be. He's a rescue flyer. They see some shit."

Phillips nodded. "Field office is monitoring your frequency, and yeah, whatever equipment you have would be good."

Agent Jones's van sat in front of me, a symbol of my failure. "Let's do it," I said. "Jude, tell them to get everything ready for when we land. The faster we do this, the better chance we have."

Chapter 27

Emma

My hands were bloody. I was already fully immersed in the panic seeing myself bleed could send me into, so it didn't make a difference anymore.

There was one sharp edge *just* within reach of one of the straps. And it wasn't easy to force the material against the metal. The action was enough to fray the strap slowly, but it was tearing up my hands in the process. Still, if I had any kind of chance to untether the cage and take them by surprise, it would be worth it.

I pushed down the voice in my head telling me that freeing the cage didn't give me a way *out* of the cage. While I was in here, I needed to do something…anything to keep myself sane.

How long had I been in the van? It seemed like it was getting darker, but it was hard to tell. It felt like a lifetime, but I knew more than anyone that fear made you perceive time differently.

The strap was frayed almost all the way. Could I…could I snap it?

No one would call me physically strong, but I was going to try. Not like the guys holding me would care if I screamed. Forcing my fingers under the tight fabric, I closed my eyes and *pulled*, letting my voice lend me strength.

The strap suddenly snapped, tossing me back against the other side of the cage. This time, it moved a little, one side free.

A *bang* sounded from the front of the van—someone hitting the divider between the drivers and me, presumably telling me to shut up. Fine. I'd gotten what I needed.

Moving to the other side, I gasped in shock, this time trying to keep myself quiet. The strap was loose, having been looped lower, in a recess I couldn't see. The cage was free. Now, what could I do with it?

Slowly, I maneuvered myself into a crouching position, using my feet below the bottom bars. Fuck, the cage was heavy, but I was able to move it. The sound of driving covered the slow scraping of my movement, and I kept going until I was pressed up against the doors. I tried the door, but it was predictably locked. Part of me had hoped they'd forgotten since I was unconscious. Too much to hope for, it seemed.

I moved again, shuffling until the edge to the cage tilted into the door well. When we stopped, maybe I could use my momentum when the doors opened to break the cage and take them by surprise. It was another long shot, but everything was a long shot now.

Sitting back, I finally let myself rest. My head still ached, and my fingers were raw. I tucked them under my arms, trying to apply some pressure to them.

It was definitely getting darker in the van. My stomach was starting to grumble. How far were we going?

I didn't know whether to wish for the drive to stop or for it to keep going indefinitely to give Daniel a chance to do whatever he was doing. Because he would be doing something. He'd saved my life three times, and he would try again.

As if I'd conjured it out of the air, the van angled, turning around a huge corner like an off-ramp. The cage slid with the momentum but not too much.

New nerves spiked in my chest. Were we almost there? My whole body went cold. I could be brave all I wanted in my head, but the reality of facing death was terrifying.

The van kept moving, still on smooth roads for a while, and I got drowsy. Lulled by my stillness and the exhaustion of adrenaline.

A sharp turn had the van on rougher terrain, which felt like a dirt road. It rumbled, but the van didn't seem to slow down at all. A bump tossed me, jostling both my body and the cage, thanks to their speed.

My heart was in my throat, and my hands shook. If they were speeding up, we might be closer to our destination… and Simon.

Pain slammed into my head. I was in the air and not sure how I got there, crashing into the bars as the cage left the floor. A *huge* bump. That's what it was. A pothole or big dip in the road.

Another one, along with a turn, tossed the cage backward toward the front, and I crashed into the bars again, a small *crunch* notable in my shoulder.

"*Fuck*," I groaned the single word, already knowing the bars would leave bruises.

Reaching back under my shirt, I felt for the tracker and peeled it off my skin. In the dimming light, it was clear the disk was shattered, broken by my impact against the bars.

"Fuck," I said the word again. My stomach dropped

down to the ground. We were still driving, and the tracker was gone. Daniel had no way of finding me now.

Tears flooded my eyes, and I blinked them back.

No. He could still find me. There had to be a way. I wasn't going to give up hope now. Not when I'd realized how much he meant to me. If I was going to die, I was going to die with hope until the very last second.

I got the cage back against the doors again and waited.

It wasn't long this time until the van slowed and finally stopped. The front doors to the van opened, and I readied myself. The lock ground open, and as soon as I heard the handle pop, I hurled myself at the front of the cage, bursting out of the doors to curses and shouts, landing on the feet of the man who'd opened them.

Blood was on my tongue where I'd been jostled and had bitten the inside of my mouth. I shoved against the cage, but it hadn't broken. There hadn't been enough force behind it.

"You *bitch*," the man yelled, kicking at the cage.

The bars were too close for his foot to make it all the way through. Small favors.

There was still light in the sky, so I could see the men above me. I remembered them. They'd been at the house and had seen me in this cage once before.

Another kick clanged against the bars. "I don't often say I'm going to enjoy grave-digging duty, but I think I might with you."

I simply moved, making myself as comfortable as I could, ready for whatever came next.

"Nothing to say? Probably for the best." I heard the rough metal sound of a gun being drawn, and I closed my eyes.

The sound was so loud, I couldn't hear anything. My ears rang, and I was dizzy. But I wasn't dead. I was still here and breathing.

Beside the cage, the man who had kicked it fell to the ground. I'd seen enough death in my month of captivity to know he was gone. The way he hit the ground told me that.

"I thought my instructions were very clear," a voice said. "Bring her to me, and no one touches her. She'll die, but I'll do it in my own way and in my own time."

Turning as best I could, I saw Simon with his arm outstretched, gun still pointed where the man had stood. "Hello, Emma."

I swallowed. "Hi, Dad."

Chapter 28

Daniel

The chopper was loud even through the headset I had on, and the sun was setting outside.

Landing at Resting Warrior had been an experience. We hadn't thought to include a helipad on the ranch, though we had plenty of room. Grant and Harlan were there waiting with all the equipment, and now I was fitted into a bulletproof vest, watching the screen as the tracker kept speeding east.

Agent Jones was safely in the hands of Charlie in the Garnet Bend jail. Grant had called him, and I was eternally grateful I didn't have to hear that conversation. I couldn't imagine that going well.

I knew how lucky we were that Emma hadn't reached her destination yet. Every passing minute felt like an hour, my mind constantly trying to drag me down into the guilt and fear I couldn't shake.

It was my fault; at least, that's what my emotions kept

trying to tell me. Deep down, I knew it wasn't, but it was hard to push logic to the front and emotions to the side. Regardless of who was to blame, we were going to try to save her.

We were catching up, but not fast enough for me. Anything could happen between here and there.

Please, I begged. *Keep driving.*

"The Seattle field office has a team on a flight to Billings," Phillips said. "And they're scrambling SWAT to get wherever the tracker ends up, but it's hard to make a plan when we don't know where we're going."

"Tell me about it."

And then there were all the elements we weren't mentioning. Almost every single factor was an unknown. Simon had nearly unlimited resources, and he knew how to use them. I was hoping because he was underground that the crew he was keeping around him was small, but it wasn't a guarantee.

On the screen in front of me, the tracker turned, leaving the highway.

"Shit." I kept the word under my breath, but the mic picked it up anyway.

"What?" Jude asked.

"It's turning off the highway."

The others were talking, but all I could do was watch that dot, following as it turned off and drove north for a while. *Hold on, Emma.*

I shoved down the unthinkable question of whether I was only following her body.

Fuck.

"This is helpful. We can give them a direction."

"It's not enough," I said. "It's not—"

On the screen, the tracker's dot went out.

I sank forward, heart skipping a beat and stomach falling all the way down to the ground below us. "No."

"Daniel?"

I couldn't stop staring at the screen. The tracker was gone. Broken. What did that mean?

Noah took the phone from me and showed the others.

"It's not a tracker connected to vital signs," Jude pointed out. "They might have found it."

"You know what it means if they did," I said. "They're searching her. They're—" Stopping, I let myself sink into the mission. "The tracker was still moving when it went out. They're still driving, and we don't have a way to find them."

Phillips was talking in a different channel on his headset. I could see his mouth moving but not much more through the noise.

"It still narrows it down," Jude said. "There's not much out here. And I don't think they're camping."

Dropping my face into my hands, I thought through everything. Any detail I might have missed—anything we could use to find out where he was. Some misstep.

"Jones brought his van back," I said.

Harlan looked at me. "What?"

"When Jones came back before we confronted him, he came back in his van. So Emma would have known."

Phillips cut in. "We've pulled the plate from the traffic cameras in Polson and are trying to track it that way. But 90 doesn't have many. Plus, it's a rental. Fake name."

"Rented from where?"

"Billings."

Okay, so this hasn't been a spur-of-the-moment decision. They'd had a plan all along, to rent a van that far away to cover their tracks.

The communication between Jones and Simon was already

a dead end. Burner phones and things he'd already destroyed. He'd known if he was caught, Simon would do far worse things to him than the FBI. "Anything on the fake name?"

"Nothing yet. Just an old alias, loosely connected to one of the shells Simon used to hide his dealings. Clearly, he doesn't care if we know about this one."

Something was nagging in my brain. There was a piece I was missing, and I didn't know what it was. I felt like Emma, sitting in that cabin for six months trying to figure it out, only to realize she didn't have enough information.

But she had more information now, and she knew how to use it. They'd set her up at that little computer shop because of her knowledge. That wasn't a lie. And—

I looked at Phillips. "Jones said she was using the computer in the store when he left her. Do you think he was lying?"

He shook his head. "I have no idea. Why?"

"Emma hasn't been on a computer since she came to Resting Warrior. There was no need, and we didn't want to risk them finding her. If she was passing time on a computer while waiting for Simon, I don't think she was shopping for shoes."

Blinking once, he nodded. "I'll tell them, see what they can do."

It wasn't much. It wasn't anything, really. I was grasping at straws, and how I wished Emma's wall of clues hadn't been so blank and I could look at it now to keep my mind busy trying to figure out the puzzle so I could save her life.

Phillips looked up at me suddenly. He was still on the other channel, but his eyes were wide in shock. "What?"

He held up a hand, still listening to the open channel he had with the field office. Finally, he clicked over. "Good call, Daniel. It's a long shot, but it makes sense. Emma tried to hack the old site she'd used to access Simon's records when he first caught her.

"The site is wiped, but it still has some things attached to it—things Emma wouldn't have been able to see if she wasn't looking. The second she accessed the site, the server sent a ping."

For the first time since I saw the tracker was in motion, I felt a spark of hope. "Where?"

The smile on Phillips's face was one of satisfaction and anticipation. "Thirty miles from where the tracker went dark."

"Holy shit," Noah said. "What do we know?"

"They need ten minutes to get more information. Any photos we might have, an idea of what we're up against."

We had the time. As much as I wished we were, we weren't ten minutes away. But this was good.

"Thank you," I told him. "Truly."

"It was your idea."

I nodded. "You know that's not what I meant."

"I know. I'll tell you as soon as I have more."

Taking a deep breath, I heaved it out and turned to the window to watch the landscape fly by.

We had a chance. Not a large one, but it was a chance. That was all I could ask.

Hold on, Emma. I'm coming.

Chapter 29

Emma

Simon looked down at me, and his eyes held no mercy. He could shoot me dead in this cage, and that would be the end of everything. I was surprised he hadn't done it already.

"I've been looking for you. You're slipperier than I expected."

"Lot of good it did me."

He smiled, and I felt sick. "Don't beat yourself up too much. You couldn't go against me having someone in the FBI. It was a good attempt, though, I'll give you that. I wish I would have found you sooner to keep you from talking, but what's done is done." Pointing to the other man he hadn't shot, Simon nodded to me. "Get her out."

I fell painfully against the bars as the man heaved the cage upright where he could open it. What did I do here? If I ran for it, Simon would shoot me in the back. But I didn't have a guarantee he wouldn't shoot me anyway.

I was pulled from the cage, and I stumbled, still dizzy

and in pain. The man now dead beside me had a hole straight through his forehead. "This isn't North Dakota," I said, betting I hadn't been unconscious long enough for us to get over the border.

Simon laughed. "No, it's not. Why?"

"Because." I straightened and looked at him, pretending to be braver than I felt. "You promised me an unmarked grave in North Dakota. You've hardly fulfilled any of your promises as a father. You might as well keep that one."

I watched his hand tighten on his gun before he holstered it. "I'll see what I can do about that. But first, you're going to help me do the only thing you're still good for. Get her inside."

The buildings in front of me were nondescript and ancient, just like everything I'd seen Simon favor. He used the natural abandonment of properties in barren locations to hide himself. I'd commend him if he weren't a murdering psychopath.

"Do I get to know?"

"Know what?"

"What I'm still good for." I swallowed. "We both know I'm not getting out of this alive. There's no harm in telling me."

"I'll tell you things you should have known. Like the fact that I knew you were at that ranch the second Agent Jones found you there, and I've been watching you ever since. Of course you would go to them, after they managed to sneak up on me like that—something I assure you will not happen again."

I didn't contradict him and tell him I didn't choose to go to Resting Warrior and only ended up there because of Daniel. "Was it you who shot at me?"

He scoffed. "If I had been the one there, I would neither have hesitated nor missed the target."

"If you tried to kill me then, why am I still alive?"

Simon smiled. "Clever, bringing it all the way around to your original question. You don't think I know the FBI will come after you? And your little band of soldiers? You're my daughter, and they'll do anything to take me down. So that's what you're good for, Emma. Bait."

"You have Agent Jones in your pocket," I said. "I'm sure he'll spin it for you."

"He'll try. But you disappearing on his watch? With a tracker? They will know, and they will come after you, which is exactly what I want."

I stopped walking, frozen in place. The man behind me tried to shove me forward, but I resisted. He knew? This whole time he knew?

Simon turned and looked at me. "Don't be so surprised. I've been doing this a long time, Emma. You think I'm so naïve that I wouldn't have my men check for trackers?"

He knew, and he wanted them to come after me. He wanted them here while I was here. So he could kill them? Take them hostage? Torture them? I didn't know. With Simon, it could be anything.

"Why not just disappear?" I asked. "You had your chance."

Yanking open the door in front of us, he shoved me inside. "Disappearing doesn't do me any good if I can't use my resources, Emma. What those Resting Warrior bastards did was shine a spotlight on me after I'd been invisible for years. You did it too. Do you have *any* idea how much I've had to restructure just to keep things afloat?"

I looked at him, making it clear with my face I didn't give a rat's ass how much of his illegal drug and gun business he'd had to restructure.

Simon nodded, and the brute following us grabbed my hands, spinning me and snapping handcuffs around them as he glared at me. I didn't fight him—there wasn't any point. He marched me into a huge empty room, one wall lined with cages, and shoved me into another one. "You really have a thing for cages, you know that?"

Simon looked at me. "You know what they did?"

All I did was stare at him. The longer I was here with him and alive, the closer I was coming to the moment when he decided keeping me alive was no longer worth it.

"They started a war. Your boyfriend and the toy soldiers. Now the ball is in my court, and you're helping with that move. That's all you need to know."

"So, you're going to fight a war? Until what? Until you die?"

"If I have to." The statement was so casual and carefree, I believed him. He started to walk away. "And if I die, it will keep going. I've built an empire that will be very hard to destroy."

"Mom was right about you." I startled, unsure why those words had come out of my mouth.

Simon whirled. "What did you just say?"

With all the fear and panic swirling around inside me, I wanted to make him feel something. Anything but the casual arrogance of inevitable victory. These were things I hadn't told him, because at the time, I'd been so relieved, I hadn't cared. "Mom was right about you. She told me not to contact you. She told me you weren't worth it and I should stay away. Then she died, I was alone, and all I wanted was a parent. Instead, I got you."

Rage cracked over his face, and he took three steps toward me, knuckles white on his gun. "That's fine, Emma. You're right. I'm not a good father, and you're not a good daughter. We're quite the pair. I'll make sure your grave has one hell of a view."

He turned again and stormed from the room, slamming the door behind him and leaving me with the brute.

I blew out a shaky breath and tilted my head back, resting my eyes for a second. Alive. I was alive. I hadn't expected to be.

The problem was Simon knew about the tracker, but he didn't seem to know the tracker was now broken. Daniel and the cavalry would be trying to locate me, but would they find me in time? And once they got here, what would they be walking into?

Simon was gearing up to throw a grenade, and he didn't hold back. He already had no respect for human life. If he thought this was a war, he would care even less.

What could I do?

I closed my eyes and ran through my memory. I couldn't do anything now to help Daniel. All I could do was rest here and make sure I had enough energy to make a move when the time came.

And it would come.

I had one single memory I was holding on to. I needed to make plans in case I could use them. It was a stroke of luck they'd handcuffed me with my hands in front of me. That meant I could use them. And reach what I needed.

Making myself as comfortable as I could, I settled in to wait and quietly prepare.

Chapter 30

Daniel

It was fully dark now, and I was losing my mind.

Two miles away from the place where we thought Simon was, we were gathered. Phillips, all of us from Resting Warrior, and local police who'd been redirected here. The FBI was still on their way—landing right now with an imported SWAT team—but the closest airport was a tiny one, still half an hour away. We'd already waited long enough. I wasn't going to delay anymore.

"We should wait, Daniel," Phillips said. "We don't know what's going on in there."

"No, we don't. But she could be dying. He could be torturing her. She could already be dead. We can't—"

"*That's right,*" he snapped. "She could already be dead."

Everything around us went silent at his outburst. Phillips stepped closer.

"Believe me when I say I hope Emma is okay. But she's been here for two hours. If she's already dead, there's nothing we can do about it. I hope to god she's alive. But if she's not, I don't want to lose more people because we went in before we were ready."

"Has anything changed?" I challenged him.

Things moved quickly when you had the full resources of the FBI behind you. They had satellites overhead, and the place was barely populated. The army they were afraid of wasn't there. Every scan they ran said the same. There were only a few people in the complex, and no more were around for miles. Were there variables? Yes. There was every chance this was a trap, but we could see that if we got closer.

Either way, in my mind, the risk of going in now was lower than waiting, because my goal wasn't Simon. It was Emma.

Phillips stared at me, and I knew he didn't want to give the answer. "No. Nothing's changed."

"You don't have the power to stop me," I said, voice low.

"I could arrest you."

"You and the cavalry that's not here yet?"

"Daniel—"

I shook my head. "Wait here if you want. I'm not."

"You can't do that."

Turning around and heading toward my men, I simply said, "Watch me."

The guys were clustered together, watching me approach. "Do you guys feel comfortable, given what we know?"

"To go in?" Liam asked.

"Yeah. It's going to take another thirty minutes for the troops to get here, and that doesn't include all the staging they'll want to do."

Noah shook his head slowly. "This is Simon we're talking about, Daniel. If we do this, we have to be careful. You know as well as I do, he already knows we're coming. He's not stupid."

"I know. Which is why I'm asking you guys. Is there truly a possibility Simon has an army stashed out here someplace we don't know?"

"Unlikely," Harlan said. "Those buildings are old. If they have a basement, it wouldn't be deep enough to avoid the infrared. And Simon is lying low. This isn't his main base of operations. He's not going to sink money into creating a bunker. If anything, he picked this place so that it can get destroyed."

"That's what I'm thinking. At the very least, I want to get closer to see what's going on."

"Daniel." I clenched my jaw and turned to meet Phillips.

"Yes?"

"Come on, I want to show you something."

For a long second, I hesitated, and then I followed him. He passed me a tablet lit up with plans for the buildings on it. "They found these. If everything is the same, the switch for the power is here. Only three entrances make for an easy breach with the seven of us."

"The seven of us?"

"Seattle has been moving fast and expediting because they know what's at stake, and everyone is still on their way. But DC got wind, and they're losing their shit over Jones. There's about to be sixty times more red tape, and I already told you how I feel about bureaucracy. But I'm not letting Simon Derine escape because people who weren't in the field decided to argue too long."

I nodded, relieved. "Thank you."

Waving everyone over, we crafted the plan. Get closer, use the earpieces we'd picked up from the ranch to communicate. It was dark now, so we'd be using night vision. The goal was simple. The satellites told us only five or six people were in the buildings. If one was Emma, that was all we needed.

Our job was to get in, grab Emma and Simon—alive, if possible—and get out. This was risky. Simon always had a backup plan, and we didn't know what it was. We had darts but not many. Real bullets would have to do if we ran out.

But even with the risks, he had to know we were coming. If he ran, he ran with Emma or killed her. Not only did we lose her, we lost our chance to catch a truly terrible criminal.

The odds weren't in our favor, but I still felt calm.

In less than ten minutes, we were moving, fanning out in the dark and jogging down the road toward the buildings. I saw nothing. No visible defenses, no signs of cameras.

It reminded me of when we'd gone in to take out Evelyn's stalker, and it had been a mistake. Something in my instincts was tingling, but I didn't know what. Liam and Noah had approached Simon's other hideout easily too. And the mission from my own past—

"Be careful," I said. "Something doesn't feel right."

The trees were clear, and other than these buildings, the nearest ones were another five miles away.

"Yeah," Grant said. "This feels wrong."

"Nothing's changed," Phillips said. "Everything shows six alive inside the buildings and no more."

Phillips and I were together, heading for the power source. Liam and Noah had paired off, heading for the front, and the last group of three was circling to the back entrance.

"There," Phillips said. On the wall of the building in front of us was the power box. Outside.

"This is too easy," I said. "Something's wrong."

We got closer, bracing ourselves against the wall. Our entrance was ten feet to the left. "Everyone in position?"

"Ready," Noah and Grant said at the same time.

"Pulling the power." I flipped the power to the building,

and sparks shattered out of it, a whining sound whirling through the wires. Behind us, an ear-piercing screech made us cringe, and a firework went straight into the sky, exploding in a giant red burst behind us.

"Fuck," Phillips said, but we were already moving, busting down the door into darkness, and…he was standing there. Simon and two of his men.

I shot a dart into the one on the left. Phillips took the one on the right, and I stopped short of shooting Simon Derine. Because he had a gun pointed straight at Emma.

In a cage.

She was in a fucking cage.

It was only adrenaline that kept my mind clear. The flashbacks were hovering at the edges of my vision.

"Emma," I said. "Are you all right?"

"I'm alive."

"Yes," Simon said. "She's alive. And you came running, just like I hoped."

"Simon Derine," Phillips said. "You're under arrest."

He laughed. "Sure about that?"

Light blazed to the left, and for a long moment, I thought it was fire. Just like that day I'd burst into the room and it exploded in flames, killing everyone but me.

It wasn't fire. It was headlights and gunshots.

Bullets hit the wall, and Phillips and I dropped to the floor. The doors burst open with Liam, Noah, and the rest, running in and dropping too.

"The firework," I said. "The fucking firework."

The next buildings were five miles away and had been abandoned. They had been *abandoned*. Every scan told us that. But it had been a signal. Somehow, they'd been hidden.

The guys made it to us, and we all managed to get into the next room, which put more walls between us and the firing guns. "*Emma!*" I called, lunging for the door.

"She's not in there," Noah said. "No one is in there."

Shit. He'd taken her and run, and we were pinned down from the outside.

"He had her at gunpoint," Phillips said. "Could have made you do whatever he wanted. But he still took her and left." He stood, looking around frantically. "Daniel, he said you came running just like he wanted."

It all hit me at once. Empty buildings. Easy access. He's already declared war on Resting Warrior, and he finally had one thing he *knew* we would try to get back. "*Get out!*" I shouted. "Get out now!"

We ran for the door, sprinting outside and to the nearby trees for cover. The force of the explosion tossed me to the ground, along with everyone else. A bright fireball rolling into the sky blinded my night vision, and I pulled off the goggles, blinking to clear my sight.

"Move, move, move," I called, getting to my feet and ignoring the fiery pain in my shoulder, hauling Liam up and getting him behind more cover. I heard shots behind us, and the others were firing back. A secondary explosion came from one of the vehicles, and then I heard boots on the ground.

Here was Simon's army. I didn't see nearly as many as we knew he had, but there were still enough for us to be outnumbered. Backup was almost here. We needed to retreat until it came.

"Use the trees," I said into the comms. "Get back to the staging point. By the time you get there, we'll have backup."

The raging fire lit up the ground, and I looked around, searching for where Simon had gone. He'd known we were coming, and he was prepared. But he wouldn't have run to the vehicles raining bullets. Not when they could explode.

Everyone started moving backward. A hasty retreat was the only option until we had better numbers.

There.

At the edge of the trees, a scrap of blue. A conversation sprang into my head.

Of course, it's easier if whatever you're tracking leaves you a trail. Broken branches, footprints. If it's human, scraps of cloth. But you use whatever you need to in a rescue.

Emma, with her perfect memory, was leaving me a clue. Thank fuck.

I ducked away from the others and flicked off my radio. Keeping my steps silent and my pace quick, I dove between the trees and put my night vision back on, facing away from the fire. Simon Derine and I had unfinished business, and I was going to get my girl.

Chapter 31

Emma

The cold barrel of the gun pressed into the back of my skull. Simon forced me faster than I wanted to go, and I stumbled. But the stumbling distracted him from the trail I was dropping behind us. My one last Hail Mary pass, trying to stay alive.

I'd spent the last while in the cage tearing my shirt. Especially once my guard got bored. Ragged pieces off the bottom of my jeans too. Every thirty steps, I dropped one, hoping it would be enough. If they were still alive.

I couldn't even think about it. Tears were streaming down my face, a reflex to the terror and everything else. As soon as those shots went off, Simon pulled me from the cage and outside. We were already in the trees when the buildings exploded.

"As soon as we get far enough away from whoever your friends left behind, you're done. Sorry, you're not going to get a grave in North Dakota. You don't deserve it."

"You bastard."

"If you think being called a bastard hurts my feelings, Emma, you're wrong."

I tried to drop another piece of fabric and dropped what felt like three instead. "Shit."

"Have something to say?"

"Nope."

He laughed, a vicious sound I was sure would haunt my nightmares if I was still alive to have them in an hour. "If I were you, I'd reconsider 'nope,' as your last word."

Another piece of fabric.

I was running out of clues.

Simon stepped over a dip in the ground, and I didn't make it, stumbling and falling this time. I caught myself, scraping my palms on the hard dirt. And the fabric in my hands went everywhere.

No.

"Get up," he snarled, yanking me up by the handcuffs.

As soon as I was upright, he froze. He bent down, picking up a piece of the fabric. "Leaving clues for your lover?"

"Can you blame me?"

He huffed a laugh. "I should have killed you a long time ago. This is far enough."

The click of his gun was loud in the darkness, and it was pointing straight at me.

"Let her go, Simon," Daniel's voice called out.

I could have cried harder at the sound, but I was staring down the barely visible barrel of a gun.

"You Resting Warrior people are surprisingly hard to kill."

"I know. Now let her go."

"I don't think so."

Closing my eyes, I raised my voice. "Daniel. I love you. I

just want to make sure you hear me say it. None of this is your fault, and I don't want you to live thinking that, okay?"

"What makes you think he's going to live?" Simon asked. "As soon as I kill you, he's next."

"Then why haven't you done it? Maybe you're sentimental and can't kill your only daughter, even if you do hate me. Even if I ruined your empire. A small sliver of you can't kill what's a part of you."

Simon stared, and then he laughed. "Your mother was right about me. I'm someone everyone should stay away from. Because you're wrong, Emma. The only thing I want to do is make it hurt more. So I changed my mind." He turned his body. "Mr. Clark dies first."

~

Daniel

Simon turned his gun on me. I could see him perfectly in the night vision. "I die, you die, Simon," I said. "I can fire just as quickly. You know that."

Behind me, I heard gunfire and shouting. The cavalry had arrived, and they were fighting the Riders.

"Then we go down together," Simon said with a shrug. "I'm just one head of the hydra I've created. You think killing me will do a fucking thing?"

"I think it will, yeah." I kept my voice steady. "I think you keep such a tight hold on everything that your empire collapses into chaos when you're gone."

"You can try. Or rather, they can keep trying. You won't be around to see it."

His body tensed, and everything happened at once.

Emma screamed, jumping on Simon to move the gun. A

force with the weight of a truck hit me from the right as the shot rang out. And another shot. I hit the ground hard, the air knocked out of me. Instantly, I rolled out from whatever it was and aimed. Simon had shoved Emma to the ground, and his gun was almost in position.

Three shots.

One.

Two.

Three.

Simon staggered, the gun falling out of his hand as my bullets struck him. I moved, grabbing his weapon off the ground and keeping mine trained on him. He was gone, body sagging and limp, but I checked anyway. No pulse. Simon Derine was dead.

"Emma," I gasped.

She launched herself at me, and I caught her, holding her to my chest. Alive. She was alive. That was the only thought in my head.

"Daniel," Emma said. "Look."

I turned and found Phillips on the ground, holding his leg. It was bleeding. The bullet had gone straight into his thigh. He'd jumped into me, taking me down and out of the way of Simon's shot.

I hit my knees beside him, Emma still with me. "Phillips. Why?"

He groaned, the words strained. "Simon shoots for the head. I couldn't let that happen. He's dead?"

"He's dead. We need to get you back and to a hospital."

"I'll be fine."

"Keep pressure on it." He was bleeding, but the bullet was still in his leg and blocking the flow. As long as he got to a hospital soon, he would be okay. I clicked on my radio. "This is Daniel. I'm with Phillips, half a mile to the south.

He's been shot in the leg. We need medical support and a stretcher. Simon Derine is dead."

For three heartbeats, there wasn't any response. Then Noah's voice crackled through. "En route to you. And when we get home and all of this is over, we're going to have a conversation about you going off alone like that, got it?"

"Got it." He had every right to call me out. It hadn't been the right move, and I knew that. The three of us were lucky to be alive. Right now, I didn't care.

I pulled Emma to me and held her while we waited for the lights to appear. Not long after, they did, the FBI reaching Phillips and helping him and then taking possession of Simon's body, handing me the keys to Emma's cuffs that he'd had in his pocket.

Time seemed suspended. All I wanted was to take Emma somewhere alone where I could hold her and revel in our passion for each other over and over again until we were satisfied—which was going to take a while.

They wanted to check us out too, but we were fine. They could check us out as long as I didn't have to move away from Emma. Still, we hung back behind the others.

I turned her to me and kissed her. I kissed her with everything that had been inside me since I'd realized that she was missing and that I loved her. I *loved* her.

And she loved me. She'd told me, and I'd barely even processed it.

"I love you," I breathed. "I love you and I have loved you, and for whatever reason, it didn't surface until I saw that tracker driving away. I've been *out of my mind*, Emma."

She clung to me, fingers digging into my shirt. "I meant what I said. I love you, and you're the thing that kept me alive. If I died, I knew it was going to be fighting because of you."

I kissed her again, wrapping her up in my arms so tightly it almost hurt. "You left a trail for me."

"It was a long shot. But you saved my life, Daniel. Again."

I pressed my forehead against hers. "Simon is gone. Agent Jones is in jail, which I'll tell you about, and you're free, Emma. You're free to go wherever you want and do whatever you want."

I knew what I wanted, and I'd never been surer about anything in my life. But Emma had all of hers in front of her, and if she wanted to go elsewhere, I would support her even if it destroyed me inside.

"I want to come home," Emma whispered. "I don't want to leave."

"Thank god," were the only words I could get out before I kissed her again. "I don't ever want you to leave, Emma. Stay with me. I'll build you a bigger house, and you can do whatever you want with your life. There are no limits. I just want you to do it with me."

She reached her arms around my neck. "It's all I've ever wanted."

"Hey!" Liam called from the direction of the camp. "You two lovebirds want to come assure people you're still alive?"

I kept my arm around Emma's body and her tight against my side as we walked. She had her fingers wrapped and her head checked, but we would be seeing Dr. Gold as soon as we got back.

Now that the FBI and SWAT were on the ground, it was nice to relinquish the responsibility. Phillips would live and had already been bundled into a car and was being driven to the nearest hospital. There were prisoners—men from the Riders who had surrendered and who I was sure would make a deal with the FBI. But with Simon's network still in place for the moment, who knew if they would be safe in witness protection?

Hours later, after the FBI took our statements, we were ready to go. They would contact me later about being the one to shoot Simon, I was sure. But I didn't regret it. He was about to kill Emma and me.

Still, we were dragging on our feet as we got back into the helicopter. Emma and I were pressed against each other, her leaning her head on my shoulder. If I could keep her in my house and in my arms for a solid week, I would.

Liam chuckled over the headset. "You guys trying to become a single being over there?"

"I didn't realize that was an option," Emma said sleepily. "If it is, we'll investigate it."

A laugh burst out of Liam. "Good to know. I'm glad you're okay, Emma."

"Thanks."

"And I'm happy you're coming back with us, and I fully reserve the right to make fun of you both later."

I raised an eyebrow. "Was there even a chance you'd do something else?"

"No."

I laughed quietly, but the rest of my brothers weren't laughing. "I'm sorry. I know it wasn't the right call."

"Damn right, it wasn't," Noah snapped. "We could have gone with you, Daniel. We would have had your back."

"I know." I didn't point out that he'd gone in alone against the Riders multiple times. Every one of the men who worked at Resting Warrior had made risky decisions to help the people we loved. And it was their right to call me out for it. He was angry, but it was also a reaction to the fear.

"Once Lucas gets back, if you guys think we need a meeting to reevaluate our roles at the ranch, I accept that."

I felt Harlan's eye roll in his voice. "No, Daniel. I don't think anyone wants that."

Noah didn't contradict him.

"But we do need to talk about it. A lot has happened with all of us, and every single one of us has more on the line now than when we first came to Garnet Bend. We have our rules, and they're good ones. But we need to talk about it."

"I agree," Jude said.

The others nodded in the faint light of the helicopter.

"You got it," I said. "We'll have a meeting once Lucas comes back from his honeymoon."

Everyone got quiet then, and I pulled Emma closer, nearly into my lap. It felt like a miracle we were both here and together. Alive, without the danger hanging over our heads. And now that we were free, we could finally start planning a future.

Epilogue

Emma

Five Months Later

I ducked through the chattering crowd and into the kitchen, looking for the extra candy I'd bought. I knew it was here somewhere, but I was still getting used to this new, much bigger kitchen.

"Need any help in here?" Evelyn asked behind me.

"I'm okay," I said with a laugh. "Just trying to remember where I put the extra chocolate."

"Sign me up for that."

I glanced at her while she took a glass and filled it with water. "Do you want me to grab you a chair?"

"No, I'm okay. Thank you, though." She downed the glass of water, cradling what was now a very visible baby bump. The Halloween party we were having was loud, but I could and would find a quiet corner for her if she needed.

"This place is really beautiful," she continued. "Makes me want to have Lucas do some updates to ours."

"Probably a good idea," I laughed. "Might keep him busy."

The men of Resting Warrior, particularly Lucas, were more worried about the pregnancy than any of the women were. Evelyn was doing amazing, and everything was proceeding picture-perfectly, but that didn't stop Lucas from treating her like spun glass. Some of the time, she liked it. Sometimes, she kicked him out of the house and refused to let him in unless he relaxed. Which meant he ended up in the lodge with Daniel and me.

I was still figuring out what I wanted to do, exploring different options. With what had happened already, I didn't necessarily want to get a job in computers, and Daniel insisted I didn't have to work at all. I wanted to, but I was grateful for the time to figure it out. In the meantime, I still helped Mara around the ranch and was learning everything I could about every job we had.

And true to his word, Daniel had built this house for us. We'd only been living in it for a week, and a housewarming Halloween party had seemed like a good idea, but now I was exhausted.

Lucas found his way into the kitchen. He was dressed as the Grim Reaper, and Evelyn was dressed as a ghost. Her pregnant belly made for a fun ghost shape under the billowing white dress. "There you are."

"Here I am."

He leaned in and kissed her, and I looked away to give them some privacy. Deciding to give up on my chocolate hunt, I decided maybe I would go find Daniel and do the same thing. Not that we could sneak away as the hosts, but at the same time…

The party was in full swing, and I was so happy everyone

had taken the invitation so seriously. Not a single person—myself included—wasn't in costume.

I'd opted for something simple. A ladybug, complete with headband antennae and black-and-red polka dots. Grant and Cori were Woody and Jessie from *Toy Story*. Harlan and Grace were a detonator and a stick of dynamite, poking fun of what had almost happened to them last year. Even Rayne was present dressed as a rose, and Charlie had dressed as a member of the fire department rather than the police.

In the corner, I saw Mara. Her costume was beautiful and delicate—a ballerina. She was talking to Liam, as I'd caught more and more lately. He was dressed as a matador, and it somehow worked between the two of them. Everyone was talking and laughing, both the people I knew and the people I didn't know. Friends from town were here, and it felt like more than just a housewarming or a Halloween party. It was truly a celebration of life.

I found Daniel on the back porch, the phone to his ear. "Yeah, that will be fine. Can you get back to me on Monday with the confirmation?" A long pause. "Okay, thanks."

"Everything good?"

He turned and smiled. His clothes were green, and he'd even been a good sport and painted his face green. Daniel was the leaf to my ladybug. "Yeah. They're moving forward with the trial. Might have to fly out and testify."

I frowned. The trial was a big one. A combination of former Special Agent Jones and the men who'd been caught that night but hadn't flipped. Plenty of people had been caught since, but that was a different story.

Daniel had been mostly right when he'd told Simon his empire would fall apart without him. It took time, and we didn't know as much since Simon was gone, but it wasn't the same without him. Huge pieces of his network had been exposed, and even only five months later, the operation was barely half of what it had been.

"Well, I want to come with you."

"If they'll let you, absolutely."

I nodded, wetting my lips and fighting against the nerves. I needed to tell him something, and I couldn't wait anymore. "I want to travel while I still can."

Daniel looked at me, face full of concern. "While you still can? What are you talking about? Did you finally snap and commit murder?"

"No, nothing like that."

Pulling me to him, he kissed me lightly. "You look worried. What's wrong?"

"Nothing's wrong, I promise. I just… I want to travel because you're not supposed to once you hit the third trimester, and I've never really been anywhere. So, I want to do some traveling with you before it gets harder."

Daniel's face went slack with shock. "Really?"

"Really." I smiled. "I'm not ready to tell everyone else, but I wanted to tell you."

"Holy shit." He kissed me, backing me up against the wall of our new home. My red makeup and his green makeup were going to be smudged together, but I didn't care. Not for one second. "We're having a baby?"

"We're having a baby." A laugh burst up and out of me. "And before you say anything else, you are not going to turn into Lucas. I am not made of glass. I can still kick some serious ass even if I'm pregnant."

Daniel had moved his mouth down to my shoulder, leaving green kiss-prints on my skin. "I absolutely know you can. I apologize in advance for any overbearing dad stuff. It'll happen."

We stood there for a minute, breathing each other in before he whispered, "I want to marry you."

My heart skipped a beat. "What?"

"I want to marry you, and I've been planning on proposing. Christmas was when I was going to ask, and it will still be when I ask, because I'm in the process of buying a ring. But I can't let this moment pass and not tell you I want to marry you, Emma Derine. I want you to be my wife."

I bit my lip, staring up at him in the semi-darkness. My savior and protector. The man I loved more than anything in the world. Would I marry him? Of course I would. "I won't answer you now if you're not asking," I said. "But I'm very much looking forward to Christmas."

Daniel's mouth crashed down on mine, and we both moaned, unable to control it. He broke away, breathing heavily. "I only wish you'd told me a little later."

"Why?"

"Because the party is just getting started, and now all I want to do is kick them out so I can take you upstairs."

I laughed, bright and loud in the darkness. "There's plenty of time for that. But we might have to fix our makeup."

"No. I want everyone to see just how much I love you. I can't keep my hands off you even as a ladybug."

Underneath all my red makeup, I turned pink with pleasure. "I love you, Daniel Clark."

He was beaming when he bent down to whisper in my ear. "I love you too."

•••

Thank you for reading MONTANA FREEDOM! The Resting Warrior Ranch series continues with MONTANA SILENCE, the story of Liam and Mara. Grab it **HERE**.

. . .

And…

Click here to join Josie's VIP reader email group and as a special gift to you, you'll receive free ebooks each month. Plus, updates on Josie & Janie's new releases, sales, and specials.

Also by Janie Crouch

All books: https://www.janiecrouch.com/books

LINEAR TACTICAL: OAK CREEK

Hero Unbound

LINEAR/ZODIAC TACTICAL CROSSOVER

Code Name: OUTLAW

ZODIAC TACTICAL (series complete)

Code Name: ARIES

Code Name: VIRGO

Code Name: LIBRA

Code Name: PISCES

LINEAR TACTICAL SERIES (series complete)

Cyclone

Eagle

Shamrock

Angel

Ghost

Shadow

Echo

Phoenix

Baby

Storm

Redwood

Scout

Blaze

Hero Forever

RESTING WARRIOR RANCH (with Josie Jade)

Montana Sanctuary

Montana Danger

Montana Desire

Montana Mystery

Montana Storm

Montana Freedom

Montana Silence

INSTINCT SERIES (series complete)

Primal Instinct

Critical Instinct

Survival Instinct

THE RISK SERIES (series complete)

Calculated Risk

Security Risk

Constant Risk

Risk Everything

OMEGA SECTOR SERIES (series complete)

Stealth

Covert

Conceal

Secret

OMEGA SECTOR: CRITICAL RESPONSE (series complete)

Special Forces Savior

Fully Committed

Armored Attraction

Man of Action

Overwhelming Force

Battle Tested

OMEGA SECTOR: UNDER SIEGE (series complete)

Daddy Defender

Protector's Instinct

Cease Fire

Major Crimes

Armed Response

In the Lawman's Protection

Also by Josie Jade

See more info here: www.josiejade.com

RESTING WARRIOR RANCH (with Janie Crouch)

Montana Sanctuary

Montana Danger

Montana Desire

Montana Mystery

Montana Storm

Montana Freedom

Montana Silence

•••

NEVER TOO LATE FOR LOVE (with Regan Black)

Collection 1: Heartbreak Key

Vanessa's Guardian

Jasmine's Guardian

Robyn's Guardian

Amy's Guardian

Heartbreak Key Boxed Set

Collection 2: Ellington Cove

Sarah's Protector

Angela's Protector

Gabby's Protector

About the Author (Janie Crouch)

"Passion that leaps right off the page." - Romantic Times Book Reviews

USA Today and Publishers Weekly bestselling author Janie Crouch writes what she loves to read: passionate romantic suspense featuring protective heroes. Her books have won multiple awards, including the Romance Writers of America's coveted Vivian® Award, the National Readers Choice Award, and the Booksellers' Best.

After a lifetime on the East Coast, and a six-year stint in Germany due to her husband's job as support for the U.S. Military, Janie has settled into her dream home in Front Range of the Colorado Rockies.

When she's not listening to the voices in her head—and even when she is—she enjoys engaging in all sorts of crazy adventures (200-mile relay races; Ironman Triathlons, treks to Mt. Everest Base Camp...), traveling, and hanging out with her four kids.

Her favorite quote: "Life is a daring adventure or nothing." ~ Helen Keller.

facebook.com/janiecrouch

amazon.com/author/janiecrouch

instagram.com/janiecrouch

bookbub.com/authors/janie-crouch

About the Author (Josie Jade)

Josie Jade is the pen name of an avid romantic suspense reader who had so many stories bubbling up inside her she had to write them!

Her passion is protective heroes and books about healing…broken men and women who find love—and themselves—again.

Two truths and a lie:

• Josie lives in the mountains of Montana with her husband and three dogs, and is out skiing as much as possible

• Josie loves chocolate of all kinds—from deep & dark to painfully sweet

• Josie worked for years as an elementary school teacher before finally becoming a full time author

Josie's books will always be about fighting danger and standing shoulder-to-shoulder with the family you've chosen and the people you love.

Heroes exist. Let a Josie Jade book prove it to you.